A.N. VEREBES

Handle With Care

Jukebox Collection Book 1

To Adam, my wonderful husband and biggest supporter.

To T & B, my boys, I hope you never read this. (Especially the sex scenes.)

Contents

Preface

Firstly, this book contains explicit content not suitable for persons under 18 years of age.

Secondly, thank you for reading Handle With Care. I genuinely hope you enjoy it as much as I enjoyed writing it.

If you do enjoy it and are looking for more, you can sign up for my newsletter via my website (details can be found at the back of this book) and receive an alternate scene that didn't make it into the novel.

Acknowledgement

Firstly, I thank my wonderful husband, Adam, for supporting my lifelong ambition to publish something. (Anything!) Without his wrangling our boys and encouraging me to write, even when I wasn't feeling like it, I might never have achieved this goal.

I also thank Mark, my writing buddy and BFF, for listening to my meltdowns while I was writing, and for helping me through everything that came after the book was written. Cover designs, publishing options, pen names - his help was invaluable. (And I doubt he's ever going to read this. It's not his jam.)

And last (but I swear not least), I thank my good friend, Claire, for reading through this before the editing, for her valuable (if slightly biased) feedback, and for being so kind and patient with my billion questions as she read it.

Okay, no, I lied - I also want to thank anyone who picks this book up and reads it, too. I hope you enjoy it as much as I enjoyed writing it (ignoring, of course, how much I detested the editing process.)

Oh! And, even though he'll never see it -and I *really, really* hope he doesn't- I'd like to thank Matt Bomer for not suing me for the blatant fangirling herein. (Seriously, please don't sue me - it's all complimentary, I swear!)

Chapter One

"Hold the door!"

Ever a goody-two-shoes, Gemma scrambled to obey the English accented voice that had come from down the hotel hallway, pushing herself away from the mirrored wall of the lift and holding her hand in place to prevent the doors from closing.

Within seconds, the owner of the voice stepped through the doors, offering an effusive "Thanks."

In retelling the story to her friends, Gemma would like to say that she said, 'You're welcome' and smiled warmly. But, in reality, she felt her face warm and the sound that left her mouth was more of a garbled, "Eep."

Sharing her lift was a man she recognised instantly, being a rather huge fan of both him and the fantasy genre TV series he'd starred in. She cleared her throat and, a second too long for her reaction to be considered anything other than unadulterated awkwardness, found her voice. "All good."

Everett Rhodes –also known as one of her bigger celebrity crushes– was sharing her lift. Nay, he was sharing her hotel. Further still, unless he was lost, he was sharing her *floor*. Gemma was suddenly thrilled that she'd splashed a little extra cash to stay in one of the top floors of the swanky hotel for a couple of nights. She did her best not to hyperventilate or go full blown fangirl on him, fiddling with her phone unseeingly and reminding herself that she was a grown woman.

Out of the corner of her eye, Gemma watched his shoulders slump as he realised that she'd recognised him. "Here for *Pop!Con?*" he asked, hesitating over the name of the convention she was specifically staying on the Gold Coast to attend. He was being wheeled out as one of their 'Pop-Stars' – one of the sole reasons she had splurged on tickets and accommodation this year. Even thinking this made her feel just a little bit ridiculous.

Snapping to attention, she nodded, brushing an errant strand of mousy brown hair behind her ear. "Uh, yeah…"

The smile he gave her was warm and genuine, those blue eyes of his sparking with a hint of mirth. "I don't bite, love."

If she'd had more confidence, she might have flirted and said something to the effect of 'What if I asked you to?' but instead she felt her face heat up further. "Sorry," she dropped her gaze, embarrassed. "I'm just…" She sighed, giving up all pretence of being *normal*. "You probably get fangirled at a lot. I'm trying to prove we're not all crazies." Especially given that she was nearing thirty and had no right behaving like a teenager. Besides, she was certain that she was far from his type and flirting would just be sad.

She glanced at her watch and then up at the screen on the lift, watching the numbers tick by extremely slowly. In fantasy, being stuck in a comically slow-moving elevator with her celebrity crush sounded divine. In reality? Not so much.

Her confession earned her a wry chuckle. "I don't think you're *all* crazy."

Unable to help herself, she smiled back at him, feeling like a bit of a lech as she sized him up in person. He was shorter than she'd expected, only a few inches taller than her respectable 5'7", but he was still extremely handsome with his artfully scruffy angular jaw and athletic physique. He practically radiated stereotypical Hollywood pretty boy at her.

Part of her cursed her decision to wear a Disney shirt today of all days, but this was who she was, and he'd forget their encounter as soon as they parted ways at any rate. This was real life and not some cheesy rom-com where the attractive actor would fall in love with his fan, after all. And, hey, at least she wasn't in full cosplay. (Not that there was anything wrong with cosplay; she just wasn't very good at it.)

"More fool you, really." Gemma had no idea where the courage to tease him had come from, but she couldn't take the words back and they hung suspended between them for a brief –but awkward– moment. She wanted to facepalm and checked again on the progress of their descent. "World's slowest lift," she murmured, silently begging the ground to just open up and swallow her.

Rhodes chuckled again, more out of politeness than anything.

Gemma went back to fiddling with her phone.

The silence stretched on as the floors seemed to inch down to the ground level. Then the lights flickered, and the lift made a strange grinding-clunking sound, stopping abruptly. The display on the screen said that they had reached the 7th floor, but the doors didn't open.

"That didn't sound too good," Gemma observed slowly, frowning at the still-closed metal doors. She pushed the 'open doors' button. They remained shut. The lights flickered again ominously.

"Pretty sure we're stuck," her companion remarked, frowning and pulling out his own phone. She assumed he had a travel sim installed or simply didn't care about exorbitant roaming charges. "I don't have any reception."

"Well, fuck," she muttered, realising that she didn't either. They must be in a dead zone, because Murphy's Law was an actual thing in her world. "Neither do I." She held up her phone to prove that, for all her joking about crazed fans, she wasn't lying to him.

She hit the emergency call button in the lift.

Nothing happened.

Gemma blinked, incredulous. "You've got to be kidding me." She hit the button a few more times with increasing frustration and just a hint of panic. She just about jumped out of her skin when a warm hand landed on her shoulder.

"Sorry," Rhodes backed up again, holding his hands up in surrender. "Are you okay?"

Fighting down a hysterical laugh, she swallowed and shoved shaking hands into her pockets. "I'm not the best with confined spaces. For short periods of time, it's fine, but…" she blew a breath out slowly. "Sorry. I promise I'm not actually a raving lunatic."

Talking to him was distracting enough from the plight of being stuck in a small metal box suspended between hotel floors, though, so she kept going. "I don't suppose you have bodyguards or assistants or handlers or something? You know, someone that knew you were getting into this lift and who will raise the alarm if you don't wander out on the ground floor in the next couple of minutes?"

He laughed at that, and it surprised her that it was a self-deprecating sort of sound and it was accompanied by a shrug. "No. No, I'm not *that* famous. In fact, you're the first person to recognise me."

Objectively, if she hadn't been such a huge fan (with a crush to boot) she mightn't have recognised him at first glance, particularly with the shaggy haircut he was sporting and if he slid his sunglasses on. Additionally, his show had been off air for two years: if he were off being successful and relevant, he wouldn't have been booked at a random pop culture convention in Australia, would he? But that thought seemed a little unkind, considering how much she –and thousands of other people–looked forward to these conventions.

"Oh." Gemma shook her head, feeling a little traitorous for her musings. "I'm willing to bet the closer you get to the Convention Centre, the faster that will change. Whether that's a good thing or not, well…" she trailed off and offered him another small smile. "We're not *all* crazies, remember."

"I thought that was my line," the actor grinned, and she felt her heart do a little flip. *Damn him and his aesthetic charm.* He stuck out his hand, officially introducing himself, "Everett, or Rhett, if you'd prefer."

"Gemma," she responded, shaking the offered appendage. Cocking her head to the side, she mused on his chosen nickname. "I never picked you as the 'Rhett' type. I would have thought it was Everett or bust. You know, if I'd given it much thought. Which I hadn't. Well, until now."

His lips twitched upwards into a smirk. "Rhetts have a type?"

"Yes," her reply was one of affected haughtiness, because she got weird when she got nervous. And *boy* was she nervous. "They wear shorts,

Hawaiian shirts, and thongs." At his raised eyebrows, she corrected, "Flip-flops, or sandals, sorry." She looked him over again, taking in the form fitting jeans, polo shirt (with sunglasses tucked in at the unbuttoned collar, offering just a hint of his dark chest hair) and dress shoes. "You're dressed like an Everett."

This earned her another laugh, but it was warmer and richer than any of the previous iterations of the sound. "You were trying to convince me you weren't crazy, remember?"

"Oh," she waved her hand dismissively, "I abandoned that plan at least three seconds after I said it. Lost cause and all that. Still," she mused aloud, gesturing to the shut doors, "I wasn't exactly expecting this."

It was probably a good thing that she'd gone to the bathroom before she'd left her hotel room, too. She pressed the emergency call button again. Still nothing. She clenched her hand into a fist and gave the button a good thump for its uselessness.

"Okay, so we're going to leave the button alone now," Everett told her, gently pulling her away from the panel. "I'd guess there's been a glitch of some kind. But I get you're a bit claustrophobic, and the talking was helping right?"

She glanced down to where his hand was still on her forearm, warm and solid and connected to his own toned arm and delicious biceps, which looked so good in the tight sleeves of the black polo and...*Fuck! Focus, Gemma.*

"Yes," she acknowledged, a blush staining her cheeks. She was a terrible person for objectifying him. And yet, courtesy of her crush, she couldn't help it. Not that that was a valid excuse, she knew. And now her traitorous thoughts were turning circular. "It was. Sorry. Trying to rein in the crazy."

"I have a fear of anything reptilian, if it helps," he admitted, surprising her with the information. "So, I get it. Your country terrifies me with its wealth of deadly snakes and lizards and even turtles! Seriously, you have *turtles* that can maim people. That's not normal."

"I mean, most of our wildlife is engineered to kill you, so I guess that fear's warranted." Who was this person that was in control of the sounds coming out of her mouth, she wondered. She needed them to stop now.

"It's the blasé way you say that that really worries me." Everett still sounded amused, though, so she figured she hadn't made too much of a fool of herself.

"I'm also afraid of snakes, don't worry," she shuddered. "I've been considering moving to Hawaii or New Zealand. Or even Ireland. No snakes there. Could get my hike on without being afraid of certain death."

"Oh, you like hiking?" There was additional animation in him now, a genuine interest with the topic. Of *course* he was the outdoorsy type – he was practically built for it.

Gemma nodded. "Yeah, I have a thing for views and scenic vistas. Don't much love the actual hiking itself, especially with Eastern Browns at every turn here, but the payoff is usually worth it."

"Yeah. There's definitely something magical and rewarding in getting to the top of a climb and looking down over the rest of the world, right?" Everett smiled conspiratorially.

"Right." Her heart was not thumping away at a billion miles per minute just because seeing his eyes all lit up and crinkled at the edges made him extra handsome. Nope. It wasn't. She swallowed. "I'm thinking of travelling to the US in the next couple of years. Any choice spots I should focus on if I do want to come off the beaten track and do a hike?" She knew he was English, but that he'd spent at least the past eight years living in America, filming television shows and movies.

"I guess it depends on where you're talking about visiting. East Coast or West Coast? Or desert? Tourist destinations, or the cities that most people dismiss because they're not famous?"

She slid down the wall, deciding that she might as well settle in and get comfortable. "I'm kind of a Broadway baby," she confessed, "so I'd love to see New York City. Not a lot of hiking to be done there, I know."

He considered this, following her example to slide down the wall beside her, resting his wrists on his elevated knees. She hated herself for thinking that even that simple action seemed sinful coming from him. "It sounds overdone, but Central Park is awesome, and huge. No hiking, but it's scenic at any time of year. You could spend days wandering around in there and still not see it all."

"That does sound like a Bucket List activity." She was even good enough to not mention the crime stats and the concept that she might get mugged.

He smiled and her heart did that flopping thing again. "There are plenty of hiking spots in Upstate New York, too." He began listing them, counting them off on his fingers, "Lake Placid, Bear Mountain, Watkins Glen…or, if you Google, you can find a few spots closer to NYC that you'd probably also love."

"Google!" She cried, startling him, and pulled out her phone. "I don't have reception, but if we can get WiFi…" Her face fell. The little metal box they were in did not get WiFi reception either. "Never mind."

Everett's hand was on her back, patting consolingly. "I'm sure someone is already on it. Fixing the lift, I mean."

Her head hit the mirrored wall with a dull *thunk*. "Didn't *Speed* start this way?"

He blinked at her abrupt change of topic. "Huh?"

"I'm sure it did," she continued. "Keanu Reeves and Jeff Daniels were trying to save a bunch of people from plummeting to their deaths in a lift."

"You're *really* not a fan of confined spaces, are you?" He was starting to sound concerned now, his cobalt eyes wider as they peered at her. "Don't pass out on me, okay, love?"

Gemma forced herself to calm, taking a few deep breaths and feeling completely embarrassed. Closing her eyes and resting her head against the cool surface behind her, she said, "I am sorry for this. I'm sure being locked in a box with a panicky random isn't quite how you imagined spending your morning."

"I'll admit," he conceded, "there was more caffeine and less claustrophobia in my original plans."

"When we get out of here, I'll owe you a coffee." The casual offer escaped her before she remembered who she was talking to. A flush immediately suffused her cheeks, and she stammered, "I mean, sorry, I didn't mean…" she winced and pinched the bridge of her nose. "Stopping talking now."

The fact that her unwitting companion was actually laughing, shoulders shaking and all, didn't help matters.

"If nothing else, I'm glad I'm able to entertain you," she snarked at him, feeling her cheeks burning. She'd probably actually seek therapy after this, the mortification of the entire encounter burning deep into her psyche. "Just promise me that when you get your next big role and start wheeling out this story in interviews as 'that time I was trapped with a crazy fan', you'll at least fib a little and say I was stunning or something complimentary alongside the humiliation, yeah?"

Everett sobered a little, a frown pulling his eyebrows down, giving him the broody expression that he'd practically patented during his run on *Happily Never After*. He opened and closed his mouth a few times, as though trying to find the right words. She cursed herself for making him uncomfortable. Well, *more* uncomfortable.

Fuck her life.

"So, I've watched you on a few panels. Online, obviously. You've got this wicked sense of humour," she found herself explaining into the awkward silence, blaming her lack of filter on an imagined decreasing amount of oxygen. However, at this point she was pretty much in for a penny, in for a pound when it came to her embarrassment anyway, and she had a point to make. "The playful narcissism is entertaining, and you *just* ride the line between knowing you're attractive and still being charming. Personally, I can't pull that off, so my style of deflection –as you've noticed by now– is more self-deprecating." She shrugged. "What a juxtaposition, right?" She swept her eyes over him again. "Of course, if I were as pretty as you, maybe things would be different."

"Hey, I can't control that this was the jawline I was born with," he defended lightly, gesturing towards his face with the back of one hand, "or my eyes. Or cheekbones. Or–"

"Yeah yeah, buddy. You're rocking your natural aesthetic," she threw her arms wide, indicating an invisible audience, "we all know. Pity about your height, right?"

He snorted, "I think I liked you better when you were starstruck. Besides, I'm five ten and a half, so I'm not exactly short."

"Of course you did." Rolling her eyes as her brain caught up with the rest of his sentence, she repeated, "And *a half*," with a laugh in her voice. "Every half-inch counts, right?" Somehow, she managed to deliver this absolutely deadpan.

She had no shame.

His lip curled upwards again at the innuendo, but he let it be. "Well, I could stretch the truth a bit and say I'm six feet tall. If I wear lifts, it's not a lie."

This made her chuckle and shake her head before knowingly observing, "There's *definitely* an element of truth to your narcissist shtick, isn't there?"

"That's the thing about landing jokes, isn't it? The best ones all have a bit of truth to them."

Gemma acknowledged this argument with a jut of her chin. "Yeah. Well, at least, that's what they say. Whoever *they* are."

"A secret society, I'm told. Very exclusive," he tapped the side of his nose with the tip of his index finger and she laughed again.

"Right. Seems legit."

There was an awkward lull in conversation, and just as she was beginning to feel the walls closing in, her companion asked, "So where would you recommend for hiking around here?"

Gemma's building anxiety receded again, and she was glad for the ongoing distraction. The guy was a saint. It did nothing to abate her crush on him. "It depends on what you're after or how far you're willing to travel," she mused aloud. "Bushwalks around here can get you to ocean views, mangrove walks, waterfalls…" she shrugged. "I've always found the short track between Burleigh Heads and Tallebudgera relaxing, but it's not what I'd call a hike. More like a nature walk. If you're looking for epic views and are happy to set aside pretty much a whole day –including the drive there and back– there's Mount Warning. It's not an easy climb, though. At least, not to get to the summit." She was proud that she'd managed it. Once, and she maintained that it had almost killed her, but she had managed it, and that was enough. "Or there's Mount Ngungun, which is a couple of hours' drive north from here and is a much shorter, easier climb with an epic pay off at the top on a clear day. Mount Coolum, also a couple of hours north, is the same."

"A relaxing nature walk sounds pretty good," Everett mused thoughtfully. "And that one's close to here?"

"Yeah, just a short drive down the highway. If you get a few hours free, you should check it out." *Unless we die in this lift,* her brain added testily.

Oblivious to her internal musings, he nodded again. "Right. I'll add that to my To Do list."

"So, you're not just here for the convention?"

"No, I've got a few days reprieve before I have to head back home. Thought I'd do a little sightseeing. Maybe even pat a koala or something."

"I guess flying halfway around the world for a three-day stay does sound a bit rough," Gemma acknowledged with a tilt of her head. Then she made a face. "You know koalas carry chlamydia, right?" They were cute, but there was no way in hell she'd ever touch one again.

Everett let out a bark of almost startled laughter. "What?! That can't be a thing."

"It is," she responded emphatically, slapping her thigh. "Koalas can carry the clap. Google it." Her brows drew down into a frown. "Once we're out of here and there's WiFi and reception again."

He snorted inelegantly. "If you're lying to me, I'll be collecting on that coffee."

Her heart skipped a beat. Was that flirting? No. The lack of oxygen was clearly getting to them both now. But her mouth fired off before her brain, "And when you realise that I'm not, *you* can shout *me* a coffee."

"You've got a deal," he told her with a smirk and extended his hand for her to shake.

Gemma did so with an accompanying shake of her head. "Sure," she told him, mild disbelief colouring her tone. As if he was even going to remember her once they were released and he was swept up in his celebrity duties. Still, it was kind of nice to pretend that he was an ordinary person and that they'd just arranged a coffee date. "I take mine white, no sugar. Preferably a latte, but a flat white will suffice."

"Confident, aren't you?"

"Eh," she shrugged, her lips quirking upwards, "I know my country."

"Well, then, if you're so knowledgeable," he shot back playfully, leaning into her space and nudging her shoulder with his own, unaware that the action set off a flurry of butterflies in her belly that had nothing to do with her fear that they were going to die trapped in the broken-down elevator, "what should I do with my free time here? Other than go for a nature walk where I might encounter a snake and die."

"Melodramatic, much?" Gemma snarked with an exaggerated roll of her eyes. "You're a big boy, you'll be fine." She only barely resisted the urge to reach out and pat his shoulder with blatant (light-hearted) condescension. "What sort of stuff are you into? We've got a bit of everything here: theme parks, beaches, botanic gardens, wildlife sanctuaries…" She drummed her fingers on her thigh as she considered what else was on offer locally. "Australia Zoo's only a couple of hours' drive north, too. That's always a favourite with tourists. So's Byron Bay, which is an hour or so south of here, but…*eh*…it's a bit hipster and a whole lot overrated, if you ask me. Which, I'll remind you, you did."

Everett affected faux offence. "Are you calling me a *tourist?*" He spoke the word as though it was a slur.

Snickering, she shrugged again. "I mean, you kind of are."

"You wound me," he continued his exaggerated act, clutching imaginary pearls. He widened his eyes, the colour more crystalline in the artificial lighting of the elevator. "I thought we were friends now."

There went the butterflies again. "Oh, it takes more than a shared near-death experience to become my friend."

Everett laughed, his eyes crinkling at the corners, and the sound delighted her. "I'll win you over yet, sweetheart."

"Yeah, nah," she responded, "not if you call me sweetheart again." She'd liked it way too much for it to be healthy.

Chuckling, he asked, "Did you just say 'yeah-nah'? What the hell is that?"

"It's Aussie slang for no."

Blinking at her, the incredulous question "Why don't you just say no?" followed, before he added, "And, what, do you say 'nah-yeah' for yes?"

"We do, actually," the corners of her lips twitched at his bewilderment.

"Honestly, it's more a bogan thing than anything, but–"

"Bogan?" The word sounded bizarre in his accent as he tested it out.

Her shoulders lifted and dropped while she raised her hands with their palms facing upwards. "Kind of our version of a redneck or a chav?"

"Right," he drew out the word, clearly amused. "And you just happen to fall into this use of slang at random?"

"When I'm comfortable enough," she responded without thinking, feeling her cheeks burn as she realised what she'd admitted.

Everett held his index finger towards the ceiling, "Ah ha!" he cried, victorious, now using that same finger to poke her shoulder. "You admitted it. We *are* friends now."

Gemma was convinced that he was running out of oxygen now. Still, his enthusiasm was contagious, and she found herself grinning and shaking her head. "Fine, okay, whatever."

"I knew I'd win you over."

"Why?" she queried, feeling bold. "Because I'm a fan? Because of your *obvious–*" sarcasm abounded "*–charm?*"

He wriggled his hips and stretched out his legs, settling in for the long haul. "A little from Column A, a little from Column B."

She hated herself a little for finding the narcissist shtick so endearing, but with his eyes glinting at her and that mischievous smirk on his sinfully scruffy face, she felt powerless to resist it. Still, she didn't need him knowing that.

"I think I liked you better when you were a mysterious celebrity," she twisted his earlier words back at him playfully.

"I've already used that joke, love," he snarked back. "Find some new material."

Gemma opened her mouth to argue, but the elevator seemed to lurch back into life, jerking and clunking and startling her enough that she squealed and clutched at her companion's arm.

"Hey, it's okay," he soothed, rubbing her hand but making no move to throw her off. He glanced up at the ceiling and then the display panel. "I think we're back on the move."

Sure enough, the number had changed to 6 and she could feel the lift descending. Everett pushed himself to his feet and offered Gemma his hand, which she took and allowed him to help her stand. "Thanks," she said softly, suddenly overcome by the realisation that their brief friendship was about to go its separate ways. "Sorry again for freaking out on you."

"What are friends for?" he cajoled, brushing the apology off, unaware of the melancholy turn her thoughts had taken.

She smiled, hoping it met her eyes, and gave his hand one last squeeze. "Well, thank you, then," she said, watching the numbers tick down. She stepped back. "I hope you enjoy the convention. I'm sure your panels will be awesome."

Everett inclined his head, "Are you going to be there?"

Given that he had been her motivating factor for attending, she'd been planning on it but, after this, did attending make it weird? Though, she supposed, it wouldn't be odd for a friend to go watch another friend perform or give speeches or answer fan questions, would it?

She was overthinking it.

"Wouldn't miss it," she informed him as the doors finally slid open at the ground floor. She was oblivious to the crowd of people assembled outside. "I'll be cheering you on from the back of the room, I'm sure."

Then, with a final (if somewhat awkward) wave, she turned around, ducked her head once she saw the large group of people gawking at them, and made her way out of the lift and across the hotel lobby.

* * *

Chapter Two

Pop!Con was a lot of fun. At first, Gemma had worried that attending by herself would be lonely and disappointing, but once she walked through the entrance gate and into the cavernous convention space bustling with people and colours and characters and *life*, her concerns disappeared.

She posed for photos with cosplayers, shopped for new books (and chatted with little-known authors offering free signings with purchases) and even treated herself to a couple of t-shirts for her favourite fandoms. The whole atmosphere felt electric.

A fabulous Ursula cos-player –complete with to-scale foam octopus tentacles and purple body paint– sauntered past her as she stopped to check her watch. She had another hour to kill before the first fantasy TV series panel. She knew that the hardcore fans of the four shows being represented by their respective actors and actresses would already be lined up, vying for the best seats.

Prior to the events of that morning, that would have included her. But she'd had her own private panel experience and she didn't feel the necessity to fight off other fans for the best seat anymore.

Instead, Gemma made her way to a nearby stand selling themed stationery. She was a sucker for funky pens and notebooks. She lost herself amongst the choices, eventually settling on a sparkly unicorn pen and a new hardcover, bound A5 notebook with a rainbow pattern to match. She had no idea what she'd use the notebook for, but she just had to have it. After thanking the vendor, she checked her watch again and realised that she'd spent the better part of half an hour browsing the stand and deliberating over her choices.

"I really need to get a life," she muttered to herself with derision. "Half an hour over a pen."

Gemma made her way across the Convention Centre to the auditorium where the panels were being hosted. As predicted, there was an epic line of eager fans snaking up and down the wide hallway. The FAQs on the website suggested that the doors would be opening twenty minutes prior to the panel's start time, so she figured she'd timed her arrival well enough.

Within a few minutes, the staff opened the doors and began processing the line of attendees. They were quick and efficient and soon she was seated at the end of an aisle in the middle of the room, the rest of the space filling up rapidly. With five minutes to go before start time, a few stragglers sauntered in and took up standing space at the back of the hall, and then the doors were shut.

The panel's host, another Pop!Con volunteer, walked onto the stage to applause (the fans were excitable, ready to see the celebrity guests) and gave a brief explanation of how the panel would run. This year, the host would ask pre-submitted questions, allowing the panel to discuss, then there would be some 'surprise' games played amongst the panellists. Finally, some lucky members of the audience, chosen at random, would get to ask questions of their favourite stars. There were rules, all common sense, and then the first actor was introduced.

The crowd went nuts as the star (a sandy-haired, middle aged man from a TV series Gemma wasn't familiar with) emerged from the wings and crossed the stage, waving and blowing kisses and riling them up further. People were on their feet, cheering and clapping and whistling. Even though she didn't recognise the man, Gemma was swept up in the enthusiastic response to his appearance.

The host asked him some generic questions and he responded in a sweet Irish accent. He was charming and witty, and then the next guest (a young

Australian actress with gorgeous bright red hair and beguiling green eyes) was called upon. The cycle repeated.

Then it was Everett's turn.

Though Gemma hadn't stood up for the previous two panellists, she found herself clamouring to her feet, whooping with delight as he crossed the stage and took his seat. He was wearing the same outfit he had that morning, but someone had coiffed his hair (and had likely dabbed a bit of makeup on him, too.)

"Mister Rhodes," the host greeted him, and the crowd cheered again. "Welcome to Pop!Con!"

Everett grinned and thanked the room for the enthusiastic greeting, exchanging 'Hello's with the other two panellists as well. Gemma imagined they'd all already met backstage but went along with the act for the audience's benefit.

"I hear you've had quite a day already," the host prompted, and Gemma found herself straightening a little in her seat.

Chuckling, Everett nodded. "Yeah," he rubbed the back of his neck, "I got trapped in an elevator this morning."

There were a few gasps and 'aww's of commiseration across the audience. The host leaned forward, "That's, like, my worst nightmare. Were you in there long?"

"Maybe half an hour or so?" Everett shrugged, sweeping his gaze over the crowd. Gemma pretended that he was searching for her. He turned his attention back to the host. "I had some entertaining company," he added with a smirk, and she tried not to let the euphemism sting. Then, in a seeming non-sequitur, he asked, "Tell me, do koalas have chlamydia?"

Raucous laughter erupted across the room. The other panellists demanded an explanation for the question between their own giggles. Even the host seemed perplexed. Clearly, that hadn't been rehearsed at any point. Some part of Gemma enjoyed the fact that she was the only person who understood the link between the subject of conversation and his question. Their own personal joke amongst a room of hundreds of people.

"Is he drunk?" the girl in the seat beside her whispered to her companion.

There was a snort from the next girl along. "Does it matter? God, he's hot."

Despite the fact that, prior to that morning, Gemma might have responded the same way, she felt her stomach turn in discomfort. Everett was a real person, with real feelings and an enjoyable personality.

Was it any wonder his shoulders had initially slumped when he'd first realised that she was a fan? If this was how most of his fans discussed him, she didn't blame him at all. In fact, hearing them objectify him felt wrong, and not just because she felt mildly possessive of him courtesy of their shared experience that morning. (Though she did suspect that might have played a *slight* part in it.)

On stage, with his legs stretched out in front of him as he reclined in his seat, Everett was briefly explaining what had prompted the question. "I said I wanted to cuddle a koala, and I was told that they can carry chlamydia. Is that really a thing?"

Someone in the front row of the audience must have looked it up. A phone was held up and Everett leaned down to look at it. "Oh, you Googled it?" he asked the owner of the phone. There was some light chuckling scattered around the room. "It's actually a thing?"

The blonde head he was addressing bobbed.

"I owe her a coffee," he muttered before he laughed and sat back in his seat with a shake of his head, grinning at the audience. "Australia, *what* is going on with your animals?"

Gemma didn't hear the laughter that followed his playful taunting of the crowd, too stuck on the words he'd murmured beforehand. She willed her heart to calm and talked herself down from the precipice of hope she'd climbed. Just because he remembered the conversation a few hours from when it had happened didn't mean a thing. Her life was not a Julia Roberts rom-com. He wasn't going to show up on her doorstep with a coffee and a smile just for her.

By the time she was paying attention again, the final Pop-Star had been introduced and was already seated on the stage. Gemma eyed the actor (a young, blond guy she didn't recognise) with interest. This was a panel for fantasy TV shows, and she was always looking for new series to get stuck into.

The host kicked off with generic questions about their individual shows, and they each had a chance to answer and bounce off each other. Each actor told tales of shenanigans while filming, they compared notes on some of the crazier things that each of their respective characters had done, and they all knew how to get the most extreme reactions from their fans in attendance.

And reactions there were! Fans laughed, cheered, booed and some even cried. Hands were raised, ovations stood, and applause issued.

Gemma did her best not to fixate on Everett. She tried to focus on the other actors –the Australian actress was vivacious and had some hilarious stories to share– but inevitably her eyes were always drawn back to him. It was magnetism.

Happily Never After had been a fun (if convoluted) fantasy series which had lasted six seasons. Rhodes had played the lead character: the son of Long John Silver, who had been kidnapped by Blackbeard as a small child and then cursed, along with the rest of the fantasy realm, to forget their fairy-tale identities and live in a modern, fictional city until the curse could be broken. His 'cursed' identity had been Detective Steel Waters, and all the cases he and his partner-slash-love-interest had to solve hinted at the fairy-tale characters' origin stories.

Gemma had loved the first season, attempting to guess the fairy-tale identities of the 'real world' or 'cursed' characters, but made no secret of her enjoyment of the second season, where the curse was broken and worlds collided, and the procedural element of the show became more and more ludicrous as time went on. Watching Everett now, she recalled why it worked so well.

He was genuinely charismatic up on the stage. He spoke animatedly, often using his hands or his body for emphasis. It was like he was built to draw focus. His enthusiasm was contagious, and he led the others in conversation, but never spoke over them or interrupted. Though it seemed effortless, Gemma imagined he'd been well coached on how to present himself over the years.

Soon enough, the host directed the panellists to play some of the pre-arranged games. A hat was procured from off-stage, and an assortment of "dares" were contained within. There was laughter as the celebrities were encouraged to sing and dance and make fools of themselves. A guitar appeared during the proceedings, and the young, blond actor was cajoled into playing it and singing for the audience. Unsurprisingly, he had a gorgeous singing voice and could play the instrument well. It smelled of a setup a mile away, but was fun nonetheless.

Finally, the audience was invited to ask questions. Hands were raised all over the room as fans hoped they'd be one of the lucky few selected. Some of the questions were thoughtful, others bordering on obscene, but the four celebrities took them all in their stride. Time was winding down when the girl beside Gemma stuck her hand in the air and one of the room's attendants thrust a microphone into her hand. The girl stood up, giggling into the mic. Heads swivelled to face her.

"This question's for Everett," the girl said, grinning up at the stage.

Gemma sank into her seat as Everett's attention zoned in on them. She watched his eyes narrow and then spark with recognition, even as he charmingly greeted his interviewer.

"My friend and I were wondering," the girl said, gesturing to her other side, where her friend waved towards the stage, "if we could come and give you a hug?"

"Ah, sorry," the host broke in, "that's against the rules–"

"It's fine," Everett interrupted, waving the host off. "A hug won't hurt." He smirked into the audience as they cheered, and the girls who had asked the question squealed. "But how 'bout I come to you?"

It was obvious that the host was not happy with this turn of events. He tried protesting, but Everett was already jogging down the side steps of the stage and up the side aisle of the audience, giving high-fives and stopping for quick selfies along the way. The other Pop-Stars laughed and shook their heads at his antics, while Gemma found herself being pushed and trodden on by the girls in the next two seats as they raced out of the row and leaped at him.

He laughed while they manhandled him, posing for photos (after having forced their phones upon random strangers) and giggling madly. Gemma's smile felt strained, though she told herself that he had volunteered for the spectacle. Besides, she had no right to feel jealous. None whatsoever.

"What about your other friend?" he asked as he finally began to extricate himself from their embrace. He jutted his chin in Gemma's direction.

"Oh," the first girl –the one from the seat directly beside her– said dismissively, "no, we don't know her."

He lifted his dark eyebrows minutely in surprise at Gemma and she shrugged back.

"Here alone?" he asked, though there was thankfully no judgement or pity in his voice. Instead, he grinned, "Then you definitely want a hug."

Her face heated up –whether due to the spotlight literally aimed at her, or the feel of a couple of hundred curious onlookers' attentions, she wasn't sure– and she shook her head. "Oh, no, that's fine. Personal space is a thing." And she felt as though she'd invaded enough of his during their elevator ride of doom earlier that day.

"You're insane," one of the girls still lingering at his side insisted, shaking her head.

Rolling her eyes, Gemma stood to allow them past her to take their seats again. "The poor guy's about to head into Photo Ops," she justified, turning back to offer Everett a shrug. "Just because people pay to meet you doesn't mean you should feel obligated to do anything you're not comfortable with, is all."

She hadn't meant to grandstand, but she was suddenly passionate about a person's right to maintain healthy boundaries. It wasn't even because she was jealous. It wasn't. Well, not entirely.

Something in his expression softened, though he shook himself and grinned wolfishly at her. "I'm not offering services that I don't enjoy myself, love," he informed her, much to the crowd's delight, if their whooping was anything to go by. "But you do make a valid point, regardless. Some of the younger talent–" here he shot a pointed stare up at the stage, where the young, blond guy rolled his eyes right back "–might feel pressure to do things they normally wouldn't."

"Speaking of," the host cut in, having made his way down from the stage himself, a couple of security guards at his side, "we really need to wrap this up now."

"Coming to Photo Ops?" Everett asked her, taking a couple of steps backwards.

Gemma had already bought the ticket, no matter how awkward that felt now. She nodded stiffly, and there was something akin to victory in his gaze as he allowed himself to be led back to the stage. He cracked snide jokes along the way, which the audience lapped up.

The host closed the panel, but Gemma was lost in her own thoughts for the remaining few minutes. It wasn't until people around her began gathering their things and getting to their feet that she shook herself and made her way out of the auditorium.

* * *

"Next!"

Standing in line for Photo Ops later that afternoon, Gemma shuffled forward. Around her, a queue of mostly women chattered and gushed about the poses they wished they could convince Everett to make with them. She considered ditching her ticket, but that would be an epic waste of money and she knew that she'd ultimately regret it. A photo to remind her of how insane this situation had turned out was probably warranted. Besides, she didn't need to touch him. Again. They could just smile for the camera and that would be that.

"Next!"

More shuffling forward. She was near the back of the line, having debated with herself for too long to just get it over and done with. Each photo seemed to be taking less than 30 seconds, though, which was simultaneously a blessing and a curse. A blessing because it meant the line went quickly and she'd only have to endure the awkwardness of their next encounter for a few moments at worst, and a curse because her anxiety ratcheted the closer she came to her own turn in the booth.

"Next!"

Gemma fiddled with the bags in her hands. She knew she was being silly. After this bizarre day was over, he'd forget all about her and she could romanticise the events in her head as she returned to her ordinary life.

"Tickets, hun?" The volunteer staffer asked her when she was the third person in line. She pulled out her phone and showed her QR code, and the volunteer scanned it. "Thanks."

Gemma nodded, her stomach now in knots. What was wrong with her? Outside of finding the whole situation beyond far-fetched, she had to acknowledge that he'd seemed almost pleased to hear that she'd be seeing him again. But that made her suspicious because she couldn't understand why.

It wasn't that she didn't think she was attractive. She was usually quite comfortable in her own skin, despite the self-deprecating jokes she cracked when she was anxious. But she couldn't compare to the women in his world, with their personal trainers and chefs and makeup artists on call. Women who had an entire team of staff that dressed them and instructed them on how to best present themselves. She couldn't compete with them.

Not that there was any actual reason to think she had to.

He'd called them friends, not anything that even remotely suggested she was in with a shot.

And she didn't want to be.

Not really.

Except…well, he was Everett Rhodes, the actor whose character she'd all but fallen in love with from the moment he'd swung onto her screen, clinging to a rope while brandishing a sword and some hilarious innuendo.

So, okay, some part of her might have liked it if he was a bit into her.

But he wasn't, so it didn't matter.

"Hun, you're up." The same volunteer from before shook her from her thoughts.

Swallowing, and hoping her nerves weren't anywhere near as obvious outwardly, she ducked into the booth.

"Gemma!" He beamed at her, "I was beginning to think you'd stood me up here."

She had no witty comeback for that, and instead blushed and shifted her footing. "You're kind of popular. There was a pretty healthy line."

Beside the photographer, a lady in a pinstriped pantsuit cleared her throat and tapped her watch. Everett rolled his eyes. "Alright, alright," he waved her off, before turning to Gemma. "My handler's a bit impatient."

"Your handler has her hands full," she responded, genuine empathy for the professionally dressed woman seeping into her tone, "if you've been pulling stunts like you did at the panel all day."

His blue eyes sparkled with mischief, and she was beginning to suspect that he actually hadn't had to do much acting when it came to the handsome rogue he'd played on TV. "Well, are you going to drop those–" he gestured to her bags "–and come pose for a photo? You're holding up the whole line now, you know."

Though she knew he was being playful, she huffed at him. "You're nowhere near as charming as you think you are."

"And yet you paid for this experience, darling."

Gemma stepped up to his side. "Don't remind me." She was fighting off a smile, damn him.

"So, am I allowed to hug you for this photo?"

"Don't people normally ask you that?"

Everett laughed and nodded, "Yeah. It's a nice change of pace, I'll grant you that." He extended his arms and batted his lashes exaggeratedly. "Please?"

Biting back the urge to tell him it wasn't fair to play on her obvious crush on him, she sighed and wrapped her arms around him. He'd been working all day, and it was a warm day at that (given that it was the middle of November and it was the Gold Coast), but he smelled amazing. His cologne was somehow spicy and sweet all at once, and there was a hint of something else –something slightly earthy that she assumed was just his natural scent– that sent a jolt of *want* straight through her.

"Okay, smiling at the camera," the photographer requested, "Three, two, one – got it!"

"There now," Everett said, slowly pulling away, leaving his hands on her shoulders as he teased, "wasn't that bad, was it?"

"Shut up," she chuckled, shaking her head. The same feeling of melancholy that she'd felt in the lift settled over her as she realised that this was it – this was the actual end – and she smiled softly at him. "But thank you for today."

Before he could respond, she snatched up her bags and raced out through the designated exit to wait for her printout.

Her heart didn't stop racing until she was back in her hotel room, staring out of the city view and daydreaming about hypotheticals and what might have been if her life actually was some sort of romantic comedy chick flick come to life.

* * *

Dusk turned to early evening, the darkening of the sky finally bringing down the heat of the day. From the vantage point of her hotel window, Gemma watched the city beneath her begin to twinkle as lights switched on, fending off the oncoming darkness. She hadn't been able to stretch her budget for an ocean view room, but at night-time she had zero complaints, finding the glittering colours against the inky blackness mesmerising.

She was contemplating climbing back out of bed –where she had face-planted after such an action-packed day– to go out in search of food when the sudden, high-pitched ringing of the phone on the bedside table almost gave her a heart attack.

"Hello?" she asked cautiously, wondering whether the front desk had an issue with her credit card or something. She couldn't imagine why anyone else would be calling her room.

A male voice cleared his throat. "Gemma?"

"Everett?" Her voice went up an octave and she cringed at how shrill she sounded. She was trying to decide whether this was weird or exciting. "How'd you get my room number?"

"I asked the front desk." He paused, then quietly added, "I just realised that this could come off as stalking, and I apologise. I'm not that guy. I don't do the creeper thing."

Which is what all 'nice guys' say, she mused silently, but chastised herself immediately for it. He'd been nothing but genuinely friendly –if a little flirty and playful once he'd realised that she wasn't going to jump him– and she thought that it was entirely possible that he was just a little lonely. She could relate to that.

With that last thought, she opted to give him the benefit of the doubt. "It's fine. A bit surprising, but I feel like if one of us was going to stalk the other, it would be around the other way."

He made a noise that sounded as though he'd snorted inelegantly. "Crazy fangirl, right?"

"The craziest."

"I'm beginning to suspect you're all talk on that front, I'm afraid."

There went her heart, fluttering again. Along the phone line, she imagined that his voice had dipped low and flirtatious.

"So, uh, why did you call?" It was an awkward segue, but she couldn't go around thinking that he was getting all sexy with her.

"I was wondering if you'd be interested in joining me for dinner?"

She pulled away from the receiver and stared at it for a moment. Had her epic celebrity crush just invited her to dinner? Was she being pranked?

"-ma?" She could vaguely hear him questioning.

Bringing the receiver back to her ear, she apologised, then said, "Um, dinner? Tonight?"

"If you haven't already eaten," he affirmed.

Was this a date? Just friends? Did he want to go somewhere fancy, or was this a 'wander through Surfers Paradise until some sort of casual dining inspiration strikes' sort of deal? "Uh…"

"You know what? Hang on."

"Wait, what?" She responded, but there was no reply, only a dial tone. Had he decided she wasn't worth the effort?

There was a knock at the door. She hung up the phone, guessing who she'd find on the other side once she crossed the room and opened it.

Sure enough, he was grinning at her when she swung the door open. "May

I come in?"

Stepping aside, Gemma swept her hand outwards. "Knock yourself out."

"I figured talking in person would be easier," he explained, striding over to the window and whistling. "Lovely view. I'm on the opposite side of the building. I get stunning ocean views by day, but by night, everything is dark and dull."

Her lips pulled upwards. What was it they said about great minds?

Turning back to face her, he asked, "So, have you eaten?"

"No, but…I don't want to impose."

"Impose?" Everett arched one of those expressive dark eyebrows at her. "I practically had to bribe the woman at the desk to patch me through to your room just to ask for the pleasure of your company, but you're afraid that you're going to impose upon my plans?" He scoffed lightly. "Love, I take it back. You *are* crazy."

She could feel her cheeks heating up with a blush. "Why me?"

"We're friends now, remember? And I'd rather dine with a friend than alone."

"I'd have thought you'd be friends with some of the other *Pop-Stars*," she argued back, aiming for nonchalant.

"And yet, you're the first person I've had a genuine conversation with here."

Gemma blinked, taken aback. "Oh. Really?"

Everett shrugged, but she thought she could read dejection in his expression. Wondering if she was going soft, she felt herself giving in. "Is this, um, I mean…do I need to get changed into something a bit more formal?" She'd brought one dress along with her just in case she decided to spoil herself with a fancy meal before she returned to the monotony of her life.

She was still wearing her jeans and Disney shirt, while he was now in black slacks and a light grey, short sleeved, button down shirt. The top two buttons were popped, and she stuck her hand into her back pocket to prevent herself from reaching out and smoothing his collar and the material over his chest.

Everett offered her an easy smile and a shake of his head. "What you're wearing is fine. There was a little Vietnamese place down the street that caught my eye." He caught himself, cocking his head and flushing a little. It was stupidly endearing. "Do you like Vietnamese food?"

"I do," Gemma nodded, tucking an errant strand of hair behind her ear. "When, um, when did you want to go?"

"Now?" he rubbed the back of his neck, "If you don't have any other plans?"

"Alright, just…just give me two seconds." She waved around the room. "Make yourself at home. I've just gotta…" she threw a thumb over her shoulder in the general direction of the bathroom. "I'll be right back."

Inside the bathroom, with the door securely closed and locked, Gemma leaned back against it and did her best to calm her racing heart with measured breathing. She still had no real idea what his intentions were. He'd mentioned dining as friends, and she had to take his words at face value. But the lengths he'd gone to in order to track her down made her suspect he might want more, and she wasn't certain she would actually be willing to go down that path with him, no matter how intense her crush was.

"Friend," she muttered to herself, making that her new mantra. She pushed off the door and went to the toilet, trained from childhood to pee before any outing. She met her reflection as she washed her hands in the basin. "Random, hot, celebrity friend who will forget all about me when he returns to his own real life."

That was the part that was bothering her the most. She couldn't afford to get attached to him as a real person, not when they'd both go their separate ways and lead separate lives and never speak again after this crazy weekend. It was much easier having a crush on an actor that she'd never get to know.

When she exited the bathroom, she found him sitting on the edge of her bed, scrolling through his phone. He glanced up and beamed at her. "Good to go?"

"Yep," she popped the 'p', rocking back on her heels. "Lead the way." She snagged her handbag –containing her phone and room key– from the bedside table as she passed it.

The walk to the restaurant was short and surprisingly comfortable. He asked about her day, and she told him about the authors she'd met, and he in turn asked questions about her favourite novels –all fantasy, which wasn't a surprise to him– and then confessed that he shared her taste in literature.

"I don't watch a lot of TV," he explained, "but I do love to read. And I agree – Neil Gaiman is brilliant."

Gemma felt herself getting excited in her usual fangirl way, only this time she was sharing her excitement and her passion with him about her favourite author. They chatted and laughed and shared their favourite quotes and, before she knew it, they were sliding into opposing sides of a booth at the restaurant, and she'd almost forgotten that he wasn't just another 'normal' acquaintance.

They placed their orders after a quick perusal of the brief menu – he went for a bowl of pho while she opted for the pork belly vermicelli noodle salad – and then they were engrossed in conversation again. She mentioned her annoying older brother, Brennan, and he snickered.

"I've an older brother as well," he said, and this genuinely surprised her. She hadn't really investigated his life story, even if she was a rabid fangirl.

"Really? What's he like?"

"Well, I'm the handsome one," Everett teased, pausing to thank the waitress as she placed their meals in front of them, and Gemma echoed his sentiments. "But he's broader, taller, blond and tanned. Star rugby player and generally my Mum's favourite. Not that she'd ever admit such a thing."

"I hate him already," she informed him matter-of-factly, and he snorted.

"Ta, love, but Charlie's alright. He stepped up when Dad shot through and helped Mum wrangle me during my wayward youth."

Without thinking, she reached across the small table and placed her hand on his forearm. "I'm sorry about your Dad," she told him, blushing and removing her hand once she'd realised what she'd done. She moved her hands to her lap, eyes downcast. "I'm, uh, well technically I was a foster kid, but I tell people I'm adopted."

It was easier that way. Easier than having to explain that her biological parents were considered unfit, but had refused to put her up for adoption until she was past the age where anyone might actually want her. She hadn't seen or heard from them since her early teens, and she preferred it that way.

She cleared her throat into the expectant silence that had met her declaration. "The last family I stayed with…Brennan's family?" She paused and shrugged. "Well, really, it was just him and his Dad, Marcus. They kept me for four years, from when I was 14 until I was 18, and then let me stay even though they weren't obligated to. They're my family, even if it's not legit, you know?"

She cursed herself for bringing down the mood and startled when he raised her chin with his index finger. "Your family sound like lovely people," he told her earnestly. "I'm glad you found them."

"Me too," she agreed quietly, then busied herself with her food.

"So…what do you do?" he asked, attempting to put their conversation to rights. When she looked up at him in askance, he extrapolated, "For work?"

"I'm a nurse," she responded, and his eyes widened in surprise and awe. "It's not as exciting as it sounds, I promise. It's mostly paperwork."

He spooned another mouthful of his soup into his mouth, and she averted her gaze, determined not to sexualise the simple act of eating pho. "But a noble profession. You help people." She didn't think she'd ever forget the way his smile reached his eyes. "Love, that's wonderful."

"I do enjoy it," Gemma admitted, chewing thoughtfully. "Every day is different and brings new challenges." She cringed as the words left her mouth. "I know, I know — that sounds like the sort of answer I'd give in a job interview, but it's true. Plus, I love the people I work with. We're pretty close-knit."

"Yeah, I miss my team from *Happily*," he nodded. "By the end there, we were basically family."

"I've never really given much thought to how transient your work is," the words left her mouth before she could filter them, but the more she thought about it, the more she realised that his life, and lifestyle, wasn't without its risks. "I mean, as a fan, I never stopped to think about the fact that if your series ends or your character is killed off, you have to move on to something else, and even then, that's not guaranteed, is it?" Now she frowned. "And Hollywood's kind of cutthroat, right? Too many actors, not enough roles?"

Everett shrugged. "It's not as though we're not paid well when we are successful, so that mitigates the risk somewhat."

"Somewhat, sure, but there are new faces popping up every day and–"

"You're definitely a glass half empty type, aren't you?" he chuckled, cutting her off. "There's always work, regardless of whether I'm currently acting or not. For example," he sat back and extended his arms, "I'm here working. I'm handsomely paid to travel and talk and enjoy myself. It's not an awful life to lead, I assure you."

"You meet crazies," she refuted, pointing at herself with her chopsticks, "and get pawed at, asked degrading or inane questions on repeat, and nothing about your life is really private. I'm guessing that you don't get to see your friends and family often, unless you're fortunate enough to work near them or with them." Her cheeks coloured, not having intended on ranting like that. "And, yeah, I know I'm part of the problem, given that I'm one of those fans with the stupid questions and the pawing…"

"You've not pawed at me yet, love. I'd recall such a thing, I'm sure of it."

Gemma rolled her eyes, trying not to be affected by his flirtatious wink. "I'm serious. Speaking as a fan, I appreciate the sacrifices you make for my entertainment."

His gaze softened. "Well, I appreciate your appreciation."

"That's ridiculous," she laughed, shaking her head.

"Why? You essentially said it yourself: without fans, such as yourself, there'd be no demand for my profession or the services that come with it."

"That's not the point I was trying to make, and you know it." She jabbed her chopsticks in his direction, punctuating her reprimand.

Blue eyes glinted with mirth. "Yes, but it's entertaining to rile you up." He smirked at her continued frowning. "Seriously, Gemma, it's sweet that you're concerned. However, I truly enjoy my life: risks and sacrifices and all. Just as I imagine you enjoy yours." He was eating the ramen from his bowl now, gesticulating with his own chopsticks. "And, to be honest," he added after his next mouthful, "I couldn't imagine doing what you do. Dealing with injured, sick, upset, or grieving people, and real blood and guts and bodily fluids?" He shuddered. "No thank you."

"Okay, you make valid points," she conceded, now at the point where she was attempting to nab the remaining dregs of her salad from her bowl, the tiny threads of remaining noodle refusing to lift. "I just really hadn't given that much thought to just how much your lives are disrupted as actors." She gave up on the last few strands of lettuce, setting her chopsticks down primly in her bowl and pushing it aside. "So now would be your opportunity to vent if you wanted to."

Done with his own meal, Everett chuckled and wiped his mouth with a napkin. "I'll admit that I do miss my family at times, but that was bound to happen whether I'd moved away to be an actor or if I'd moved away to be an accountant." She crinkled her nose at the latter suggestion, causing him to smirk. "I'm shit at maths, so that was never going to pan out."

"Oh, what a shame you couldn't follow that dream," she responded, tone dry.

"Guess I'll just have to settle with fame and fortune instead."

"Devastating, I'm sure."

Everett nodded with a grin, then stretched, closing his eyes and making a sound of satisfaction that Gemma decided was not appropriate for their current setting. "Well, that was a delightful meal," he said, unaware of the turmoil his simple action had caused within her. He smiled warmly across the table at her. "Thank you again for joining me. I suppose another casualty of my career has been my social life."

Words. You need to use words now. She cleared her throat and fought back her blush, the sound he'd made still echoing around in her brain. "Uh, yeah, no...thank you for inviting me."

His eyebrows drew downwards. "Are you alright?"

"Yeah, yeah, totally fine," she brushed his concern aside, feeling ridiculous for how quickly her thoughts had turned creepy fangirl. "I just lost myself in thought for a second there, I'm sorry."

"Should I be offended that I'm no longer holding your attention?" He teased.

If only you knew, she thought at him before shaking her head and forcing a light laugh. "I promise it won't happen again."

Cocking his head, he mused, "Somehow, love, I don't believe you."

* * *

They had a brief argument about paying the bill. Gemma didn't like the idea of him paying for her because it made her uncomfortable. They weren't dating and they'd only met that morning. She wasn't the sort of person who liked to feel beholden to anyone else, either, nor did she want him to think that she expected him to pay because he was presumably rather wealthy.

"If it's that big an issue," he eventually huffed in frustration, waving his credit card over the contactless reader while she squawked indignantly, "*you* can buy *me* dinner tomorrow night."

Her hazel eyes went wide, and she could feel herself gaping at him, which he ignored, nodding at the restaurant staff before turning on his heel and waltzing out the door. She hastened after him. "That's presumptuous of you."

They fell into step alongside each other leaving the restaurant. Instead of taking the direct route to the hotel though, Everett looked both ways across the esplanade and crossed the road to the oceanside footpath. "Presumptuous, yes, but am I wrong?"

Trotting a little to keep up with his long strides, she scowled. "There's that narcissism."

"You said you liked that about me."

He had no business smirking at her like that, lit up as he was by streetlights, his dark hair artfully ruffled by the sea breeze. Gemma shrugged, aiming for nonchalance. "Well, that was when you were an abstract concept built up in my head and not a real person that I actually know."

"I think you *like* the real me." He teased, bending to nudge her shoulder with his upper arm.

Bolstered by his casual touch, she paused her strolling and reached up and patted him condescendingly on his scruffy cheek. "You tell yourself that, bud." And her hand did not tingle, and her stomach did not do a somersault at the thrill of having touched his pretty face. Nope. Not at all.

God, she should have had wine with dinner.

There was mischief in his eyes, but he didn't challenge her. Instead, he swung his arm around her shoulders, recommencing their walk, and asked, "What are your plans after tomorrow?"

"Uh…" she blinked, wondering if he was for real, "I'm going home?" Technically, she would be checking out of her room before 10 a.m. the next morning and storing her belongings in her car while she attended the final day of the weekend convention.

"Oh," her stomach did that flip-flopping thing at the obvious disappointment in his tone, "and directly back to work? Or would you be able to play tour guide to a hopelessly lost new friend?"

"Surely your agent or assistant or whatever could organise you an actual tour guide."

"I suppose they could," he mused, but he sounded disinterested. "I was hopeful that you might be interested, though."

That statement sounded more loaded than it appeared, and she wondered if maybe her crush on him was inventing a subtext that didn't exist.

Still, she answered cautiously, "Don't get me wrong, I am very interested," and she was glad that they were walking, and that it was mostly dark, and that he couldn't see the blush creeping up her neck and suffusing her cheeks, "but I'm checking out tomorrow. I mean, I guess I could still make the drive back." It was about an hour and a half from her home on the north side of Brisbane to Surfer's Paradise when traffic was flowing. Inconvenient, but she already knew that she'd kick herself for eternity if she didn't give in to his request.

"Hmm," he mused, his fingers drumming against her shoulder as he considered how he might proceed, "we'll cross that particular bridge when we come to it, then. You're not expected back at work immediately?"

"No, I took a few extra days off." The thing was, she was kind of a workaholic. Her boss had practically forced her to take an entire week of her accrued annual leave, demanding that she go out and live a little.

"Excellent!" Everett was livening up again. He reminded her of an overgrown five-year-old. "And will I see you at the convention tomorrow?"

She shook her head. "No. I'll attend your final panel, but I don't collect autographs, so I won't visit the signing booths, and I've got my photo for the weekend." It felt strange to say such a thing so coolly. Part of her wondered if maybe she'd passed out in the lift that morning and this was all some sort of oxygen-deprived hallucination.

"Wait for me after the panel, then. That's my final obligation for the weekend."

Gemma knew she was going to agree, even though she considered at least pretending to think over her options. "Alright. Here," she walked them over to a nearby garden bed, surrounded by a concrete wall which sat about knee height. She sat down on top of it, pulling a pen and little notepad from her handbag. Using the space beside her as an impromptu tabletop, she scrawled her number and tore the page from the notepad. "Here's my number," she informed him, handing it over. "I'll loiter after your panel, and you can text or call and let me know where to meet you."

Everett took the paper and pulled out his phone, immediately typing the digits in and calling her. "And now you have my number, too."

She pulled her phone from her pocket and smirked at the Australian number, confirming the suspicion that she'd had all those hours earlier in the lift. "Not even handsomely paid Pop-Stars can afford exorbitant roaming charges, huh?"

He just shrugged.

* * *

Chapter Three

Gemma was climbing out of the shower the next morning when there was a knock at her door. She glanced at the clock on her bedside table as she wrapped her towel snugly around her, scandalised to find that it wasn't even yet 8 a.m.

Towel secured, she opened the door and then wished she hadn't.

Once again dressed as sin personified in a form fitting polo and jeans, Everett Rhodes stood in front of her holding out a takeaway coffee. He blinked in surprise. "Um, good morning."

It was early, she was barely awake and not at all caffeinated, and she was standing naked in front of her crush, save for a towel. Not to mention the fact that she wasn't wearing a lick of makeup, and her hair was wet and bedraggled from the shower. "Hi?"

He seemed to shake himself. The tips of his ears turned pink, and his gaze softened, turning sheepish. "I apologise," he extended the coffee cup. "I just wanted to bring you this. I believe I owe you, after all."

"Uh," she was still clutching her towel, now starting to feel awkward, "thank you. That's sweet. You didn't have to. Just, um, pop it down on the coffee table there." She stood aside to let him in, regardless of her state of undress. She wasn't certain why.

He complied and then rubbed his palms on his jeans, seemingly anxious now himself. "Right, well, I'll just…" he gestured back towards the door.

She nodded, not sure what else to say or do.

As he opened the door, she managed to find her voice again. "Everett, thank you. For the coffee." She smiled, hoping that he understood that, as awkward as she was being, she wasn't backing off from their odd friendship. "I'll text later."

"I look forward to it."

***

'Thanks again for the coffee!' Gemma typed into her phone after the caffeine hit had started to sink in. *'I needed it.'* She added a zombie emoji, then pressed send, slipping her phone into her pocket and doing a last sweep over her hotel room, making sure she wasn't leaving anything behind.

She felt a little sad to be leaving her home of the last couple of nights, but another full day at the convention awaited her, as did another evening with Everett.

She'd made more effort with her appearance based on that last fact, wearing jeans that she felt made her butt look amazing, and a soft pink, flowing blouse. She'd even worn mascara and eyeliner and a bit of lip gloss, forgoing her usual 'foundation only' makeup regime. She felt pretty and much more confident than she had the previous evening.

Wheeling her suitcase out of her room, she stepped into the lift and hoped that this time there wouldn't be any surprise stops between her room and the ground floor. Fate seemed to smile upon her, because the trip was smooth and without any interruptions, and it wasn't long before she was handing over her room key and checking out.

She hopped back into the lift, travelling down to the basement car park, and tossed her suitcase into the boot of her little SUV. Then she was off.

It was a short drive from the heart of Surfer's Paradise into the Convention Centre at Broadbeach. The car park beneath the Convention Centre was filling quickly when she arrived, and she took a photo with her phone to remind herself of which section she'd parked in. (Brennan still hadn't let her forget the time she'd called him in a panic because she'd 'lost' her car in a shopping centre car park.)

She joined the line of ticket holders waiting to enter and was soon swept up in another day of panels, shopping and admiring cosplayers.

When she stopped for lunch, she pulled out her phone and realised with a start that Everett had replied to her text.

'My pleasure, love. Enjoy the con. See you tonight.' A simple enough text, but it was followed up with the 'kiss blowing' emoji.

He was quite a tactile person, Gemma reasoned, and generous with his affection. She was the opposite, finding being demonstrative difficult unless she was truly comfortable with the other person. Many people had accused her of being cold, prickly, and standoffish, but it was a fear of being hurt, ridiculed, and rejected that had her walls up so high. The curse of the foster child, she supposed.

And yet it hadn't stopped Everett from persevering with his displays of easy warmth. In less than 24 hours, he'd gotten her to unwind enough to playfully reach out and touch him (and when she closed her eyes, she could recall with clarity how surprisingly soft the scruff on his cheek had felt against her fingers) and that scared her.

She was becoming far too attached to him. Gemma was under no illusions that they'd maintain their 'friendship' once he went back to Hollywood. She was a nobody, and he was a celebrity. Why would he want to keep in touch? She was just entertainment for him while he visited a strange country on his own. He probably picked up a random girl to toy with at every port.

But still she wished they could be more: that she could somehow live out her rom-com fantasy and become his friend, keep in touch, and eventually fall into a relationship and live happily ever after.

With a sigh, she shook her head free of the silly thoughts. *Just enjoy what you can get while you can get it,* she told herself, typing back a message wishing him an enjoyable afternoon, then sinking her teeth into the burger she'd bought.

Her afternoon went as quickly as her morning, and –as promised– she lined up for the last of the fantasy TV show panels for the weekend. There were a couple of different actors in this one, and it was more structured than the previous panel, with a theme and guided discussion from the host.

As with the other panel, Gemma's eyes were glued to Everett. He was in his element, his arms and hands waving as he excitedly answered questions or responded to something another panellist had said. He winked and flirted with the others on stage, waggling his eyebrows at the audience and playing up that narcissistic shtick that she found amusing.

It was almost startling to realise that he was being genuinely himself –if a little more polished– because he was no different when it was just the two of them. And, while he was an actor, she didn't think he was that good that he could keep up the act 24/7.

The panel closed with another Q&A segment with the audience but, to Gemma's absolute relief, the excitement of the previous day's session was not repeated. She chatted with a couple of other audience members on the way out the door and checked her watch. It was half past four, and the convention ended at six, but Everett had told her to check in after the panel was over.

Her phone buzzed in her hand as she slid it from her pocket and she answered the call, "Someone's eager," she teased.

"What can I say, love? You look delectable in those jeans."

She swallowed, her heart rate increasing as she looked around, wondering where he was that he could see her, but she couldn't see him. "I know," she tried to draw on the confidence that she'd felt when she'd pulled them on. "That's why I'm wearing them."

There was a moment of silence and his voice lowered, "For me?"

"Well, I mean, for me, really," she coughed, her cheeks burning, "but… maybe a little for you?"

Why was she being honest here? Why couldn't she deny her actual motivations and just tell him that she wore them because they made her feel good and just leave it at that?

There was more stunned silence and she panicked. "I mean," she added, her mouth doing that thing where it worked before her brain could filter her words, "you can't be seen out in public with someone who looks like a homeless person."

"Gemma…" She couldn't work out his tone, and she'd previously thought herself an Everett Rhodes expert.

"So, are we going to meet up in person, or are you leaning in to this new stalker vibe?" Cutting him off and teasing him saved face. The wide hallway outside the auditorium had emptied out and she spun around slowly, looking for him once more.

There was a chuckle down the phone line, but she jumped at the murmured "Behind you, love," that was very much decidedly spoken in person.

With her hand to her chest, Gemma spun around. "Jesus," she hissed, slapping his chest, "don't do that!"

He caught her hand, having the grace to duck his head and blink balefully at her. "I apologise."

"Don't do the puppy-dog eyes," she demanded, looking away to fight off her amusement.

It was unfair that he could get under her skin so easily. Unfair that he had such a penetrating gaze and a jawline that undermined all of her inbuilt defences. Unfair that –though he knew he was attractive– he wasn't arrogant and easy to dismiss based on a hideous personality.

"Why, darling?" he asked, pulling out the big guns, his accent curling around the endearment and sending her nerve endings skittering. Hell, he could probably feel her pulse jump, given that he was still holding her hand, his thumb smoothing over the backs of her fingers.

Gemma summoned her pride and indignation. She was not humiliating herself for this man. Jutting her chin, she attempted to regard him with disdain. "Begging for compliments doesn't suit you."

The actor's lips spread into a wide grin, and he took pity on her, releasing her hand. "I love how feisty you get."

"You're a strange creature, Rhodes."

"I've never claimed otherwise." He shrugged, smiling maddeningly at her.

(That smile was going to be the death of her, she just knew it.)

"Anyway, you're out here in public without a handler," she observed, beginning to walk down the hallway towards the nearest exit. He followed her lead without question. "Does this mean you're officially a free man?"

From the corner of her eye, she watched him nod happily. "For the next four days, at any rate."

"So…you fly out on Friday?" The thought was upsetting, further proof that she was far more attached than she had any right to be. She hoped that her question came off light and airy.

"Early Thursday afternoon." And now she was imagining a hint of disappointment in his tone. She was clearly projecting again.

"From Brisbane? I'm assuming you're going back to LA?"

This time his nod was slower, less jovial. "Yeah. I've got a couple of auditions lined up when I get back."

She turned her head, smiling genuinely at that revelation. "That's awesome! TV roles or movies?"

"You know I'm technically not supposed to give out any of this information, don't you?"

"And here I was, thinking that you trusted the random stranger you met less than 48 hours ago with all of your deepest, darkest secrets."

Everett chuckled. "Alright, alright, there's no real harm in giving you vague answers anyway."

"I'm touched, Everett, truly," she snarked back, enjoying the snicker it earned her before realising they were standing in the middle of the foyer.

It was late in the day, so there weren't many people milling about, but someone would recognise him before too long if they stayed there.

"But before you satisfy my curiosity–" and she ignored his mutterings about other things he could satisfy, finally coming to realise that he was just flirtatious by nature "–what's the plan from here? My car's parked downstairs, but we can leave it and come back later if you wanted to stay local. Or…I don't know, it's still too early for dinner, so…" she trailed off gracelessly, shrugging.

Being that it was the middle of November, even though it was inching towards five o'clock in the evening, the sun was still high in the sky outside. She bit her lip, then offered, "Have you had a chance to see much of the Coast?"

The actor shook his head ruefully. "Sadly, no. I only arrived Thursday, slept most of the day –and night, boring sod that I am– and then it was work from Friday morning onward. Until a lovely woman almost had a heart attack in my lift yesterday morning, anyway."

Snorting, she rolled her eyes. "That was bordering on cheesy, bud. You're losing your touch."

He appeared set to respond with another vaguely naughty rejoinder, but stopped himself and smirked instead. "I believe you were about to suggest a way for us to entertain ourselves before that dinner you promised me?"

"Nothing special," she insisted, "just a drive down to Burleigh. We can walk along the esplanade, you can get a feel for the slightly less tourist-y beachfront, and then maybe we could grab some fish 'n chips or seafood for dinner? Unless you're allergic or don't like it, or aren't in the mood–"

"That sounds perfect, Gemma." He took up her hand and offered her a warm smile. "I haven't been to a proper chippie since my last trip home."

Something electric seemed to pass between them in that moment, and she had to fight off the sudden urge to pull him down for a kiss. She cleared her throat, and the spell was broken.

"Just don't desecrate our chips with vinegar," she found herself finding her footing again. "I won't stand for that."

"Fine, but no tomato sauce," he bartered back.

"Tartare?"

"On the side."

"Of course!"

* * *

Gemma was glad that she'd cleaned out her car before she'd driven down for the weekend. She wasn't a messy person, but it was nice to not have to apologise for a pile of clothes and paperwork cluttering up her passenger seat as he slid into it.

It was five o'clock on a Sunday, so the traffic wasn't too terrible, and Gemma zipped up the Gold Coast Highway easily, the trip taking about

41

fifteen minutes including the barrage of traffic lights along it. She'd never really understood why it was called a highway when it was more a suburban road, lined by shops and restaurants. A couple of years earlier, the council had put a tram line in, running parallel to the main road as well, which also often slowed down traffic.

Her newfound friend amused himself by flipping through the music on her phone –connected via Bluetooth– and choosing songs from her library that he quite enjoyed.

It wasn't until she was about to pull into a park along the esplanade that he chortled.

"Gemma, really?" Everett sounded equal parts fond and incredulous.

"What?" she asked, concentrating on putting the car in park and turning off the engine before she turned in her seat to face him.

He held up her phone.

Oh, she realised, once more feeling herself blushing. Still, she attempted defiance. "What?"

"*Me*. You have *me* on your playlist."

The song was from the sole musical episode of *Happily Never After.*

"It's a fun song."

"Love, it's ridiculous." He was shaking his head. "I'm this close," he held up his free hand, pinching his index finger and thumb closely together without allowing them to touch, "to suspecting you are actually one of the crazies. Should I be concerned that you're going to kidnap me and tie me to a chair somewhere?"

"Don't be stupid," Gemma scoffed, unbuckling her seat belt, "you'd probably enjoy that." She reached for her phone. "Besides, I like musicals of all sorts. You'll find I have quite the selection on here, including the entire series soundtrack of *Galavant.*"

He cocked his head to the side, curious. "What's gallivant?"

"I can actually hear you spelling it wrong," she laughed, opening her door to climb out of the car. He did the same and she locked her car with the press of a button, tucking her keys into her pocket as she extrapolated, "*Galavant* was a musical sit-com about knights and kings and princesses that lasted all of two short seasons but was hilarious and wonderful." She considered the fact that he shared her taste in literature and added, "I think you'd enjoy it."

Instead of mocking her like her ex-boyfriend had when she'd suggested he watch it with her, Everett bobbed his head thoughtfully as they began to wander aimlessly down the footpath that ran alongside the beach. "I'll try my best to remember it."

"It's streaming on Disney plus at the moment. Well, at least it is here." She barely refrained from suggesting they grab some snacks after dinner and go back to his hotel room to watch it, lest he think she was suggesting the old 'Netflix and Chill' routine.

His lip curled upwards, and she felt as though he'd read her mind anyway. "Well, perhaps I've found my post-dinner entertainment."

They walked further up the headland, towards the hill that overlooked the coastline. The wind whipped Gemma's mousy brown hair around her face until she stopped and turned her ponytail into a quick bun. At the top of the hill, Everett went straight to the bench seat positioned to take in the view and sat, intending to do just that.

"So, this is Burleigh Heads," Gemma told him, sitting beside him as he watched the waves crashing against the nearly white sand and into the rock formation directly beneath and in front of their vantage point. "And straight out there," she pointed along the beach to the cluster of high-rise buildings on the horizon, "is Surfer's Paradise. It's not a bad walk along the beach or the esplanade on a cooler day."

The beach was still fairly busy, but that wasn't surprising given the heat of the day and the inviting blue colour of the water. Children built sandcastles and splashed in the shallows, people spread out on towels sun-baked, while others in the water body-surfed and rode boogie-boards. Closer to the headland end, where Gemma and Everett were perched, there were even a handful of surfers hoping to catch a few more waves before the sun began to set.

Gemma could feel herself relaxing effortlessly. After Marcus had fostered her, she'd spent a lot of time at Burleigh Beach. It was like a second home to her.

They sat and chatted about their respective days, Gemma beginning to feel as though his job was just another job. He was just like any of her other friends, if more distractingly attractive (and she sent a silent apology towards her friends for thinking it). It surprised her that they actually had a lot in common. That said, she hadn't initially given much thought to what he might be like as a person, and now she regretted having objectified him to the point of dehumanising him.

The sun was finally beginning to dip behind the buildings to their left, the sky turning orange and pink. "This is my favourite time of day," Gemma found herself saying, feeling as though she was a walking, talking cliché.

"I can understand why," he responded softly while she continued to look out over the horizon. "It's lovely."

Gemma nodded, then turned to respond, the words dying on her lips when she realised that his intense gaze was trained on her. Decided that now she was definitely imagining cheesy rom-com moments that weren't actually happening, she pasted on a smile and got to her feet, wiping her sweaty palms on her thighs as she asked, "So, ready for some fish 'n chips?"

"Lead the way, love."

Setting off back down the footpath, instead of following it along the way they had travelled, she led him to jaywalk left across the road and then down the hill, past the old, brick arcade building to the set of traffic lights at the bottom of the street, which met with the Gold Coast Highway. She pressed the button that would hopefully trigger the lights to turn in their favour and once the 'walk' light was all lit up, they made their way to the other side of the road. There was an old lawn bowls club to their left and a small public park to their right, and then another street to cross before they hit James Street – the bustling hub of Burleigh Heads' hipster cafés, boutique stores and small restaurants, and also the home of Gemma's favourite fish and chip shop.

Being a Sunday night, the street wasn't nearly as busy as it was during the day, though the restaurants and cafés were beginning to fill with dinner patrons. Gemma strode with confidence towards the dark green facade that housed their destination, sighing when she realised there were a number of people ahead of them in line.

"So, what do you feel like?" she asked her companion as they surveyed the menu on the large, chalk backboard above the counter.

Everett shrugged. "Whatever you suggest. I prefer my fish battered, but beyond that I'll leave it in your fair hands."

"Alright," she mused turning to look at the fresh fish on ice in the display box and settled on snapper, which she hoped was caught somewhat locally. When it came time to order, she ordered the meal for two, with one piece of snapper battered and the other grilled, a serve of calamari and a tub of tartare sauce. She eyed the fresh oysters, and added half a dozen of those as well, watching her companion's lips quirk.

"What?" she asked, passing her debit card over the card reader and accepting their numbered ticket with a quick thank you to the young guy behind the counter.

She led Everett out the door to wait for their meal. "Oysters?" he queried, amusement glinting in those mischievous blue eyes. He leaned against the glass window with his arms folded and his eyebrows raised.

"You don't eat them?" she asked, curiously.

The actor shook his head, still smirking. "You know what they say about oysters."

"That they're delicious?"

He unfolded his arms and ducked his head to murmur into her ear, "That they're an aphrodisiac, darling."

His words had her heart racing, and she felt her face flush. She swatted at his chest, refusing to get side-tracked by how firm and solid and warm he felt under her hand, and huffed, "Stop that. You know that's not fair."

"Why? Because your crush on me–"

"On Detective Waters," she interrupted defensively, uncomfortable at having her feelings called out, especially by him directly. "I don't really know you. I know your character. Your fictional, professionally made-up, scripted character with embellished abs. That guy. Not you."

He arched a single eyebrow. "Is that how we're going to play it?"

It was how she *had* to play it because it kept her safe. "Yep," she stared defiantly back at him.

Everett chuckled and backed off, hands up in surrender. "Alright," he acquiesced, but was unable to resist the parting shot, "but I'll have you know there's *nothing* embellished about my abs."

She made a dismissive sound, "Now you're just being a tease."

"You wound me, Gemma."

"Somehow, I think you'll survive."

* * *

"That was fantastic," he told her later, reaching for a napkin to wipe his hands and mouth following their meal by the sea. It was properly dark now, and they were perched at a picnic table in the park near where they'd left the car. The space was lit by the moon and a few streetlights, and the night was clear and warm. "Almost as good as back home."

"What do you mean 'almost'?" Gemma laughed, turning her head from where she'd been watching the inky waves crashing into the shore, the whitewash almost eery in the slivers of moonlight.

He tossed his napkin into the pile of paper that had held their meal and now contained nothing but crumbs, oyster shells and traces of salt. "Nothing beats real English fish and chips, love."

"Well, I wouldn't know, having never been," she shrugged, "so I'll just have to take your word for it." She reached for the pile of rubbish and balled it all up together, climbing out of the bench seat. "But I am glad you enjoyed this, anyway." She made her way further down the path to the nearest rubbish bin and got rid of their mess.

Everett got up as she returned, and she wasn't quite sure what to do next. "So," she asked him, rocking back awkwardly on her heels with her hands in her back pockets, "do you want me to take you back to your hotel now?"

He shook his head. "The night's still young, unless you're eager to be rid of me."

"No, I'm good, I just thought…well, I'm hardly the life of the party. I'm sure you could find more entertaining company."

He stood in front of her, placing his hands on her shoulders and staring her in the eye. He seemed uncharacteristically serious. "Gemma, it might have escaped your notice, but I'm not exactly drawn to…" he tilted his head, attempting to find the right words and coming up short, "whatever stereotypical behaviour you're imagining. I prefer a pint at a pub to nightclubs or anything of that nature. Spending time with you has been enjoyable because you seem to share the same sort of interests as me. I assure you, if I wanted to be elsewhere, I would be – but I don't, and I'm not."

Blinking at him and feeling somewhat stunned by the gentle lecture, she nodded. "Alright, sorry. I'm just making sure you're where you want to be."

There was a flicker of some unidentifiable emotion in his gaze before he smiled that disarming smile of his and reiterated, "Trust me, love. I am."

* * *

They ended up at a mini-golf facility in Surfers Paradise. It was slightly dated –having been there for as long as Gemma could remember– with three courses (two indoors, one outside), all themed and heavily decorated. Everett insisted on paying, though Gemma told him that he was wasting his money because she was absolutely shit at putt putt.

"I have zero spatial intelligence or hand-eye coordination," she warned him, taking her putter and golf ball from the attendant, "and my grasp of physics is shaky at best."

"I promise not to mock you too much when I wipe the floor with you, then," the actor grinned, leading the way towards their first course – a Jurassic themed round of 18 holes, heralded by a towering tyrannosaurus rex statue.

Gemma rolled her eyes. "Oh, good."

Despite her protests –and her warnings– she found herself having fun. He was a big kid, whooping with delight whenever he sank a putt, and taking photos with the dinosaur decorations along the way.

"This hole," he said seriously as they stepped up to the thirteenth, "will be a hole-in-one."

"Didn't you say that about the last five?"

"Shut it, Fox." He'd finagled her surname out of her somewhere around the sixth hole, when she'd been attempting to psych herself up into achieving par. She rather liked hearing him say it. Then again, he could read from the phone book and she'd be rapt.

They'd spent the better part of forty-five minutes acting like carefree teenagers, and she had thoroughly enjoyed it. It turned out that in addition to their mutual taste in literature, they shared similar opinions on most topics they broached and had similar senses of humour. Spending time with him was easy, and not just because of her initial fangirl infatuation. They just clicked, and it was beginning to sink in that he might actually feel the same way.

Gemma hated to admit that he might have been right all along – they did make good friends.

"C'mon, Rhodes," she teased back, completely unrepentant, "make the shot while we're still young."

A bark of laughter escaped him before he pointed his putter in her direction. "You're getting awfully impatient for someone with an average par of six." They were on a course where the par for each hole had been three. "Becoming impatient to lose, are we?"

The corners of her lips tugged upwards, and she leaned her hip against a plaster triceratops. "So, where's your hole-in-one, again?"

Rolling his eyes, Everett gauged the angles and obstacles in front of him. She couldn't help but find the look of intense concentration on his face equal parts hilarious and charming. (And if she checked out his butt as he bent forward, swinging the putter at the ball, who could blame her? She was only human, after all.)

"Alright, this damn course is rigged," he muttered, watching the ball pass directly over the hole, having hit it with too much force.

"I've only been saying that for twelve holes now," Gemma commiserated, her tone dry as she lined up her own shot. She shot wide, her ball bouncing off a plastic dinosaur egg and rolling in the opposite direction. "Definitely rigged."

Everett snorted.

Three holes later, Gemma was about ready to throw in the towel completely. They'd abandoned their score cards and were instead playing purely for fun. Everett still had yet to score his hole-in-one, but was still hopeful that the next would be his chance at glory.

"Please tell me the humiliation will end after this course," Gemma muttered, finally sinking her ball on her fourth shot – proof that she'd been gradually improving.

They'd only paid for the one game, thankfully, with the thought that they'd give the others a go if the mood struck them. As far as Gemma was concerned, there was no mood. She was moodless. Entirely mood free. Besides, her watch told her that it was close to nine p.m., and she still had to drive back home to the opposite side of Brisbane, which would take at least an hour and a half after dropping Everett back at the hotel.

He bobbed his head. "Yeah, I don't think it would be very gentlemanly to thrash you so soundly a second time around."

The image that assaulted her at his playful words had nothing to do with golf and make her cheeks go pink. She had no idea where it had come from –especially because spanking was definitely not one of her kinks– but she was glad the indoor course was dark enough to hide the worst of her blush.

"Whatever helps you sleep at night," she shrugged, mentally reprimanding herself. Hadn't she only recently decided that it was a bad thing to objectify him? *Damn his pretty face and his sexy accent straight to hell.*

Whatever reply he was going to make –and she thought it might have been a fun one, judging by the sly expression on his face– was cut off by her phone's loud ringtone. She pulled it from her pocket, unsurprised to find her brother Facetiming her.

"I've gotta take this," she apologised, moving off the course to a nearby bench seat, still flanked by dinosaurs, "otherwise he'll send a search party for me. It's happened before." She was convinced Brennan thought she was still a teenager sometimes.

"Sounds like a fun tale," her companion responded, while she brought the phone up and swiped to answer.

"Hey," she greeted as her foster brother's face came into focus, "what's up?"

He furrowed bushy dark eyebrows at her. "Is that a dinosaur?" he asked, followed quickly by, "Where the hell are you?"

"Putt putt with a friend," she answered easily, shooting a quick glance in Everett's direction, her heart fluttering at the way his expression lit up with glee.

He'd been attempting to get her to admit that they were friends all evening. She'd been holding out purely to stir him up.

Brennan's frown only got deeper. "At nine o'clock on a Sunday night? I'm guessing this is a friend of the 'has a penis' variety."

Resolutely not looking in her companion's direction, she sighed. "I haven't verified it," and she ignored the salacious 'Happy for you to do so, love' that came from the man in question, "but, yes. I'm playing putt putt with a male friend. Happy?"

"Can I interrogate him?"

"Brennan." There was no way she was allowing her brother to see who she was hanging out with. She'd never hear the end of it. He'd sound just like all her internal fears and conscience personified.

With understanding that she actually liked her mini-golf companion blooming in his brown eyes, Brennan backed off. He offered her an easy smile. "Sorry, Gems, I'm just playing. I'm glad you're out having fun. It's been too long." Alongside his supportive words, there was something in his expression that said 'be careful' and it warmed her. He cocked his head to the side. "Wasn't this your big Con weekend?"

"It was," she nodded, unable to contain her smile. "It was great."

"And weren't you going alone?"

This time, it was her eyes that narrowed. "I'm not loving this game of twenty questions."

"Ah, so you met this mystery golf guy at the convention, then?"

"The *mystery golf guy* can hear you," she sighed, finally looking back over to Everett apologetically. He was leaning against a large plaster rock formation, arms folded across his chest, amusement dancing across his face. Stifling a groan of annoyance, she looked back at the phone in her hand. "So why are you calling?"

Brennan chuckled. "I just wanted to make sure you'd gotten home safe, but seeing as you're still out, that's moot."

"It is," she agreed, not bothering to argue with him over the fact that she was almost thirty and not a teenager who needed to check in with her parents. Though it annoyed her, she also secretly loved that her foster brother –despite being almost five years her senior and having been leaving for university when his father had begun fostering her– loved her and cared about her enough to still be so close, even well into their adult years. "But if it makes you feel any better, I'll call you tomorrow morning to confirm I'm still alive, okay?"

"Okay," he agreed. "Have fun. Don't do anything I would do." He cleared his throat and raised his voice, "That goes for you, too, Mr Mystery, *especially* when your date is my sister."

"Alright, that's it, you're done. I'll call you tomorrow. Bye." She ended the call before he could say any more. Sliding the phone back into her pocket, she smiled awkwardly in Everett's direction. "So, that was my brother, the comedian."

"It's sweet that the two of you are so close," he unknowingly parroted her earlier thought. "Charlie and I speak once or twice a month, at best."

"Yeah, I consider myself lucky most days."

"Except for when it comes to mini-golf, eh?"

She laughed and stood up, wincing a little at how stiff her legs and back felt. She'd been walking all day, so sitting for a spell hadn't been the smartest choice. "Right. You've still got a game to win."

"We all know I've already won, Fox," he swung his arm around her shoulder and guided her towards the seventeenth hole, "but I appreciate the sentiment."

Rolling her eyes, Gemma allowed herself to be led down the course to complete their game.

Everett finally sank a hole-in-one on the eighteenth hole, raising his putter into the air and cheering himself as though he'd won some sort of prestigious tournament. Gemma applauded, squealing when he turned to her mid-victory dance and lifted her off the ground, spinning in a circle.

"Well done, Rhodes," she congratulated drily after he set her back down, trying not to be too distracted by the feeling of his hands still at her waist. "I take it all back; you're a putt putt legend."

"And don't you forget it," he instructed, finally stepping back and releasing her. He gestured to the final hole, making a wide, sweeping motion with his hand. "Let's see you at least make par on this one."

"Oh, sure, no pressure or anything." She sighed and teed up her shot, hitting the ball with what she hoped was enough power to get her somewhere near the 'green'. She blinked when her ball landed within tapping distance of the hole. "Well, I'll be damned." Turning to face him, she suggested, "Do you think this one is deliberately easier than the others?"

He arched an eyebrow. "Are you trying to take the impact of my achievement away?"

She tapped the ball in, and it disappeared down the tube that led to the front desk. "No," she responded cheekily, "never."

* * *

"Well," Gemma said later as she turned into the driveway for the hotel, "here we are." The same feeling of melancholy that had struck her when she'd left him in the lift the previous morning began filling her. She tried to shake it off, forcing a bright smile, "Thank you for tonight. It was fun."

"I should be thanking you," he refuted, smiling softly back at her. "You've chauffeured me about and organised dinner."

"Yes, it was such hard work, too," she joked.

He chuckled but made no move to unbuckle his seat belt. "Stay tonight," he blurted, and she blinked owlishly.

"I checked out."

"With me." For the second time in the two days that she'd known him, she watched as spots of colour appeared on his cheeks. He reached up to rub the back of his neck in what she now recognised was a gesture of embarrassment. "I'll sleep on the sofa. I just…well, I can't see the point in you driving all the way home if you're returning in the morning."

"You were serious about that?" Some part of her thought he'd have tired of her attention by then.

His expression turned from sheepish to affronted. "Why wouldn't I have been serious? And I swear to God, Fox, if you suggest that you're boring again…" he let the threat hang, not really having anywhere to go with it.

Her nerves were turning jittery. Once again, this entire situation felt surreal. But he was staring at her so earnestly that she found herself agreeing before she could overthink it. "Okay. I'll just need to pay for a parking space because I checked out."

"My room should have one allocated. Hang on." Everett unclipped his seat belt and left the passenger seat, and she watched him through the glass doors as he sauntered over to the reception desk and began speaking to the concierge. He gestured towards the car as he presumably explained the situation –and her cheeks burned because she knew exactly what it looked like from an outside perspective– and then nodded and accepted some paperwork, which he filled out on the spot. Then he turned on his heel and headed back towards her.

He looked far too pleased with himself as he slid back into the seat beside her. "Done. You're all set to stay until Thursday."

"Thurs…*what?*" her hazel eyes were wide with surprise. "You said tonight. Just tonight. I'm not prepared for *four* nights." Not mentally, and not physically either. She needed fresh clothes and underwear, having only brought enough for her planned weekend.

"I assumed that we'd be travelling past your home at some point during our adventures," he shrugged, clearly not seeing the same dilemma she did. "We could do that tomorrow: swing by, allow you to pack some new things, and then continue on."

Her mind short-circuited at the idea of Everett Rhodes in her little townhouse. The place she lived. The place where she'd discovered him on TV. Where she wrote goddamn fanfiction about his character (not that she would *ever* admit that out loud, and certainly never to him.) She wanted to tell him that he was being presumptuous again, that he'd been out of line for just deciding her plans for her, but the words that came out were, "Well, you're not sleeping on a sofa for four nights." When she realised that the alternative meant sharing the bed with her, she flushed and quickly extrapolated, "I will. It's your room. I'll be fine on the couch."

"We'll see," was all he said, and the tone suggested that he was going to do as he liked anyway.

She sighed and started the car back up, making the familiar drive to the basement car park. Everett handed over his room card to swipe and then informed her of the car park number she'd been assigned during her surprise extended stay. After parking, he pulled her suitcase from the boot and insisted on carrying it (or rolling it, considering it was on wheels) for her. Her protests echoed off the concrete walls and were ignored.

"Ah, memories," he jested as they stepped into the lift and he hit the floor number.

The look she shot him was nearly scathing. "I'm still slightly traumatised, I hope you realise."

"From being stuck with me?"

"From being stuck, period." She shuddered, and his expression turned sympathetic.

"I'm sorry," he apologised, placing his hand on her shoulder. "I know it wasn't pleasant for you."

Just as she couldn't stand watching Detective Waters become upset on TV, she found she couldn't abide Everett being morose in reality either. Trying to lighten the mood, she quirked her lips upwards. "I guess it wasn't *all* bad," she told him shyly. "I mean, I came out of it with a new friend."

"Of the 'has a penis' variety and all."

She snorted. "I'm going to kill my brother."

✳ ✳ ✳

Everett talked her into sharing the bed. She didn't know how it had happened. One second, she'd been determined to take the couch, but by the next, he had convinced her that they were friends, and adults, and it was a huge bed, and it didn't have to be a big deal.

He had his laptop out when she exited the bathroom wearing her pyjamas, after she had brushed her teeth and her hair, and had spent a few minutes psyching herself up for the inevitable bed sharing. She was genuinely starting to suspect her life actually was a ridiculous, clichéd rom-com full of expected tropes –'and there was *only one bed!*'– because this sort of thing didn't happen in real life. Certainly not to her, at any rate.

But there he was, propped up against the headboard, wearing cotton boxer shorts and *nothing else* (he was evil – he had to know that not wearing a shirt when she'd already complimented his abs was just plain cruel) with his laptop balanced on his thighs. She took a moment to take him in, feeling lecherous but unable to stop herself.

He hadn't lied: there was no makeup or trickery involved in his onscreen shirtless scenes, though perhaps they trimmed his chest hair a little to make him more universally palatable for the show. (Not that there was anything unpalatable about the way it was naturally, all thick and dark and gloriously masculine.) He had abs, and defined pecs, and his skin was tanned, and she wanted to follow that tapering trail of chest hair down its dwindling path to whatever she could find beneath the cotton shorts he wore.

Her cheeks burned when she realised that he'd caught her staring.

Instead of teasing her, though, he patted the space beside him, the covers already turned down. "I don't bite, love," he reminded her, grinning cheekily, adding the flirtatious "not unless you ask nicely" that she'd only fleetingly considered during their first meeting.

Rolling her eyes, she forced her feet to move across the room, climbing up onto the side of the bed. He had *Disney+* open on his laptop screen and he shrugged, "I thought perhaps you could introduce me to that television show you mentioned – the musical one."

"Do you like musicals?" she asked. He'd called the musical episode of *Happily Never After* 'ridiculous', so she wouldn't force him to suffer through anything similar if it wasn't his thing.

"I do," he nodded, smirking as he picked up her train of thought, "I just don't enjoy performing in them. Choreography is not my strong suit."

"But you sing well," the compliment slipped out before she could overthink it. "I like your voice." It was a lovely, mid-range tenor that she found soothing, but she kept that part to herself.

Everett's answering smile was warm and gentle. "Thank you." He waited a beat before he asked, "So, this show of yours?"

She snagged the laptop and typed '*Galavant*' into the search bar, and then loaded up the first episode, placing the computer back down on the bed between them. She mouthed along to the opening song while watching him out of the corner of her eye for his reaction, and he didn't disappoint, laughing out loud.

"You've certainly got a type, don't you, Fox?" he asked her after the first song, an eyebrow winging upwards. "Don't think for a second that I can't see the similarities between this Sasse fellow and myself."

"Well, I mean, okay, you're both English, and you've both got the square jaw and perfectly trimmed beard and the dark hair and…yeah, alright, you got me." However, attractive as Joshua Sasse was, he didn't have Everett's intensely blue eyes, and he just didn't make her heart squeeze like Everett did.

He was smirking at her, the bastard.

"But, you know, you have to admit that you fit a sort of Hollywood aesthetic, right? I mean, I can name at least five other actors with similar features." All of whom she thought were hot. That wasn't going to help her case.

"If you say the bloke from *Grimm*–"

"Well, yeah, there's him. David Giuntoli, if you wanna get technical," Gemma nodded, loving the way he frowned because she knew that being in the same genre (both even working with twisted fairy-tales) that comparison might have been made a lot, "Or Jamie Dornan–"

"*Fifty Shades*?" he asked derisively. "Really, Fox?"

"Or Colin O'Donoghue–"

"Well, *Irish*, but I suppose–"

"Tom Ellis, or Hiddleston."

"Okay, yeah, both also English, so–"

"Liam Hemsworth–"

"Australian? Besides, I look *nothing* like a Hems–"

"Ooh, Matt Bomer, particularly the early *White Collar* years. You know, back when he had that constant –but subtle– five o'clock shadow going?"

Everett didn't seem to be on the same page. "*Ooh?!*" he echoed with overstated incredulity. "*He* gets an 'ooh'? Where's *my* 'ooh'? He's not even close to English! What happened to your accent fetish?"

Somehow, she managed to keep a straight face, merely blinking before she attempted to continue. "Or–"

"Alright, I get it," he rolled his eyes and pouted, sulking exaggeratedly, "I'm not *special*. Easily interchangeable with a bunch of others. I understand."

She snorted, patting his cotton-clad thigh a little condescendingly. "You're still my favourite."

"Didn't 'ooh' over me, though, did you?" He grumbled and wriggled himself into a slouch, turning his attention back to the laptop.

"I 'eep'ed, remember," she laughed, knowing that he was still playing. "You stepped into that lift yesterday and I made the most humiliating sound ever."

He was struggling to keep his expression sullen, amusement pulling at his lips. "That was adorable, love."

"Ugh. Embarrassing, more like it."

Everett chuckled and shook his head. "We'll agree to disagree. Now, shall we continue?" He gestured to the laptop, where Galavant was being let down not-too-gently by his former lover, Madalena.

Gemma nodded and got herself comfy, and they continued to watch. They made it through half of the first season before she couldn't contain her yawns and he shut it off.

"You were right," Everett told her, speaking quietly into the darkness as they settled in for sleep with their backs to each other. "It's entertaining. And catchy."

She smiled, despite the fact he couldn't see it, and snuggled into her pillow. "I'm glad," she responded. "Goodnight, Everett."

"G'night, Gemma."

* * *

Chapter Four

Gemma was the first to wake the next morning. Disoriented, it took her a moment to get her bearings and recall where she was and why. Following that, she became aware of the fact that they'd travelled in their sleep, both migrating from their respective edges of the mattress to the centre of the bed. She wasn't surprised to find that he was just as tactile in sleep as during waking hours. She'd stayed facing the window, but he had rolled over and pulled her back flush against his chest, holding her in place with one toned arm and a leg slipped between her own. His other arm was stretched out under her pillow, his chin atop her head. It felt awfully intimate – and she blushed as she realised that she could feel another part of his anatomy jutting into the small of her back.

Attempting to extricate herself only served to stir him, and he seemed to reel her in tighter on instinct. Clearly still in the foggy space between sleeping and wakefulness, he ground against her and pressed a kiss into the junction where her neck met her shoulder. "Mmm," he murmured, "Morning, darling."

It was so tempting to just go with it. It felt good to be in his embrace, with his strong arms holding her and his chest warm and firm behind her, but she just couldn't do it.

"Everett," she cleared her throat, "I don't think I'm who you're thinking of."

"Hmm?" he asked, the arm wrapped around her middle shifting, the hand travelling to cup her breast while he nuzzled at her neck. She felt wrong for enjoying it, knowing that he wasn't entirely aware of what he was doing, or to whom.

"*Everett,*" she said a bit more urgently. "Wake up."

He made a sound of complaint and stretched, and she could feel him tense up as his brain kicked into gear and he took stock of what was happening. "Gemma," he removed his hand and scooted back a bit, dropping a pillow into his lap. "I apologise. I…I didn't mean…"

No longer pinned in place (and telling herself she did not miss the feel of him pressed up against her), she rolled over and took in his flushed, embarrassed face. "It's fine," she told him, calmed by how flustered he seemed. He hadn't been feeling her up deliberately, and he didn't seem like the kind of man who would do anything that made her uncomfortable (unless she asked him to, and it was a good kind of uncomfortable).

She imagined that the behaviour was just his usual approach to waking up with someone he'd taken to bed. And now she needed to get *that* thought out of her head, because it was taking her places that made her chest tighten painfully with seething (unwarranted) jealousy.

The sunlight was streaming in from the window, and she chanced a glance at the clock on his bedside table. It was only just after 7 a.m. She bit her lip, feeling a bit guilty for waking him so early, and told him so.

"I'm usually early to rise," he shrugged her apology off, and she tried desperately to not hear the double entendre in the statement, being an actual adult and not an immature teen. Thankfully, he carried on, oblivious, running a hand through his messy bed hair. "So, what's the plan for today, tour guide?"

"Well, seeing as you've kidnapped me for the better part of a week," she teased, her heart fluttering at the shameless grin he shot back, "I liked your idea of heading past my place to pick up some clothes and stuff. So, with that in mind, it depends on what sort of activities you'd like to do. We could go and spend the day at Australia Zoo, and you can even fulfil your dreams of getting chlamydia from a koala–" he rolled his eyes "–and pat a kangaroo. Or we could go and do one of the Sunshine Coast hikes, but it'll be hot, and I can't promise there won't be snakes."

Everett considered his options. "Is it really a visit to Australia if I don't pat a koala?"

Gemma's lips pulled into a smile. "The zoo's a good choice," she agreed, "and most of the snakes there are behind glass."

"Most?" he repeated. "That doesn't fill me with confidence."

Even as she shot him a cheeky smirk and started climbing from the bed, she felt a pang of longing for him. He seemed younger like this, with his mussed-up bed hair and the blue of his eyes so bright in the morning sun. Carefree and within her reach – just a man she'd befriended (was possibly falling for, which seemed silly because it had been less than three days and she barely knew him) and not a somewhat famous actor that she'd have to let go of within a few days.

She said something about grabbing a shower and gathered her clothes, leaning against the closed bathroom door once she was safely inside the tiled room. *Thursday*, she told herself. *Life will go back to normal after Thursday.* And then her only concerns would be work and what TV shows to binge when she got home.

It was such a pity that her solitary life didn't sound anywhere near as enjoyable after a taste of a morning with *him*.

* * *

Having Everett Rhodes in her home felt even more surreal than anything else she'd experienced since Saturday morning. Gemma lived in a little two-bedroom townhouse in a suburb on the far edges of the northern side of Brisbane. It was small, but modern, and perfect for her needs. Being that it was a fair distance from the city, it was also affordable enough to rent on her own, even if it meant travelling to and from work was a bitch some days.

Entering via the front door, you were immediately greeted by the stairs that led to the two bedrooms, single bathroom and small lounge area upstairs, and also to the open plan lounge/dining/kitchen area on the ground floor. Offside to the kitchen, tucked in under the stairs and backing on to a tiny private courtyard, was a small powder room and laundry. It wasn't much, but the space was hers.

"You have a lovely home," he told her, inspecting the buffet unit where she'd tossed her keys, taking in the photos she had lined across its top. They were mostly of her family and a couple with her best friend, Sara. She was minimalist by nature and didn't like a lot of clutter.

He seemed out of place, even if he had dressed for a day of walking in the Queensland heat, wearing simple cargo shorts and a white t-shirt. He had a baseball cap in the car, and she'd teased him about practically being a boy scout. (She'd then had to endure his flirtatious "Well, darling, I *am* always prepared." and the imagery it brought with it.)

"Thanks," she replied to his compliment, gesturing to the two-seater couch at her left. "Make yourself at home. I'm just gonna go switch out some of my clothes and pack some new ones. I shouldn't be long. There's a toilet through that door," she gestured to the space beneath the stairs, off to the right of the kitchen, "if you need to freshen up before we get back on the road."

He made a sound of acknowledgement and she headed upstairs to pack and get changed into a pair of leggings and a long, loose cotton singlet top. She also snagged a broad-brimmed hat and dug around for a bag to toss in her sunscreen and water bottle. She knew how hot the zoo could get, especially in the summer months.

When she returned, he was scrolling through her Netflix watch history. Her heart skipped a beat, because she knew exactly what she'd watched in preparation for her weekend away.

"Alright, *this* is the part where you tie me to a chair, isn't it?" he teased from the couch, gesturing to the list of films and shows she'd last viewed. "I'm starting to see a theme, love."

"Shut up – I was psyching myself up for seeing you at the Con. I never lied about being a fan."

Everett's smirk grew into a Cheshire Cat grin, wide and knowing. "I know,

Fox, I'm just playing."

"Yeah, well, don't." She huffed, setting her repacked suitcase down by the door. "I feel…weird. Almost like a creeper or a stalker or something. And I'm not that person."

"I know you're not," he replied, contrition lacing his tone. "And I'm actually rather flattered that you've sought out some of my smaller roles."

Biting her lip, she shrugged. "It's interesting seeing you play vastly different characters. I mean, I know as an actor that's what you do, but, y'know, some do it better than others and I was kind of surprised with some of your more serious stuff. Especially with the accent changes."

"Oh? And which of my accents –outside of my natural one– did you find the best?" He was genuinely curious, cocking his head to the side and leaning towards her expectantly.

"The Southern American drawl was the biggest surprise, I think," she answered. "The one from the historical drama…plus you were all clean shaven. It took me an episode or two to reconcile that it was actually you. It could have gone really badly, but you pulled the accent off, and, by the end of the series, I'd almost forgotten you were English."

He laughed. "Well, I'm glad it didn't sound as ridiculous as I felt doing it to start with."

"What? You're telling me you're not super confident all the time? Outrageous!" She teased back.

"And are you telling me you prefer the beard, Fox?"

She blinked. "Pardon?"

"Just now – you didn't seem overly impressed when you said I was clean shaven."

"Well, isn't it a proven fact that beards –or, at least, neat, trimmed beards that highlight the angles of your jaw and cheekbones– make men hotter?"

Beneath the stubble that proved her point, his cheek twitched. "Are you implying I'm not as attractive without this?" He scrubbed his hand over the trimmed beard.

"That's exactly what I'm implying, yes." His ego could take the taunting, she knew it.

He smirked. "But the takeaway from that is that you still think I'm hot, even without it."

"There's my narcissist," she cooed, patronisingly reaching out to ruffle his hair. After watching him spend ten freaking minutes styling it earlier that morning (even while he knew he'd be putting a cap over the top of it), she knew it would irritate him.

She wasn't disappointed as he scowled and then attempted to reshape the mess she'd made. "Bad form, Fox."

"Come on, we've satisfied your ego long enough, let's–" she began, but was interrupted by a sudden knock at her door.

Frowning, she turned on the spot and opened it, then sucked in a surprised breath. "Brennan! What are you doing here?"

"Making sure you're still alive," her brother groused, pushing his way past her and pacing between the little lounge area and the dining table. "You said you'd call, and when you didn't, I tried to call you, but you didn't answer and..." he trailed off, having finally noticed Everett on the couch. "Oh. Uh, hi?" His brow furrowed and he asked, "Have we met? You look really familiar."

Gemma tried surreptitiously to take the television remote from Everett's hand with the intent of switching the TV off, seeing as her viewing history was still on display. Brennan took in the amusement on the guy's face and turned his head, catching a glimpse of the screen before it went black. With wide, surprised eyes, he turned back to his sister. "Just how much did you spend on the Con for this?"

She rolled her eyes, and gestured between them, "Everett, this is my brother, Brennan. Brennan, this is Everett, aka Mystery Golf Guy."

Everett extended his hand, with a cordial "Pleasure to meet you," but Brennan was still processing.

"I see." Gemma could see the cogs turning in her brother's head and she knew exactly what sort of conclusions he was leaping to. "Hey, Gems, could I maybe have a word with you? Um, upstairs? Or outside?" He gestured to the door on the opposite side of the kitchen, which led to her tiny courtyard.

Sighing, she leaned her hip against the back of the couch. "Brennan, it's not what you're thinking. And, even if it was, I'm practically thirty. I'm a big girl and I can look after myself."

"Be that as it may," he shook his head, "you can't just go about bringing your celebrity crushes home."

Everett snorted and she hit him upside the head. "You're not helping, bud."

"Well, we've established that you have a list," he responded, eyes glinting with mirth, "and that Matt *bloody* Bomer outranks me, so, really, I can understand your brother's concerns."

"You're such an idiot," she laughed, while Brennan's gaze shifted between the two of them like he was watching a tennis match. "I never said he outranked you. Besides, he's got a husband and kids – that makes him off limits anyway."

"You still *'ooh'*ed!"

Gemma moved to banter back, but Brennan cleared his throat. "How did this even happen? No offence, Gems, but you're...*you*. And he's–"

"Well aware that he's somewhat well-known in some circles," Everett interrupted with a frown. "Also, offence very much taken. Gemma's wonderful, and she's certainly been far more entertaining and accommodating than anyone else I met this weekend. Why wouldn't I want to spend time with her?"

Gemma blushed, but folded her arms and nodded, staring at her brother expectantly. "Yeah, Bren, why wouldn't he? Or anyone else I bring home, for that matter?"

"You don't usually..." Brennan shook his head, trailing off at the warning look she shot him. Hands up in surrender, he tilted his head downwards and took a step backwards. "Alright. Sorry. I'm just...this is a weird situation, alright? And excuse me for being concerned that my little sister's gonna get hurt. Even if it's not...*ugh*...even if you're just being friendly – I *know you*, Gem."

She could feel her cheeks burning as her blush crept over her face, down her neck and up to the tips of her ears. He wasn't wrong, though. These were all the same concerns she had. At least he hadn't continued from there. "Well, thanks for making me feel like a kid, brother mine." She shifted uncomfortably. "Don't you have a job to get to?"

"One of the perks of being the boss is that I get to set my own hours," he informed her. "And I'm not trying to treat you like a kid, I just–"

"I get it." Gemma knew he was only looking out for her. She'd gone through some serious shit relationship-wise, and he'd been there to pick up the pieces for all of it. Neither one of them wanted to go through that again. But it still rubbed her the wrong way that he was pulling the Big Brother act now, in front of someone he knew she respected (and, yeah, had a bit of a crush on.) "But now I regret not humiliating you in front of Jeff when I had the chance."

Brennan's expression turned goofy at the mention of his long-term boyfriend with whom she worked. "I think I do enough of that myself as it is," he shrugged. "And you know he'll back me up on all this," he gestured between Gemma and her guest, "too."

"True." Sometimes it sucked having two men who considered themselves big brothers to her. (Of course, she'd never give it up for anything – she'd grown up without family, so having an abundance now was worth cherishing, even when they gave her the shits.) "But can you just drop it for now?" There was no point pretending that he wasn't going to bring the topic back up later. At least it wouldn't be within earshot of the man they were talking about.

"Fine." He ran his hand through his short, dark hair, then pinned Everett with a piercing glare, "I'm glad you think Gem's awesome, because she is, but if you do anything to hurt her–"

"*Brennan!*" Gemma had opened her front door and gestured for her brother to go through it. "*Jesus.* Stop. I've got this."

He snagged her wrist and pulled her out the door with him as he moved past her. "Just be careful," he spoke quietly, staring into her eyes beseechingly. "I don't know how this happened, or even what exactly is happening, but I know you're already attached and…well, you know nothing permanent can come from this, right?"

"I'm not an idiot," she whispered back, "and I'm aware of the fact that we live in two different worlds. But…it's been *so long* since Scott and I just…well, it's just been really nice getting to know him."

She hated the sympathy that filled her brother's brown eyes at the mention of her last ex, and the way he sighed, all deflated and defeated. "Okay," he pulled her in for a tight hug. "I promise not to say 'I told you so' after he's gone and you're heartbroken."

"You're such a dick," she scoffed, pushing away. However, she still smiled, "But thank you."

Gemma bid him goodbye then slipped back inside, instantly finding herself cornered by concerned blue eyes.

"Alright, love?" Everett asked, awkwardly adding, "Your brother seems… nice."

She appreciated his attempt to normalise the situation, but it fell flat.

"I'm fine. He's just good at sticking his nose where it doesn't belong." Her lips twisted into a facsimile of a smile, and she felt tense and uncomfortable all over again, with Brennan having reminded her that whatever was happening between them was strange and temporary. She tried to cover with humour. "Anyway, shouldn't you be more offended that he was insulting your honour or whatever?"

He levelled her with a gentle expression. "I've had far worse said about me –or to me– than anything your brother implied." He chuckled lightly. "Have you ever read comments on the internet? Or *anything* from film critics?"

He wasn't real. How could someone like him be real? Where were his flaws? Why wasn't he an arrogant, chauvinistic pig? Why couldn't he go and kick a puppy or something so she wouldn't think him anywhere near as lovely as he seemed?

With these thoughts swirling about in her head, she smiled back, relieved that he wasn't bothered by the implications of her brother's impromptu lecture. "Speaking of film critics," she attempted the world's clunkiest, lamest segue, "Should we head off to the zoo, then?"

* * *

At the zoo, Everett was just as hyperactive and enthusiastic as he'd been at putt-putt. From the second they made it through the ticket booths (where he'd taken a selfie with the young guy manning the ticket desk they'd chosen, because he'd recognised Everett and had asked with excitement if that would be okay), the actor had pulled out the paper map and plotted out where he most wanted to go.

They headed up the first path to the left, passing a large, grassy area with a couple of wombats milling about in the morning sun. He took photos of the wombats with his phone, declaring that the animals were bigger than he thought they'd be, and then turned into the reptile exhibit.

It was a large, darkened room, almost like a cave, lined on either side with glass enclosures, each lit up with heat lamps. In the very centre of the room was a display of a python skeleton poised to eat the skeleton of a smaller animal, its jaws stretched impossibly wide. Gemma startled as Everett reached out and gripped her hand, suddenly tense and serious.

"You're really afraid of them, huh?" she asked softly, squeezing his hand as he peered into a glass cabinet containing an Eastern Brown snake and shuddered.

He nodded, his jaw set, his eyes not leaving the reptile lest it somehow magic itself out of the glass, *Harry Potter* style. "Yeah. It's an actual phobia."

He'd been so sweet and supportive during her claustrophobic meltdown in the lift when they'd met, and she didn't think it fair to subject him to this if he was genuinely terrified. "Why don't we skip this one, then? Go find the prettier animals?"

"They're behind glass," he argued, but still refused to get too close to any of the enclosures, hovering more at the path in the middle of the room, "let's just not loiter."

Agreeing, Gemma led them through, allowing him a chance to look if he wanted, but not forcing the issue. He seemed to hold his breath until they made it through the exit, but he kept a hold of her hand as they moved towards the aviary entrance further down the path.

Inside the aviary, he loosened up, looking at the signs that told them which species were flying about and then trying to catch a glimpse of each one. He made a competition of it, and by the time they left, she was the victor, having been able to spot more birds more quickly. And he was still holding her hand.

* * *

"Alright," she said as they passed through the gate to the kangaroo area, "you're allowed to touch these ones. Go nuts."

Everett grinned but stayed at her side. She'd half expected him to behave like the five-year-old in the group ahead of them – bouncing on the balls of his feet until his mother gave him a handful of roo pellets, at which point he'd cheered and raced towards a group of resting kangaroos, his mother close on his heels, reminding him to be quiet and gentle. But Everett had turned down the earlier opportunity to purchase the food, content to walk through the large containment area and hopefully pat a roo or two if the opportunity arose.

Further down the path, there was a large kangaroo lazing on the grass. He was a light grey colour and stared up at them with dark eyes, completely unbothered by their presence. Everett approached carefully and crouched at the roo's side, experimentally patting the fine fur of the animal's neck. The joy that lit up his face had Gemma's heart aching. Pulling her phone from her pocket, she snapped a few shots of Everett patting the peaceful creature, sending him one for his own memories (and likely for his assistant or agent or whoever managed his social media presence to post on Instagram later).

"He's surprisingly soft," Everett told her, sounding slightly awed, still stroking the kangaroo carefully.

"And very cute," she added, finally caving to give the marsupial a pat herself. This brought her right up close to Everett, and his free hand –which had been sitting on his thigh– moved to her lower back, steadying them both. She imagined she could feel him searing her skin through the cotton of her top, and her heart fluttered again.

After a few more moments, Gemma stood up, and Everett followed her lead. "They're the strangest looking animals, aren't they?" he mused, reaching for her hand as though it was the most natural thing in the world to do.

"I guess I'm kind of used to them," she shrugged, trying to ignore the racing of her heart. "But platypi –platypuses? No, it's definitely pi, right? – anyway, *they're* strange looking. But very cute as well."

"Despite your wealth of deadly reptiles, I will admit that you have your share of cute creatures as well."

They were walking towards the gate that led to the koala exhibit, though she paused to disentangle their hands and use the hand sanitiser provided. "Oh, did you not know that the platypus is venomous as well?" She asked casually, rubbing the alcohol gel into her hands and wrists.

Copying her motion, he rolled his eyes. "Now I know you're having me on."

"I'm not! They have these little barbs on their webbed feet that have a toxin in them that can cause epic pain," she explained, laughing at the twisted expression on his face. "I saw a whole thing on the Discovery channel about it." She pushed open the first of the two gates that they needed to pass through with her butt, still facing him so she could add, "I honestly had no idea, either."

"I'm not betting you on this one, then," he responded, waiting for the first gate to close before he pushed open the second one, "seeing as I lost so spectacularly with the first."

"Speaking of – look," she pointed to the tree beside him, where a sleeping koala was nestled in the lowest branch, maybe two feet above his head.

His eyes widened, not having expected to see one up so close. "I can see why they're likened to bears. They have a teddy quality about them."

"Yeah, but their fur is coarser," she crinkled her nose, "and they smell gross."

"Oh, so you have patted one before?"

"When I was in school. It was part of an excursion –or field trip, whatever you want to call it– and they made us pat them, then they had us research and write essays about them. That's where I found out about the chlamydia."

It had taken Brennan weeks to convince her virginal, fourteen-year-old self that she didn't need to get tested for the STD, but she didn't share that with Everett, feeling embarrassed enough by the memory itself.

"I'm fairly certain they wouldn't allow any risks to the public here," he argued playfully, already striding down the footpath towards the little area designated for patting the koalas. She followed him with a fond shake of her head, knowing that he wasn't going to be swayed in his choice.

He struck up a conversation with the zookeeper while he waited for the go-ahead to pat the koala that was being kept out amongst bunches of eucalyptus and branches tied to logs at about head height. Gemma stood back and was once again struck by his almost youthful exuberance.

She couldn't help the laughter that bubbled over when he turned, his hand on the koala's back, and declared, "Fox! This fellow says that the likelihood of catching chlamydia from an infected koala is practically non-existent."

"And yet, I'm not risking it today, thanks."

She'd admit to herself that she was mostly holding out just to stir him up.

"Suit yourself," he shrugged, turning his bright blue eyes back on the creature he was cautiously patting. She snapped another couple of photos, choosing the best to text through to him while he mused, "You're right though – definitely coarser than the kangaroo."

* * *

The rest of the day seemed to fly past. They went and saw the other animals, with Everett posing in front of a lemur in *Bindi's Treehouse* and Gemma doing her best to not sing *'I like to move it, move it'* much to his amusement, and the two of them opting to not go and see the famed 'Wildlife Warriors Show' in lieu of spending more time just walking and really watching the creatures in the exhibits.

Everett began narrating their antics in the style of David Attenborough, which thoroughly amused her, particularly when he decided to give them all human names and melodramatic plot lines. (The tigers were apparently a promiscuous bunch, and the meerkats appeared to have some sort of underworld mobster situation going on.) Gemma eventually joined in, but she refrained from 'doing the voices', leaving the acting itself to him.

In their adventuring, the pair skipped lunch, so by the time they returned to the car, they agreed that stopping for an early dinner on their way back down the coast would be the best option.

"Alright, so nothing fancy, because we're both kind of gross and sweaty…" Gemma decided as they drove. "Is there anything in particular you feel like?"

"Perhaps takeaway of some description? I'm rather partial to the idea of eating in front of the telly tonight."

Perfect.

Everett Rhodes was *utterly* perfect for her. And she hated him for that. Hated him with his gorgeous face, and his sweet disposition and his knowing exactly what to say in any given moment.

Keeping all of that to herself, though, she nodded. "Agreed. Sounds awesome. What sort of takeaway?"

He considered this for a moment. "Well, you made me a little homesick last night by taking me to that chippie…why not continue the trend and get Indian? If you like Indian food, of course."

"Oh, I love Indian," she agreed, while simultaneously trying to convince herself that she was definitely hallucinating this man. "Why not be super lazy and have it Ubered to the hotel room? I could probably do with a shower before we eat anyway."

She didn't think she deserved the look she caught him shooting her – the one that made it seem like she'd hung the moon. "That sounds like a fabulous idea, love."

So that was what they did. They got to the room –Everett once again insisting on carrying her bag up from the car park– and toed off their shoes, both making matching sounds of relief and then laughing at each other. Gemma pulled up her Uber Eats app and found a local Indian restaurant that would deliver, and together they chose their meal (Everett insisted they were going to share everything because that was how Indian was supposed to be eaten) and she placed the order, brushing off his concern that she'd paid for dinner twice in a row.

"And you paid for the zoo, and the petrol," she informed him, "so it's all swings and roundabouts, really."

The expression on his face was indecipherable, but he seemed to realise he was fighting a losing battle. "Alright, then tomorrow everything is on me."

"Okay," she acquiesced, "I can deal with that. But right now, I'm going to shower. I'll be out before the food gets here."

With the hot water raining down on her, taking away the grime from the day, she closed her eyes and convinced herself that she could do this – she could be his friend without getting hurt at the end.

She could.

She would.

She hoped.

* * *

Chapter Five

The next couple of days flew past. It was almost too easy how well they got along, like kindred spirits. Gemma had woken up in Everett's arms again on both Tuesday and Wednesday, and each time it was harder to acknowledge that, after Thursday, it wouldn't happen again. Ever.

So, to stave off the melancholy, she threw herself into being the best tour guide that she could be.

On the Tuesday, she took him to Byron Bay and Cape Byron, the eastern most point of Australia's mainland, where he entertained himself by taking photos of the coastline from the tip of the cape, and then forced her to take some selfies with him. (She then had him text her the photos afterwards.) Following that, she took him to Burleigh Heads for the walk through the headland and the mangroves that they'd discussed during the incident in the lift, and he commented on how different the scenery was, despite being part of the same coastline. They were exhausted by the time they returned to the hotel, heating up leftover Indian and practically passing out while they watched the last of *Galavant* together.

On the Wednesday, she decided to take him to a theme park as a last hurrah. He'd said he wasn't a huge adrenaline junkie, and she didn't really think Movie World would be his thing, so she chose Sea World (not affiliated with the American theme park of the same name). The benefit of Sea World was that it was the closest to their hotel, as well, which meant more of a sleep in in the morning.

They patted stingrays, stared at the sharks in the large underground aquarium, visited the polar bears and penguins, and she even coaxed him onto a couple of rides on the roller coasters (where she found herself grabbing his hand and screaming, much to his entertainment). In the heat of the afternoon, they got ice-creams and settled in on the grassy hill beside the grandstand to watch the jet-ski trick show, both of them howling with laughter at the poor acting and even worse scripting, but applauding the skill it took to do the stunts performed.

They returned to the hotel early in the evening, and Everett grasped her wrist, turning her to face him. "Fox, these last few days have been truly fantastic," he told her, making her heart squeeze. "And I owe that all to you. I can't imagine what I would have done if I hadn't met you."

There was too much subtext for her. Clearing her throat, she shrugged. "Sure you do – I'm sure you would have Googled or had someone sort out an itinerary for you."

He frowned, but clearly read something in her expression –or her stance– that prevented him from arguing. "Well," he tried to lighten the mood, "why don't we finish this week off right? Let's go out somewhere fancy for dinner. Get dressed up, get an Uber so we can both have some wine – the whole shebang. My treat."

It sounded dangerous to her. He'd be in a suit. Or at least dress pants and a dress shirt and tie. She had enough trouble staying in the friendzone as it was. But he was looking at her with that damn pleading expression, his cerulean gaze melting her defences, and she found herself agreeing without any argument. Damn him.

At least she'd packed a nice dress.

"Okay, then I'm going to have a quick shower," she told him. "You can Google restaurants and find something that sounds good and will let you book at late notice." Not that she really thought he'd have a problem on a Wednesday night.

Her hands shook as she applied her makeup once she was in her dress – a black cocktail dress, with a pencil skirt that clung to her curves, a peplum-styled top with two pairs of spaghetti straps that crisscrossed over her chest, and a low cut back. She couldn't wear a bra with it, but it was well fitted and had padded support in the breast area that negated the need for one. She loved this dress, always felt good and confident in it, but she still wondered whether it would be enough, and then chided herself a little because it shouldn't matter. It didn't matter. He was leaving the next day. She'd never see him again.

Oh, God, that hurt to think.

She'd never met anyone she clicked with as easily as Everett. It wasn't just that he was attractive – though, *boy*, was he sinfully attractive! No; it was that he made her laugh, that conversation between them flowed easily and (aside from when she overthought things) never became stilted or awkward.

They shared the same taste in books, TV shows and leisure activities. He wasn't pushy, he was content to just be her friend, though there were moments where she thought he might (inexplicably, in her opinion) be attracted to her as well. And in the mornings, snuggled in his arms, she felt *right* in a way she'd never felt before, which both thrilled and terrified her.

And it was all about to end.

Gemma tried to tell herself she was being ridiculous. She'd spent more time with Everett than she'd ever dreamed possible, but she wished she could have more. There was a part of her that so badly wanted to believe they really would continue a friendship via email, or Facebook, or some form of communication, but she knew better to believe that would actually happen.

She finished with her makeup, keeping it light and mostly natural, and fidgeted with the long braid she'd put her hair into after her shower. One last glance at her reflection and she steeled herself for the night to come, pasting on a smile and stomping down on the pangs of loss that were settling in.

She had one night left with him, and she was determined to enjoy it.

"About time, Fox," he teased as she opened the bathroom door, releasing a cloud of steam into the main room, "I was beginning to think I'd need to send a search–*bloody hell.*" He rose to his feet from the couch, two strides closing the space between them. He swallowed roughly as he stared down at her. "You look stunning, darling."

The epithet rolled off his tongue with the same ease as it had since she'd met him, but his voice had lowered, and his eyes seemed darker as they took her in. She didn't think she was imagining it this time. "Thank you," she answered, then, feeling the tension mounting, offered a crooked smile, "I've seen you in a suit – I knew I had better step up or step out."

"Gemma, you could wear a hessian sack and still be beautiful," he sighed, stepping back out of her personal space, "but I don't know many restaurants that will allow that in their dress code."

She was relieved that the tension was broken. With a light laugh, she gestured to the bathroom. "It's all yours. Suit up."

When he emerged less than twenty minutes later, she had a hard time not swallowing her tongue. He wore tailored charcoal dress pants, a white dress shirt with the collar unbuttoned, and a dark grey vest, and he looked as though he'd just stepped off a catwalk somewhere, his shaggy, raven-coloured hair coiffed just so, up and away from his face. His stupidly handsome face.

"Fuck me," she muttered to herself, and he smirked. Cheeks flushing, she rolled her eyes. "Oh, shut up, you know you're hot."

"And more than happy to oblige," Everett responded wickedly, and she swatted at his chest. A chest she'd been pressed against every morning but had yet to run her hands over. It was getting harder to understand why.

"You're supposed to be taking me to dinner." It came off a little petulant, but it was either that or climb him like a tree at this point. *Friends,* she forcibly reminded herself, *just friends.*

Those azure eyes sparkled with mirth and something she couldn't put a name to. He fiddled with his phone. "Our Uber should be arriving in about ten minutes."

Gemma tried not to think of the things she could do to him in those ten minutes.

She failed.

* * *

Dinner was lovely. The restaurant hadn't been intimidatingly fancy, but it was certainly a big step up from the meals they'd shared to that point. He'd booked a table overlooking the waterfront and hadn't mocked her for ordering a glass of Moscato (something her ex, Scott, had always rolled his eyes at, telling her that her tastes needed to become more refined). In fact, he'd smiled and ordered the bottle, agreeing that a sweet white wine was a nice change occasionally, and had happily shared it with her. They'd then shared a second bottle after that.

They'd dined on fresh seafood –this time she had teased him about the oysters and had bitten her lip at the almost predatory grin he'd offered her in return– and talked and laughed as easily as all their other time spent together. She would have expected him to be sick of her by that stage, but conversation still hadn't become stagnant or repetitive, and she didn't know whether to cheer or to cry.

How could the one person that she'd felt genuinely connected to in so long be so fucking unattainable?

Almost as if sensing the shift in her thoughts, Everett tossed his linen napkin over his plate and extended his hand. "Dance with me?"

Being a Wednesday night, the restaurant was quiet, and there were only a few other couples at tables scattered around the room. Usually, Gemma would feel self-conscious at being the only people dancing, but this was her last night with him and she couldn't give a shit what anyone thought.

Besides, she reminded herself, *you'll never get a chance like this again.*

Blushing lightly, she placed her own napkin over her plate and accepted his hand, allowing him to lead her to the small, cleared space that was obviously designated for dancing.

The music was slow and melodic, and she found herself leaning against his chest as they swayed to it. He still held her hand with one of his own, the other now settled low on her back. His chin rested atop her head, and his cologne –mixed with the masculine, earthy scent that was just him– was spicy and smooth and intoxicating. She had no other way to describe the feeling of the moment, other than to think that it was romantic. And it hurt.

"You're thinking fairly loudly, love," he murmured, and she relished in the rumble of his voice up his chest.

A lump had lodged itself in her throat and she swallowed to try and get rid of it. "I feel like I must have passed out in that lift," she responded, "because these last few days have been surreal."

She felt, more than heard, the light snort of laughter that elicited, but he seemed to pull her even more tightly against him. "I've really enjoyed our time together, Gemma."

God, it felt like a breakup. How pathetic was she that she was getting teary-eyed over a non-relationship ending? They'd been friends, nothing more, and it had only been a handful of days. She had no right to be so sad that she had to let go.

And yet, there was a wobble in her voice as she responded, "Me too."

"Hey," Everett pulled back a little, the hand that had been holding hers letting go and tilting her chin so he could look her in the eye. He smiled, but something in his gaze seemed to mirror her own feelings, even as he playfully insisted, "Don't go getting soft on me now, Fox."

She'd fought her attraction to him from the start. Had shot down his flirting and had deliberately (if somewhat mischievously) tried to undermine his ego at every opportunity. And for what? To prevent herself from the pain of having to let him go? Well, she was still feeling that pain.

After searching his gaze for perhaps a moment too long, one of her hands moved from its spot around his neck, her fingers toying with the hair at the nape of his neck before she pulled his head towards hers and pressed their lips together.

It only took him a moment to get with the program, his hands tightening their hold around her waist while his lips moved against hers. One of his hands moved to the back of her head, angling it back while his tongue reached out, deepening the kiss. She could taste the wine they'd shared over dinner in his mouth, sweet and refreshing, and she chased after more of it.

She couldn't help but feel as though their kisses were just an extension of their friendship – they fit together with ease. There was no awkwardness or nose bumping or teeth clashing. It wasn't sloppy or too forceful. And the way he worked his tongue against hers had her rocking her hips towards his as jolt of want and arousal shot through her.

When they finally pulled apart –his lips chasing after hers with chaste little pecks of affection– and rested their foreheads together, his pupils were blown wide, and she could see the same desire and urgency she felt reflected in them. The feel of his breath coming in short, shallow pants against her lips had her clenching her thighs together.

She didn't just want him, she *needed* him.

"Should we go back to the hotel?" she suggested, not sure where her confidence was coming from, but absolutely certain that she wasn't going to spend her last evening with him pretending to keep things platonic. Fuck that.

Or, rather, she hoped that *he'd* fuck *her*.

Everett's eyes bore into hers. "God, yes."

He sprang into action, signalling a passing waiter for their cheque while he ordered them a return Uber. With the warmth of one of his hands searing into the bare skin of her back, he kissed her again as they waited outside the restaurant for the car to arrive.

Everett's kisses were heady and addictive. Gemma suspected they were a good indication of what was to follow. He held her hand in the Uber, his thumb tracing soft, sensual patterns on the inside of her wrist. Her heart felt like it was going to beat right out of her chest.

They strode through the hotel lobby hand in hand, purposeful yet not rushed. However, the second they were inside the lift and mercifully alone, he was on her, pressing her into the mirrored wall while he captured her lips hungrily. There was more urgency to his kisses this time, his hands sliding down her sides, cupping her backside and sliding under her thigh, silently encouraging her to wrap her legs around him.

Sadly, the nature of her pencil skirt made the manoeuvre impossible, unless she hitched it up to her waist – something she wasn't going to do, especially considering how close they were to the room. If the lift broke down again, though, that might have been a different story.

"You're a goddess, Gemma," he informed her huskily as they parted for air, "and in that dress…do you have any idea what you do to me?" He shifted his hips forward, illustrating his point, and she smiled coyly back up at him.

"I have an inkling," she teased, before biting her lip, pressing herself into his clothed erection, "and soon you'll feel what you do to me."

He sucked in a breath, his voice husky when he spoke. "Minx," he accused, before ducking his head for another kiss. Though this time he held back from his earlier fervour, teasing her by barely kissing, barely dipping his tongue against hers, their breaths mingling together. It was the most erotic kiss she'd ever experienced, and she simultaneously adored and hated him for it.

She hadn't been lying – she could feel her own arousal pooling at the apex of her thighs, and this last kiss had her whimpering with need for some sort of friction.

She almost cheered when the elevator finally stopped at their floor. She practically dragged him to the door of his room, and his laughter echoed down the hall.

"Oh, *God,*" she all but moaned once they were inside with the door locked behind them, and his lips were at her neck, leaving a trail of fire in their wake, "why the hell have I been avoiding this all week?" She wriggled under his ministrations while she attempted to kick off her shoes, still moving towards the bed.

He chuckled against her skin, where he was kissing and licking a path down towards her breasts, still covered by her dress. "Your guess is as good as mine, love," he answered, though they both really knew why.

Between not wanting to get hurt and also feeling as though she wasn't good enough for him, she'd played it safe. But no more. It was going to hurt to say goodbye either way. At least this way, she reasoned, she'd have no regrets (other than the regret of not sleeping with him sooner and truly enjoying the last few nights, she supposed).

Gemma didn't want to think about what she'd been missing out on, though, nor about the painful farewell that she'd have to go through the next day. Instead, she wanted him naked, right then and there. Her fingers plucked at the buttons of his vest, trembling while he distracted her with his tongue, his hands grazing the undersides of her breasts over the thick, constrictive material of her dress. She tugged his shirt from his pants, moving for the column of little white buttons next, and she could feel him grinning against her skin.

"Impatient, are we?"

She loved seeing him like this, she decided. All tousled and impish and genuinely aroused, and all by her own doing. It wasn't just some act he was putting on; he was genuinely excited by her. There was a definite difference in his expression now to anything she'd ever seen from him on TV or in film. His eyes were dark and smouldering –not a word she'd ever thought would ever apply in reality– and his chest was rising and falling quickly as he attempted to maintain some semblance of control for the moment. He was beautiful.

Grinning back, she shrugged, still working on the shirt buttons. "You can't possibly blame me."

His eyes sparkled and he laughed at that, telling her she did wonders for his ego.

"Even if you're not Matt Bomer?" Gemma couldn't help the jibe, using it as a distraction of her own as she popped the last of his buttons and parted his shirt, revealing his chest and abs. *Hers.* He was hers for the night. It didn't seem real.

"Really?" he asked, still amused, helping her shrug the shirt and vest over his shoulders before tossing them into the middle of the room, indifferent to where they landed. "You're finally getting me naked, and you want to talk about bloody Bomer? Should I be concerned? Are you going to be imagining him while I'm fucking you, darling?"

How he could be so charming and so crude at once and have it work for him, she'd never know.

Unable to stop herself, she splayed her hand across his chest, toying with the hair that had captured her interest from the first time she'd seen him on screen. It was so much sexier in person than she could have anticipated, and who the hell knew she had a thing for chest hair? It had never interested her before (none of the handful of men she'd been with in the past had had much more than a bare smattering of coarse hair over their chests) but with Everett –as with the rest of him– it was glorious and perfect.

Maybe it wasn't the hair. Maybe it was just him.

"Oh, no," she finally answered him after her momentary distraction, her fingers scratching down his chest, over his nipples then down his delicious abs, coming to a stop at his belt buckle. "I promise, you've got my complete attention."

"And you certainly have mine," he agreed, his hands swooping down her back, "and I feel we're a little unbalanced here. Where's the zip for this thing?"

It was a hidden zip on the side of the dress, but as she moved to unzip it, she was finally struck by nerves. What the fuck was she doing? He was an Adonis, and he worked with some of the most attractive women in the world, and she was –as her brother had reminded her– *just Gemma*. She had no abs to speak of: her belly was soft with a bit of an apron paunch, and she had stretch marks on her stomach and breasts, and cellulite on her thighs, and–

"Gemma? What's wrong?" The playful tone was gone, replaced by concern, and she flushed under his gaze, closing her eyes.

God, he was going to think she was a tease, or be frustrated and disappointed or–

"Love, look at me."

With a sigh, she did as he asked, and once again found her heart squeezing at the expression on his face.

"We don't have to continue this," he told her, and there was no hint of censure or frustration in his tone, "not if you're uncomfortable. Certainly not if you don't want to."

"I do…*God*, I do. I just…"

"Just?" He led her over to the bed, sitting her on the edge so he could crouch in front of it to look her in the eye, reaching for her hand and squeezing it. "Talk to me."

"This dress is just really flattering, and it hides a *lot* of sins, and–"

His eyes widened with understanding, then narrowed. "You're a fox, Fox." He pointedly ignored her rolled eyes. "And, newsflash, I've spent the last few days and nights with you. While I've been a gentleman," this earned him a watery giggle as he'd intended, but he continued on, his tone serious, "I'm aware of what you look like. What you feel like in my arms. And I want more of it. More of you. But only if you do, too."

She supposed he made a valid point. Her pyjama shirt had a tendency to ride up at night with the way she tossed and turned, and when they'd gone to the beach during their trip to Byron, he'd seen her in a one-piece swimsuit, the cellulite on her thighs and the shape of her stomach more than visible. But it was the honesty in his gaze that really convinced her, and the way his hand was still holding hers, supportive of whatever answer she chose to give him.

Instead of answering verbally, she removed her hand from his and stood up, prompting him to stand, too, and she held his gaze while she located her zip and pulled it down. The material of the dress went slack, and she let it slip down her arms, pulling them free before she pushed the whole thing down over the prominent curve of her hips and to the floor.

"Gorgeous," he reiterated, before kissing her tenderly.

This time, she swore she could feel his reassurance through his kiss, the languorous strokes of his tongue against hers somehow affirming how much he wanted her, how much he wanted to extend this moment with her. The action also reignited the fire in her veins and the coil of tension in her belly. Then his arms were around her back, pulling her flush against him, and the sensation of her bare skin against his sent her into overdrive.

"Now who's unbalanced?" she complained, feeling only slightly uncomfortable in nothing but her sexiest panties (and she thanked deities she didn't believe in that she'd thought to pack them at all) while he was still in his trousers.

She fumbled with his belt, a combination of nerves, adrenaline and lust making her slightly uncoordinated, and he moved to help, deftly unbuckling it and pulling it free from the loops, then unbuttoning and unzipping his pants. He stepped out of them, now kicking off his own shoes while she brought her hands back down his chest to the waistband of his boxer briefs. If she'd had any remaining doubts about his interest in her –in what they were doing– they were assuaged by the evidence of his arousal straining against the confines of his underwear, a tiny damp spot near the tip betraying the level of his excitement.

"Are you a socks on or off kinda guy?" she asked him, startling another laugh out of him.

"Off," he answered with blatant amusement, "but you've not given me a chance to get there."

Holding her hands up where he could see them, the smile she gave him was cheeky. "Well, by all means, go ahead."

He bent forward, raising his left foot first, quickly pulling the grey argyle sock off and throwing it to parts unknown before repeating the action with his right foot. When he righted himself, she was once again sitting on the edge of the bed, and his breath hitched at the position she'd put herself in while she reached for the band of his underwear.

"*Gemma,*" he breathed, and she shot him a coquettish look through batted eyelashes.

"Is this okay?" she asked him, not expecting to be rejected, but not wanting to just assume either.

His expression turned incredulous, as though he believed he should be the only one asking that question, and she supposed he might actually feel that way. There was a flash of something akin to tenderness in his gaze before he nodded, the lust dominating his expression again.

That was all the permission she needed before she tugged his underwear down.

She should have expected that she'd even find this part of him attractive. He wasn't intimidatingly huge, but he was certainly more well-endowed than her previous lovers had been. Reflexively licking her lips –and barely registering the groan that provoked from him as he watched her– she reached out to take him in hand.

Like silk covered steel, his cock was hot and hard and heavy in her grip, and she stroked him from base to tip experimentally before she brought her lips to the flushed, purple head, her tongue darting out to lick at the drop of precum gathered at the tip.

"Fuck," he hissed, and she surprised him by pressing a tender kiss to the velvety soft tip before taking as much of him as she could to the back of her throat, her right hand pumping the base while her left fondled his balls. His hand came to the back of her head, but he didn't push or guide her, and she assumed he was just steadying himself. "Gemma! *Christ.*"

It was an intoxicating feeling, to know that she was controlling his pleasure. That he was at her mercy. The feel and taste of him, combined with the way he was trying not to thrust into her mouth while a litany of curses and praises escaped him, had her shifting her own hips in search of relief.

She should have guessed he'd be just as talkative during sex as he was while doing anything else. It was a new experience for her. In her two actual relationships, Brett had been a grunter, and Scott had attempted to make as little noise as possible, essentially hissing through his orgasms. And yet, instead of annoying her, Gemma found Everett's verbosity only turned her on more.

She released him with an obscene *pop* when he cupped her cheek and informed her that he needed her to stop unless she wanted things to end too soon. Gemma couldn't help the satisfied grin she responded with.

"Minx," he censured once more, pulling her to her feet and hungrily claiming her mouth again. He cradled the back of her head with his left hand while he fucked her mouth with his tongue, his right hand squeezing her left breast, his thumb toying with her nipple. He didn't linger long there, though. His hand moved quickly, skimming her abdomen and waist, slipping between them and down the front of the scrap of black lace she still wore.

She couldn't describe the sound she made as he rubbed slow, sure circles over her clit before dipping his fingers lower, groaning appreciatively into her mouth as he encountered just how wet she was for him.

"Everett, please," she urged, and he didn't need any further encouragement, sliding two fingers inside her and pumping them to the same languid rhythm that his tongue had set in her mouth, while the heel of his palm applied pressure to her clit. "*Yes*," she sighed, clenching around his fingers, and closing her eyes, "there. More."

"It doesn't surprise me that you're bossy in bed," he whispered hoarsely into her ear, sending a pleasant shiver down her spine.

In retribution, she brought one of her hands down from where she'd been tightly gripping the backs of his shoulders and pumped his cock. "We're not in bed," she argued the technicality, sounding equally wrecked, and he snickered.

"That can be remedied, love." But he made no move to do so, only thrusting his fingers faster.

She could feel herself getting close, the coil inside her tightening, and she drew a leg up his, trying to find a better angle. He took pity on her then, withdrawing his fingers and reaching to help her remove that last piece of clothing that separated them.

Everett kissed her sweetly as he backed her onto the mattress and stretched out over her. He supported his weight with an elbow on either side of her and slotted perfectly between her open thighs. Once again, she marvelled at how well they fit together.

She mewled into his mouth, bucking her hips, and he teased her with the tip of his cock, running it through her folds, smearing a mix of precum and her own moisture in a trail as he taunted her. She cried out as he pulled away from the kiss and suckled at her right breast, then her left, one of his hands snaking down to rub at her clit.

"Please tell me you have a condom," she begged, clenching around air while her hands fisted the sheets, wanting nothing more than to finally have him inside her.

"Of course," he nodded, rolling off her to dig around in the bedside table (and she refused to think about how presumptuous that was, content to be happy that he was prepared). He emerged victorious, plucking a foil-wrapped square from the box in his hand and carefully tearing it open.

Gemma watched with hooded eyes as Everett rolled the prophylactic on, and she spread her legs invitingly once it was done. He was surprisingly tender as he crawled back over her, peppering quick butterfly kisses over her thighs, then stomach and breasts, before lining himself up and slowly –torturously slowly– sliding in.

It had been a long time for her since she'd last been with anyone, and it took a moment to get used to the stretch and drag of him inside her. "You feel amazing," she heard herself say, then instantly felt ridiculous.

He only smiled down at her, though, and pecked a chaste kiss to her lips, rocking his hips slowly. His jaw was clenched in concentration. "As do you."

She didn't want to close her eyes. She wanted to memorise how he looked –debauched, a slight sheen of sweat over his chest and shoulders as his slow pushes morphed into deeper, harder thrusts, his expression stuck somewhere between pleasure and pain– but when he propped himself on his left arm to reach between them and rub her clit, she couldn't help the way her eyes rolled back and her body jerked with pleasure.

He shifted the angle of his thrusts and not only did the coil of tension inside her tighten, but it also snapped suddenly and without warning, sending her careening over the edge of the orgasm that had been building since their first toe-curling kiss. White light sparked behind her closed eyelids while her heart practically beat out of her chest.

"*Shit*," he cursed out in stammered warning, "You're so...*Gemma*, I'm — ah, *fuck*."

She opened her eyes just in time to watch his expression shutter as his hips jerked before he stilled and came, dropping his face into the crook of her neck while the aftershocks of her own orgasm still fluttered around his softening cock.

His cheeks were flushed as he withdrew from her and disposed of the condom. "That...was not my finest moment," he informed her, flopping down onto his back. He turned his head smirked at her. "I blame your mouth. I don't think I want to know where you learned to use your tongue like that."

Sure, it wasn't the longest sexual experience of her life, but she also cut him some slack, considering they'd spent days flirting and taunting each other. And he'd still managed to give her a mind-blowing orgasm before he'd come himself, so it wasn't as though she wasn't satisfied, and she told him as much.

"Besides," she murmured, "there's still a whole night ahead of us, right?"

It was his turn to blink. "You are insatiable." His lips curved upwards. "I love it."

Gemma grinned and inched closer to him, feeling a little awkward being naked now that the endorphins were fading. He had the uncanny ability to read her, and he reached out an arm, "C'mere, love."

"Of course you're a snuggler," she aimed for derision, but there was a sense of affection to her words, and she complied without any real complaint.

She had woken up in his embrace since Monday morning, but it was a whole new experience being curled against him, completely skin to skin. She pillowed her head on Everett's chest, her fingers automatically toying with the hair between his pecs, and he pressed his lips to the top of her head. "Sleep, Fox."

Her lower lip trembled and the tears from earlier sprang back into her eyes. "I don't want to," she confessed quietly. If she didn't go to sleep, then she could almost pretend that they had more time together.

Everett was quiet for a moment, and she dared to believe he might feel the same way. "Neither do I."

She wanted to look up at him and ask him whether he also felt the connection that she did, but at the same time she was terrified of his answer. He might think her a deluded fangirl after all, and she didn't want to risk that. But if there was a chance that he felt the same way, shouldn't she fight for it?

Her cowardice won out.

"I'm sorry," she apologised, swallowing back the melancholy. "Tonight has been amazing and I just don't want it to end."

"Then we shouldn't let it. Not yet." He ran his fingers down her bare shoulder and shoulder blade. "How does a nice bath sound to you?"

Her brows drew together, and she craned her neck to look at him, repeating, "A bath?"

"Don't tell me you didn't notice the tub in the bathroom." There was mischief in his eyes. "It's big enough for at least three people – and now *there's* an idea!"

She hit his chest and he chuckled.

"I don't share, Rhodes."

He kissed the tip of her nose. "It's alright, love. Neither do I. Well, except for that one night in Prague…" he waggled his eyebrows and she laughed.

Distracted now by the thought of sharing a bath with him, she mused, "A bath does sound relaxing."

With his gaze turning predatory, he nipped at her earlobe and had no business sounding as devilish as he did when he whispered, "Relaxation wasn't what I had in mind, darling."

* * *

The water was just the right temperature as Gemma sank into the bubbles with Everett already seated behind her in the almost comically large rectangular spa bath. While they could each sit on opposite ends, legs stretched out parallel to one another, he'd insisted she recline against him, his renewed erection pressing against her backside. She'd rolled her braid up and secured it with a scrunchie in a bun at the nape of her neck, and Everett took advantage of having her skin bared to him, sucking, licking and kissing everything he could reach while his hands fondled her breasts.

She lamented that she had her back to him. Seeing him wet (in photo shoots or fan-pandering, indulgent TV scenes) had always been an absolute weakness for her. Once again, there was something about seeing his chest hair plastered against him, water tracking down the peaks and valleys of his toned abdomen, with the hair on his head swept back and away from his face, highlighting the sharp angles of his jaw and cheekbones. Getting to experience the fantasy in real life and not being able to properly take it in was cruel.

That said, she *had* gotten to see him frolicking in the surf the other day, which had ticked all the boxes of her 'Wet Everett Rhodes' fantasising, even if she'd been trying to deny herself the enjoyment of it at the time.

"What *are* you thinking about, Fox?" he asked with a low voice roughened with need.

There was no point lying. "I was thinking about how hot you are when you're wet," she answered, finding that her own voice seemed to match his.

She could feel his smirk against her skin. "Funny," he mused, his right hand abandoning her breast and slipping under the bubbles, fingers teasing their way inside her, "I was thinking the same thing about you."

He had effectively ruined her for any other man at this point, she decided as her head fell back to rest on his shoulder. She thrust her hips and fucked his fingers, gripping his thighs under the water. "Oh, *God.*"

"Everett, actually."

"Cheesy," she reprimanded, before moving one of her hands to rub her clit while he continued his ministrations.

He sucked in a sharp breath and rocked his cock into her backside. "You'll be the death of me," he informed her.

"But what a way to go, right?" she panted, already teetering on the edge of her orgasm.

"That's it, love, come for me," he encouraged, shifting her higher into his lap, his erection now directly under her, bumping against his fingers as she rode him. The very idea of those fingers slipping out and his cock replacing them was all it took to push her over the edge, and she cried out as she rode the resulting waves of bliss.

"Gemma," his voice was tight, "may I–?"

She nodded, still swept up in the afterglow of another amazing orgasm, and he did exactly as she'd just imagined – removing his fingers and sliding inside her with a deep, satisfied groan.

The water lapped at the edges of the bath, some spilling over and splashing onto the floor as she adjusted to the completely different sensation of him moving inside her under its surface. She knew that water was less lubricating, but it was a surprise that she swore she could feel every vein and ridge of his skin. She wondered if it felt as intense for him as it did for her, and once again lamented that her back was to him.

Deciding that she couldn't take not seeing him any longer, she stilled his hips and pulled off him, turning and straddling his lap before she lined him back up and sank down again. With his hands on her backside, his mouth was on hers in an instant, panting into her parted lips while her breasts rubbed against his chest with her movement. She'd never really understood the appeal of breath-play before until that very moment. If she'd had more time with him, she would have certainly explored that.

"You're a goddess," he breathed, closing his eyes and resting his forehead against hers while she continued to bounce in his lap. She put her pilates exercises to good use as she deliberately squeezed around him. *"Gemma."* He spoke her name like a prayer.

Everett looked wrecked, the steam from the bath causing sweat to bead all over his exposed skin, his shaggy hair falling into his eyes. She loved that she was responsible for this, for seeing him at his most vulnerable and flustered. His thumb moved to her clit and she gasped at the unexpected sensation, tightening as another orgasm slowly grew, and he opened his eyes, his pupils blown wide, watching her expression intently.

"I don't think I can come again," she muttered, despite the slow burn building inside her.

He huffed a short laugh, clearly still distracted by the feel of her wrapped around him. "Challenge accepted."

This time when his lips met hers, the kiss was languid – a portent of his intention to take his time with her, whether to prove his stamina was better than he'd originally demonstrated or because he, like her, didn't want their time together to end was anyone's guess.

Gemma made a sound of complaint as he slid out from her, but his kissing continued, his tongue stroking hers as his hands swept over her body. He kneaded her ass and lower back, swept upwards and then around to her breasts, cupping them before tweaking her nipples while he released her mouth to suck at the hollow of her throat.

She let out a breathy "Oh!" as his mouth moved down to her right breast, lavishing it with attention before shifting to the left, one of her hands now tangled in the hair at the back of his head.

He'd slowed his pace right down, worshipping her, mapping her, memorising her. The only sounds in the room were the quiet lapping of water against the sides of the tub, and the small, husky moans and exclamations his attentions drew out of her (or the reciprocal sounds he made in return as her hands reached for him beneath the water). She was addicted to him now, utterly ruined for other men, and she worried that she may have genuinely fallen for him.

Everett rose from the water, pulling her up with him, bringing life to every fantasy she'd ever had as water dripped down his toned form. He held her hand as she climbed over the edge of the tub, then dropped to his knees, towelling her dry from her feet up, pressing kisses into her skin as he went.

"You're not real," she told him, softening the words with a smile as she slung her arms around his neck and pecked at his lips. "You're too perfect."

"Well," he joked, "secretly, I'm a serial killer, so there's that."

"Meh," she shrugged, trying not to laugh, "I'll learn to live with it." She didn't stop to think that she was speaking as though there was a future for them, too caught up in the moment.

He offered her a lopsided smirk. "Or you won't, because, you know, serial killer."

Gemma shook her head and grabbed the second towel, moving to reciprocate his actions. His cock bobbed in front of her as she knelt, and her lips pulled into a smirk as she stared up at him before licking a stripe down the shaft and tonguing at the slit.

He groaned and leaned into the contact, enjoying her actions for a few moments before he seemed to recall how it had affected him earlier that evening. "Fox," she could tell he was aiming for discouragement, but it came off as more of a whine. "I've other plans for you yet."

Taking pity on him, she released him, giving him one last stroke with her hand before continuing to towel him dry. The dark hair on his chest matched the hair on his legs and arms, but his back was bare. She wondered whether that was an unlikely gift of nature or whether he waxed. Either way, he was all over perfect in her eyes.

Kissing once more, Everett led her back to the bed, stretching out alongside her and once again exploring her body with his hands and mouth. This time, though, he paused as he reached her legs, guiding her to spread them for him as he moved his kisses closer to the glistening apex of her thighs.

She bit her lip and fisted the sheets at her sides, tensing. Despite her previous relationships, this wasn't something she'd indulged in often. Brett had hated it –selfish bastard that he'd been– and Scott had sucked at it, to the point where she'd enjoyed their sex life more if he just left it well enough alone. That really should have been a sign they weren't meant to be together, but she'd been convinced that sexual chemistry wasn't the most important part of a relationship. She knew now that, while that remained true, it was still important (to her) that she and whichever person she was with had some degree of success in the bedroom…but her thoughts had spiralled way off track and Everett could definitely sense her distraction.

"Gemma?"

Oh, God, she did not want to have to explain to this man –this far too perfect man– that she was an almost-thirty-year-old woman who could count on one hand the number of times she'd enjoyed oral attention and still have most of her fingers left over.

When she exhaled and opened her eyes to peer down at him, there was curiosity and concern reflected back at her. "Where'd you go, love?" he asked, as though he wasn't poised right over her most intimate area.

Well done, Gemma, for ruining the mood, she chastised herself, while trying to summon a reassuring smile. "Nowhere. Nothing. I'm fine. It's fine."

Yeah, that was convincing.

Not.

Those damned expressive eyebrows of his rose. "Pull the other one," he responded, "it plays *Jingle Bells.*"

Flopping backward into the pillows, she sighed, then told him everything she'd just been thinking, unable to look him in the eye as she did. She felt the mattress move as he crawled back up to lie at her side, and she felt her cheeks burning.

"It's not your fault that your exes have been less than satisfying, you realise," he informed her, and she startled as he splayed his hand across her abdomen, just over her ribs, his thumb rubbing at the space between her breasts. "In fact, I now consider it my absolute duty to prove that my entire gender isn't completely useless. Just some of us. Sometimes."

She chuckled, "Oh, I think you've done your gender proud," she responded, once again musing that she couldn't imagine being with anyone after him. Who would compare? But she kept those thoughts to herself because they were certainly the sorts of things that would ruin the mood they'd set together.

"You *think*?" He echoed playfully. "We're not stopping until you *know*, Fox."

Everett's smile was wide, his eyes sparkling, and she felt as though the wind had been knocked out of her, an awful realisation sinking in.

She'd only known him five days.

Five insignificant little days.

But she'd *definitely* fallen for him.

And she had to let him go.

Fuck. Her. Life.

* * *

Chapter Six

Everett Rhodes was an idiot. That's what he kept telling himself, anyway. A complete and utter fool. Because only he could get himself into the sort of mess he was in.

It had started innocently enough. It was his first time visiting Australia, he was on his own, the woman in the lift had been entertaining, and he'd hoped to make a friend and some company for a few days. He hadn't anticipated that he'd rapidly become interested in her, or that they would have so much in common. He certainly hadn't thought he might actually develop feelings for her. Especially not in five measly little days.

But he had.

His mother had said it best many years earlier: Everett Rhodes didn't fall easily, or often, but when he did, he fell hard and fast.

And, Christ, had he fallen for this one.

Sadly, it was also part of his modus operandi to fall for women who were completely unattainable. Marie had been married when they'd gotten together (and he'd been young and stupid), and Gemma was a bloody fan who lived on the opposite side of the fucking planet to him.

In five days, he and Gemma had talked about everything and nothing. They'd shared the tragic tales of their respective childhoods –something he never discussed with anyone other than his mother and brother– but had also laughed and teased one another in ways he'd not experienced in years. They had recommended books to each other, watched television together, shared Indian takeaway and dropped all pretences around one another. They'd essentially been having a whirlwind relationship for the past five days, but without the romance.

They'd flirted –well, he had flirted until he'd worn down her defences and she'd bantered back– but he'd never imagined that things would progress beyond that. Yes, he knew that she found him attractive (and he'd made no secret of the fact that he returned the sentiment), but he'd also known that she was extremely guarded and had some emotional skeletons in her own closet. (The hyper-overprotective big brother had also made that abundantly clear.) It made sense that she didn't want to open up and become attached, only to have to part with him come Thursday. He'd understood. Hell, he'd even related.

Then she'd kissed him.

He didn't have the willpower to step back and be rational. Despite his rakish charm, it had been longer than he cared to admit since the last time he'd been with a woman, let alone a woman he was developing feelings for, and when she'd gathered her courage and pressed those soft, delicious lips to his, all bets had been off.

When she'd wrapped those same lips around his cock and almost sucked his damn brain out, it had been all he could do to not declare his undying affection for her. Then he'd spent himself like he was fifteen again and it was his first time. At least he hadn't left her unsatisfied. And he had redeemed himself afterwards. Numerous times throughout the night, in fact.

And that, ultimately, confirmed the fact that he was an idiot.

He cared for her, far more than he should considering they'd only met five days earlier and she'd been a fan. He shouldn't have slept with her. Not once, not at all. All he'd done was make it harder for them both to part ways.

He planned to keep things light and jovial as they woke to the sunlight streaming in through the window, the clock declaring it past nine am. They were still naked (it had been an extremely enjoyable night) and she nuzzled at his jawline, sighing contentedly before she stretched and blinked up at him sleepily.

"Hey," she greeted, offering him a sweet smile that did all sorts of things to his insides.

"Hey yourself," he responded, unable to stop himself from pressing a kiss to the top of her head, then another to the juncture where her neck met shoulder.

She leaned over him to check the clock and groaned. "We're going to have to get up if you wanna make checkout on time."

Checkout. The first step to leaving. God, he didn't want to leave. He wanted to stay wrapped up in bed with her, with her legs around his waist while he showed her how she deserved to be treated by a lover.

Her confession the previous night had created an ache in his chest unlike anything he'd ever felt – how could someone as wonderful as her not have been worshipped by her previous partners? They hadn't deserved her. At least she seemed to have agreed with that assessment.

"You okay?" Gemma asked, her fingers toying with the hair on his chest (she seemed mesmerised by it, which he found amusing and endearing in equal measures), "You're uncharacteristically quiet."

"Just getting my bearings, love," he answered, twisting the truth a little. He forced a wicked grin, tickling her side, "*Someone* kept me up all night."

She squealed and rolled away, and under any other circumstance he would have followed – would have chased her into the shower and fucked her under the warm spray. (His libido apparently knew no bounds when it came to her.) But his heart was heavy, knowing that in a few short hours they'd part ways, likely never to see one another again.

"I didn't hear you complaining at the time," she refuted, full of cheek, and gathered her clothes for the day.

Everett watched her saunter into the bathroom and scrubbed his hands over his face before he forced himself to get up. He was usually a bit of a neat freak, so the majority of his belongings were already packed. It was just the clothes he'd worn to dinner scattered throughout the room –another reminder of just how badly he'd fucked up– that he needed to collect. He did just that before he slipped on a fresh pair of underwear and clothing for the new day. Then he located the bin in which he'd disposed of the previous night's prophylactics and corresponding packaging and tied the bag off, ducking out of the room to throw the whole lot down the rubbish shoot.

When he returned, Gemma was towelling her hair dry, dressed for the day in a summery dress that made him want to unbuckle his jeans, bend her over and take her one last time against the window, overlooking the sparkling ocean water. He did none of that, but he did smile and tell her how breathtaking she looked.

(He was an idiot who couldn't help himself.)

After scouring the room one last time for any missed items, they rolled their suitcases out in tandem, each lost in their own thoughts.

* * *

After breakfast in the hotel's restaurant, Gemma insisted on driving him back to Brisbane and to the airport. "I live there anyway," she said when he tried to decline, suddenly guilty for having imposed on her time, "I drive straight past it on my way home if I take the Gateway."

Everett knew she was trying to prolong the last of their time together, and he appreciated the sentiment, but it just made his agitated mood more apparent.

She didn't ask him if she'd done or said anything wrong –and he would have ardently assured her that she hadn't if she did ask– but she kept shooting him sideways glances filled with worry while she drove.

"I'm not going to freak out that you're leaving, you know," she told him after a stretch of silence that seemed to be building in tension. She tried to offer him a reassuring smile, "I knew what I was signing up for."

His lips pulled into a short, tight smile. It wasn't her that he was worried about. It was him. It had taken him years to get over Marie, and the stirrings he felt for Gemma were somehow just as strong as his feelings for Marie had been. He'd set himself up for heartbreak and he had absolutely nobody else to blame for it.

"I apologise, Fox. I'm just…" he searched for a reasonable excuse for his

99

poor behaviour, "anxious about my return flight." Again, it wasn't a complete lie. He was just omitting the part where he regretted having slept with her because now he really didn't want to leave.

He didn't deserve the look of empathy she threw his way, or the way she reached over to squeeze his hand. "I hate flying, too. But you'll be there before you know it, and, hey, I wore you out, right? So you should be able to sleep."

Her easy, playful smile had him swallowing over the lump in his throat. "Thank the Powers That Be for small mercies, hey love?"

He could have sworn he saw his pain mirrored in her hazel eyes, but it was gone within a blink.

* * *

"You don't have to do this," Everett told her as she paid to park her car so she could keep him company in the long hours between his check in and when he had to make his way through customs and to his boarding gate. "I'm sure you've better things to do than waste your time waiting about in an airport."

Gemma pulled into a spot, switched off the engine, and turned in her seat to face him. "You really don't want me to, do you?" And, damn it, he could hear hurt in the inflection of her voice –could see it swimming in her gaze– and that was exactly what he'd wanted to avoid.

He reached for her, but she drew back against the driver's side door. "No, Gemma, it's not...that's not it."

"Do you think I'm going to become like a stalker now? One of the actual crazies? Is that it? Because, yeah, the sex was fantastic, and I really like you, but I thought...well, I thought you knew me better than that by now." Her eyes were downcast as she completed her declaration, and her voice was tight.

"Darling, you've always been one of the crazies," he attempted levity, but it fell flat. As well as he thought he could read her, it turned out she could read him, too.

"Everett," she sighed. "Just...what's wrong? Because I liked our dynamic.

We always knew there was an expiration date, and–"

"We shouldn't have had sex." The words tumbled out of his mouth before he could hold them back and, in the stunned silence that followed, he wished more than anything he could take them back.

Her eyes filled with tears, and she couldn't hide how hurt she was by his declaration. "What?"

"I don't mean…Well, I do, but I only regret–"

"*Regret?*" Shrill. He'd not heard her turn shrill before.

"No! Gemma, of course not, but–"

"Get out."

He blinked, rushed to explain, "Wait, love, I–"

"Out!" She cried, pointing at the passenger door. "Take your shit and go."

"Just let me–"

"No, trust me, I get it," she laughed mirthlessly, the sound choked and wet and miserable. She looked away, clearly not wanting him to see how shattered his piss-poor word choice had made her, but he could tell anyway. "You had your fun –turned out to be exactly what I hoped you weren't, but, hey, you proved you're not actually perfect, so good for you– and you don't want to hear from me again. And you won't." She stifled a sob, and it turned his stomach to lead. "So, *get out.*"

"Darling–"

"No," she shook her head, and there were tears on her cheeks, and he'd been the one to put them there, and he was an *idiot*, "No, you don't get to call me that. Or anything else. I'm done. We're done here."

"Gemma, please–"

The fight left her, her shoulders slumping, but she still refused to look at him. Her voice wobbled as she repeated herself, practically begging him, "Out, please, Everett."

Feeling guilty and awful, he nodded and unbuckled his seat belt, sliding out from the passenger seat and retrieving his suitcase from the boot. He tried one last time to catch her gaze, but she was having none of it, and any remaining attempts to explain that he'd misspoken were shot down before he could begin. He stepped away from the car, feeling like a broken man as she reversed out of the park and drove away without a backwards glance.

He was an idiot.

* * *

"Alright, that's it," Samuel Becker, Everett's former castmate and best friend declared, flopping down on the couch at his side, with a sweating bottle of beer extended towards him. "The hell is going on with you? You've been in a funk for *months*, man."

Accepting the beverage with a nod of thanks, the Englishman sighed. How was he supposed to explain to his friend that he'd done the unthinkable and had somehow fallen for a fan? Worse still, that he'd slept with her and then ballsed the whole thing up by saying the wrong thing in the wrong moment, and had then managed to lose his only means of contacting her? That it had been *months* and he still couldn't get her out of his head?

For a fangirl, he'd discovered that she had no online presence that he could find. No social media with an obvious profile picture, no blogs, or Twitter, or Tumblrs – not even a public phone listing in her name. (He'd even had a look at the thousands of people following his public Instagram and Facebook accounts, which were managed by someone in his agent's employ, but none had leapt out at him as belonging to her.)

He knew that she probably had such things, but he didn't know which Gemma Fox she was out of the multitude of options that had come up in his searches, or if she even used her real name at all, and he truly wanted to contact her to straighten out the misunderstanding they'd had. In the eight months since he'd seen her, not a day had passed where he hadn't kicked himself for not attempting to contact her immediately after she'd peeled out of the airport car park. Any attempts to distract himself –with alcohol, or work, or meaningless sex– had failed miserably.

He wondered how she was, and whether she missed their easy connection as badly as he did. They probably could have made a long-distance relationship work if he hadn't opened his damn mouth and broken her heart with badly phrased regrets. (Oh, how he loathed the word 'regret' now.)

Sleeping with her *had* been a mistake, but only because he'd really liked her –had quite possibly fallen in love with her, as ridiculous as that sounded– and one night of lovemaking had only made him fall harder. It had been a mistake because it had made getting on the aircraft that would take him halfway around the world all that more painful. It had been a mistake because he hadn't told her how he was feeling before he'd essentially confirmed that he was just as she'd feared – a womanising cad who had gotten what he wanted from a besotted fan and then discarded her.

Sam was staring at him expectantly, waiting on a response.

Everett took a swig of his beer, hissing through his teeth after the first swallow. He closed his eyes and sighed heavily. "It's a long story," he eventually said.

"I've got time," the other man shrugged.

With no more excuses at hand, Everett launched into his tale of woe and stupidity.

"A fan?" They were onto their third beers at this stage, and it appeared that Sam couldn't quite wrap his head around that part of the story. "Of all the women in the country, you had to fall for a fan?"

"Shut it," The English actor was in no mood to hear the lecture. "I know, alright? I know about the horror stories and shit ending up in the tabloids… but it's been eight months and nothing. Not one tweet. Not one hint to TMZ. *Nothing*. She was the real deal and I messed it up."

His friend sighed and shook his head, tilting his head back to take another drag from his bottle, hissing after he swallowed. "Well, you're going to the Sydney Con in a few weeks, right? Can't you look her up then?"

Everett shrugged. Picking at the label on his beer, he said, "Sydney's so far from Brisbane, though. I might've had more chance if I'd been able to make the Brisbane Con with you." It had been a couple of months earlier, but he had been filming one of the roles he'd successfully auditioned for –a stereotypical brooding soldier with a heartbreaking backstory– and could not finagle the few days away to go chasing after a pipe dream.

"Well, there's always the Gold Coast again in a few more months, right?"

"As long as I don't pick up another role, sure."

He had to be honest with himself, though. It had already been eight months, and by the next Gold Coast convention it would have been just over a year. Gemma was spectacular and he had broken her heart: why should he assume she'd give him the time of day if he did manage to miraculously find her again, assuming she hadn't been discovered and treasured by someone else in the meantime?

The thought made him broodier, and he reached for his fourth beer.

"Hey," Sam gave his shoulder a nudge with his own, "fate shone on you once, didn't it? Maybe it'll do it again?"

With an incredulous snort, Everett downed half his beer.

His luck didn't work that way.

* * *

The Sydney convention was just like every other where Everett had attended as a guest. However, he was unhappy to be back in the same country as Gemma but in the wrong city. So close and yet so far. He didn't feel the same enthusiasm for the fans as usual and, for the first time in his convention career, he found himself having to put on an act rather than have his participation come effortlessly.

The Saturday dragged, then he drank perhaps a touch too much from the mini bar once he returned to his hotel room (because being in the same country didn't seem to help when it came to trying to locate her, and now he was beginning to feel like a stalker). To make matters worse, the Sunday seemed to stretch on for eternity, exacerbated by the pounding in his head.

By the final mid-afternoon autograph signings, he found himself acting on autopilot. He greeted each fan with a tight, robotic smile, signed the photos hastily, and barely participated in the playful chit-chat that he knew he had a reputation for. (He just knew he was going to wind up on one of those 'Why You Should Never Meet Your Idol' blog articles.) Further down the line of tables, Sam kept casting him concerned glances, but he was oblivious to them.

When a piece of paper was slid across the table with nothing but a phone number on it, he found himself biting back a sigh and sliding it back, "Sorry, love," he muttered mechanically, "but we're not allowed to–" he glanced up to at least offer an apologetic grimace, but felt his eyes widening in recognition and surprise. He clamoured to his feet, sending his chair flying backwards with a clatter. *"Brennan?"*

Three tables down, Sam was now also on his feet, and people all across the signing area were staring. But Everett's focus was purely on the tall, frowning man in front of him.

"Rhodes," Gemma's brother greeted, his tone hard and unforgiving. He pushed the piece of paper back into Everett's hand. "Obviously you're busy now, but when you get a moment, call me. We need to have a chat."

Everett's handler for the day was already trying to usher Brennan along, but the actor reached out, grasping the other man's sleeve. His heart was racing. "Is Gemma here?"

There was a flicker of something he couldn't quite interpret in Brennan's dark eyes, and the man's frown only appeared to deepen as he shook his head minutely. "No."

Everett released his hold on the shirt, unable to hide his disappointment. Still, the fact that Brennan had travelled here from Brisbane had to mean *something.* "I finish up here in about twenty minutes," he said, "and I've got an hour's break before the final panel."

Brennan nodded his understanding. "Call me when you're done here."

Though his curiosity was killing him, the actor bobbed his head, picked up his chair and sat back down. He apologised to the next few people in line, now acutely aware of their openly curious stares. "I apologise, ladies," he affected his most charming smile, finding that it suddenly came easier to him again, "that was an old friend, and I was surprised to see him."

They twittered and brushed aside his apologies, and he signed their photos and answered their questions distractedly, his eye on the clock. As soon as he'd signed the last of the autographs from his line, he tossed his pen down and scrambled to his feet. Refusing to waste one more second, he pulled his phone from his pocket and dialled the number Gemma's brother had left him.

"Where am I meeting you?" he asked as soon as the other man answered, not bothering with pleasantries as he pushed through the crowds, heedless of anyone calling after him. He was a man on a mission.

Brennan cleared his throat. "Somewhere private, preferably."

There were no private, quiet places at the convention. Not even behind the scenes. Everett ran his hand through his hair. "I'm staying at a hotel a ten-minute walk from here. Is that acceptable?"

After a moment's silence, the other man agreed. "Which one? I'll meet you there."

He gave the hotel's name, and, after a grunt of acknowledgement, Brennan terminated the call. Everett slid his sunglasses on and ducked his head, zig-zagging through the masses of convention attendees until he found an exit. He practically jogged once he hit the main street, determined to get as much out of Brennan about Gemma as he could.

He was a little out of breath as he entered the hotel lobby, unsurprised to find the other man waiting. Brennan fell into step with him, and they made their way in silence towards the bank of elevators. As they stepped inside, Everett couldn't help but reminisce on how he'd first met Gemma.

Her awkwardness when she'd recognised him had been cute, but he'd paid her no mind until their lift had glitched and broken down. Watching her attempting –and failing– to fend off a panic attack had startled him, but that very first conversation they'd shared had sparked something inside of him.

She hadn't been 'just a fan' after that. They'd shared interests, she'd made him laugh, and he'd been captivated by her wide, hazel eyes and coy smile. He'd loved that she was snarky and feisty and unafraid to attempt to put him in his place, and the entire exchange had been a breath of fresh air for him.

That he was now sharing a tense lift ride with her older brother, presumably to be (understandably) berated for having broken her heart a few days after that first meeting just felt ironic. But it was one step closer to clearing the air with her and getting closure, and that meant he'd happily endure it.

They reached his floor, and he led the way to his suite, opening the door and gesturing for Brennan to precede him.

"Take a seat," Everett instructed, pointing towards the lounge area as he headed towards the kitchenette, "Water? Tea? Coffee?" He hesitated, then asked, "Something stronger?"

"Water's fine," Brennan answered, and Everett grabbed two bottles from the fridge, handing one to the other man and then sat awkwardly across from him in one of the plush armchairs.

"Gemma's not in Sydney?" He couldn't help that the first question that left his lips was about her. "Brennan, you must understand, I never intended–"

"Stop. Shut up." Brennan toyed with the label on the water bottle in his hands, making no attempt to open it. He glowered across the small space that separated them. "You have no idea what you did to her."

Everett set his own unopened bottle down on the coffee table. "I know. I…what I said to her was awful and I tried to explain–"

"Explain what? That you're a jackass? Because she got that." The other man huffed, then pinched the bridge of his nose and took a calming breath. After he got his temper back under control, he glared back into Everett's gaze once more. "She tried to get in touch with you not long after you left. I wouldn't be here if she wasn't completely desperate now."

Everett felt his heart seize. His head fell into his hands, and he groaned. "My phone was stolen in LA the day I got back." He'd been devastated once he'd realised that he'd lost his only possible means of contacting her. At least the photos he'd taken on the device had been backed up into the cloud. He'd just never thought to back up the contacts, given that it was a prepaid SIM, idiot that he was.

"Yeah, she worked out that it didn't exist anymore." Brennan's tone was still laced with derision. He moved to say more but was interrupted by the ringing of his own phone. His expression morphed into concern as he raised it to his ear. "Gems?"

Everett sat up straighter in his seat. "Gemma?"

Brennan scowled at him, then paled as he listened to whatever his sister had to say on the other end of the call. "*What?* But you're not–" his eyes flitted around the room, and Everett felt rising horror at the panic that seemed to be in the other man's gaze. "*Shit.*" Brennan closed his eyes and winced as he told her, "I'll have to get Sara or Jeff to get you."

Though he couldn't make out the words, Everett could hear the volume of Gemma's voice escalating.

"Because I'm not in Brisbane right now." A beat. Brennan stood up and began pacing like a caged animal. Presumably, she asked him where he actually was, because he sighed and said, "Sydney."

Everett heard the loud "Why the *fuck* are you in *Sydney?*" that came down the line after that, even with the phone pressed against Brennan's ear across the room and he jerked back in surprise.

He couldn't hear what she said after that but suspected she might yell again when her brother glanced at him and quietly admitted, "I went to Pop!Con."

Instead of more yelling, though, the tiny sounds of her voice that he'd caught previously seemed to disappear, but Brennan was still answering questions, so she must have quietened down. He hated that he was only hearing one side of their conversation, especially when Brennan's concern for Gemma seemed to be mounting.

"Yes." "No." "Because I thought we still had two weeks!" "*Okay*, okay. Are you alright?" He swallowed roughly. "I'll call Dad and Sara as soon as I hang up." A longer pause. "Yeah, I found him." A sideways glance in Everett's direction. "I haven't said anything but–" Mild, indiscernible squawking down the line again. "Yeah, well, you've just thrown a spanner into my original plans, so either I tell him now, or…no, *fuck*, don't cry." Brennan resumed his pacing, and Everett could feel his own anxiety rising. "If…if he wants to—okay. No, I won't—Nobody's forcing *anyone* to—Gemma, *breathe*. Do I need to call you an ambulance?"

"*Ambulance?*" Everett got to his own feet at that, demanding, "What the hell is going on?"

Brennan scowled and waved him aside, still concentrating on the call. "Look, I'll get the next flight home. Sara or Jeff will come get you and take you to the Royal and I'll meet you there. Hopefully, I'll get back in time." His voice turned gravelly and tight. "You've got this, Gems. I love you."

Gemma's brother hung up and leaned his forehead against the glass of the window, squeezing his eyes shut. "Fucking *fuck*." Breathing out, he shook himself and, holding a finger up to silence the onslaught of questions he knew Everett was about to throw at him, he scrolled on his phone screen and brought the phone back to his ear.

"Pick up," he muttered. "Pick *up*, Sarz—Oh thank *God*. Sara, just listen, I don't have time to explain, I'm in Sydney and Gems just called to tell me it's go time. Can you pick her up and take her to the Royal?" Brennan's shoulders relaxed minutely, and he exhaled. "*Thank you*. Call Dad. Get him to meet you there. I'll call Jeff later." High-pitched, excited babbling seemed to assault him. "Yes. Look, I need you to be there until I can. I'm gonna try make it back in time, okay?"

Everett wished he could hear both sides of the call, but some part of him was beginning to piece it together anyway. His unease mounted as he listened to Brennan wrap up his conversation. "Thanks, Sara. Look after her."

"What…" Everett's voice was higher than he would have liked, so he paused to clear his throat. He tried again. "What's happening?" Despite everything, he wasn't actually an idiot, and he'd participated in enough melodrama in his career to pick up on the gist of what hadn't yet been said aloud. But the brain was a funny thing, and it was refusing to put the pieces together until Brennan spelled it out for him.

Brennan sighed and scrubbed a hand over his face. "Look, I'd planned on lecturing you, giving you her number and hoping that you'd call her so she could tell you herself like she wanted to. But, as usual, Gemma's timing is fucking impeccable, so she's screwed that plan." He shook his head and stared Everett in the eye. "Gemma's pregnant." He gave an almost hysterical laugh and wiggled his phone in the air between them. "She's in labour now, actually, so…there's that."

Everett's mouth attempted to form the word 'pregnant', but all that came out was a pathetic puff of air, which was ironic because it suddenly felt as though he couldn't breathe. He was glad that Gemma wasn't there to witness the sheer panic that stole over his features, lest she take his unfortunate reaction the wrong way.

Of course, it wasn't as though she would have expected him to jump for joy at the news. However, she probably would have hoped that he'd have been stunned, yet supportive. And he was. He would be. But in that initial moment, he could only focus on the negatives.

They'd had a one-night stand. They barely knew each other. As much as he'd connected with her and had felt himself falling for the idea of her to the extent of contemplating a long-distance relationship, saddling himself with a lifetime of responsibility was a completely different issue altogether. He hated himself a little for even thinking those words, but there they were.

He had never wanted children. He'd never wanted to risk subjecting a child to his family history of paternal abandonment. Given this inauspicious start to fatherhood, and his somewhat transient lifestyle, he wondered if he was doomed to repeat his father's actions, or his grandfather's before that.

His brain skittered to a halt.

Fatherhood.

His mouth went dry. That word applied to him now. He wasn't deluded –or stupid– enough to question the baby's paternity. Not with Brennan having flown to Sydney and pulled him from the Con to inform him of it. His agent, Rowena, would think him gullible for just taking them at their word, but this was not the moment to request a DNA test at any rate. When it came time to update his will, his lawyer would likely insist upon it, but he was getting ahead of himself.

With his thoughts ticking over again, Everett began to process the rest of the bomb Brennan had dropped on him. Gemma was in labour as they spoke! Pulling his wallet from his hip pocket, he slid a credit card from within it and held it out. "Use whatever means necessary to get us both on the next flight to Brisbane," he said, surprising himself with how level his tone was, even as his hand shook. "I've got a couple of calls to make. I'm not returning to the Con."

With begrudging approval in his expression, Brennan took the card, though he did look Everett in the eye to add, "She doesn't expect anything from you. You're off the hook if you want to be. She just wanted…" he stopped and corrected himself, "needed you to know."

Steeling his jaw, the actor shook his head. He'd never forgive himself if he took the out he'd just been offered. "Get me on that plane."

Brennan nodded and began searching for flights on his phone. Everett slipped into the bedroom and shut the door behind him, leaning against it for a moment to regulate his breathing before he dialled Rowena, mentally calculating that it would be close to 8 p.m. on Saturday night in LA.

"Everett," his agent picked up on the third ring, immediately concerned, "what's wrong?"

"I've got to pull out of the final panel of the Con," he told her, putting the phone on speaker so he could hastily pack his belongings into his carry-on case. What wouldn't fit he'd either have to send for at a later date or replace. He'd flown enough in his lifetime to know that checking a suitcase and having to retrieve it from baggage claim on the other end would take up more time than he could spare in this situation. He hoped Brennan would do the same, or that he'd travelled light to begin with.

"What, *why?*"

He deliberated sidestepping the question, but ultimately decided against it. She was his agent and had the right to know that there was likely a PR storm brewing in his life. He paused midway through tightly rolling up a pair of jeans, hesitating over the best way to explain his situation. "I've just learned that I'm about to become a father," he confessed quietly, the panic bubbling up inside him again as he spoke the words aloud. "She's just gone into labour an hour's flight away and I...I have to be there, Rowena."

"Well, that's convenient timing. How can you be sure it's yours?" she demanded, barely bothering to gentle her tone.

"I just am," he wasn't going to argue the point with her, "and you're wasting your breath trying to convince me otherwise. Just pull me from the final panel. I won't be there."

"Everett–"

He'd moved on to rolling up shirts. "I've got to go, Rowena. Tell them it's a family emergency. I'll call you later." He didn't bother waiting for her response before he terminated the call.

Next up was a courtesy call to Sam, also set to speaker.

"Okay, where the hell did you disappear to?" his best mate answered, sounding harried and concerned. "You do know we have a panel this afternoon, right? In, like, twenty minutes?"

"About that…" Everett sighed, carrying the phone into the bathroom to collect his toiletries and toothbrush. His voice echoed off the tiles. "I'm not coming back."

"What do you mean you're not coming back? What's going on?"

His hands shook as he placed his cologne into his toiletries bag, his shock beginning to wear off and give way to nerves. "The woman I told you about? The one I wished I could track down?"

There was a groan of disapproval. "Don't tell me you're leaving the Con early for some woman, Rhodes. It's an hour. She can wait."

"No, she can't," he fished his shampoo and conditioner out of the shower, giving them a cursory wipe with the towel hanging by the door before they followed his cologne. A lump lodged in his throat, and he attempted to swallow over it. "She…Sam, she's in labour. In Brisbane."

"Labour?" His friend echoed, sounding confused before the penny dropped. Everett could almost picture the scandalised expression on the other man's face as the volume of his voice dropped to a frantic whisper, "As in *giving birth?*"

"Yeah," his voice broke and he stopped to clear his throat into the stunned silence. He took his toiletry bag back into the bedroom and sat on the edge of the bed while the other actor processed the news he'd just been given.

"*Everett,*" Sam sounded sympathetic, horrified, and seriously worried all at once. "Dude, that's insane. What…God, you're going to her, then? Are you okay?"

"Next flight I can get, yeah." It felt good to talk to his best friend about this huge –terrifying– change in his circumstances, and he genuinely appreciated the fact that Samuel hadn't questioned the paternity like Rowena had. He'd just trusted Everett's judgement, and that meant the world to the Englishman in that moment. "I'm…fuck, Sam, I don't know what I am."

He scrubbed his hands over his face, knowing that he'd face no censure from the man on the other end of the line. "I never wanted kids," he continued quietly, shooting a careful look towards the closed bedroom door. The last thing he needed was Brennan hearing him venting his concerns. "And as much as I liked Gemma, I'm suddenly more than aware that she's a complete fucking stranger and none of this is ideal. I mean, Christ, she lives in *Australia* and I live in LA. How am I supposed to co-parent from halfway across the world?" Shaking his head, he lamented, "A little more notice would have been helpful. Her brother said she's been trying to get in touch with me, but obviously couldn't."

This time the silence had a touch of tension to it, extended as it was. "Shit," Sam hissed to himself, barely audible over the phone line. His tone turned apologetic. "I, uh, I think I might have been part of the problem."

"What? *How?*"

"Well, uh, you know how I did the Brisbane convention back in April?" He continued on before Everett could acknowledge the question. "There was a woman during photo ops who was insistent that I pass on a message to you, but...you know the rules. I couldn't accept the letter she was trying to give me. She was devastated. I just thought, you know, she was just another crazy Everett Rhodes fan wanting to send you fanfiction or a love letter or whatever. She didn't even stay for the photo she'd paid for." He sighed heavily. "I didn't think anything more of it...but...I mean, it fits, right?"

Slightly frustrated by what sounded like a missed opportunity to reconnect with Gemma, Everett reminded himself that Samuel hadn't had any idea back then about the woman Everett had met and become besotted with, and it was definitely best practice to not accept gifts or letters from people at these events.

"It's fine, Sam. It might not have been her." It likely was, but there was no point dwelling. "The main thing is that her brother's found me and now I...well, I hopefully won't miss out on my kid entering the world."

On the other end of the line, Samuel coughed. "That's a sobering thought."

Everett's answering chuckle was dry. "You're telling me."

* * *

Brennan had managed to get them both on the next flight to Brisbane. He had them both flying Business class, but on opposite sides of the aircraft. Everett was glad to have the space away from the glowering presence of Gemma's brother, still trying to process his entire world shifting on its axis.

He sat in his aisle seat lost in thought, absently running the pad of his thumb over his bottom lip, his index finger curled under his chin.

This shouldn't have happened. They'd been safe. Even if she hadn't insisted, he'd always been a stickler for being careful.

Not careful enough, clearly.

With his eyes closed, he leaned back against the headrest, reliving that night in his head as he had on numerous occasions – once again for self-recrimination, but of a completely different kind this time.

With a lurch, he recalled the bath. He could vividly recall how amazing she'd felt riding him in the water, and he could also recall not having a condom on hand when he'd slipped inside her. She'd been warm and tight – a wet vice that had called to him like a siren.

He hadn't come until she'd been laid out on the bed again –and they'd been safe– but that hardly seemed to matter now. While aware that precum carried sperm (thank you, Year Eleven biology class), he obviously hadn't considered it at the time. What the hell had he been thinking?

(He knew the answer: he hadn't been.)

Christ, Gemma was pregnant.

Unless one of their condoms had suffered some sort of catastrophic failure, this was all on him and his inability to think with anything other than his dick.

Scrubbing his hand over his face, he allowed the guilt to wash over him.

He was an idiot.

* * *

Chapter Seven

Brennan led the way through the main doors of the hospital, heading directly to the bank of elevators off to the right. He seemed to know exactly where they were headed without having to consult any signage.

"I am –or I was– Gemma's designated birth partner." Brennan told him by way of explanation as he hit the up button, and Everett realised that his question must have been on his face. "So I know where to go because I did the orientation tour with her."

"Ah." The actor nodded, unsure what else he was supposed to say. He bit his lip. "I'm glad you were there for her. If I'd known…" He trailed off, allowing Brennan to fill in the blanks however he wanted.

Honestly, Everett didn't know what he would have done. He couldn't have dropped everything to come and spend her pregnancy with her, but he wanted to think that he would have been somewhat involved, and that he would have been more prepared for this moment. However, that was all moot now, anyway.

Nothing more was said as a lift to their left opened its doors and they stepped through in a small group of people, with Brennan pressing the button to the fifth floor. The journey up was mercifully quick, and Everett followed the other man down the short hallway to a reception desk and a glass door declaring the space beyond the Obstetric Review Centre. A matronly woman sat behind the Perspex screen at the desk and arched her eyebrows at the two men as they approached.

"We're here for Gemma Fox," Brennan informed her, "I'm her brother, and this is the baby's father. We just flew in from Sydney."

The nurse, whose name badge read 'Anne', pursed her lips and typed into the system. "Okay, she's still here in the birth suites, but we'll need to confirm with her that she's happy for you to come through. Can I see your ID?"

Both men reached for their wallets and slid their driver's licences from their respective sleeves and through the little window under the screen. She barely batted an eye at the fact that Everett's was issued in California and took them with her as she left the desk to a hallway beyond their line of sight.

"They'll probably make us swap out with Sara and Dad," Brennan thought aloud, adding, "can't have too many people in the room, getting in the way or whatever."

Becoming more anxious with every moment that passed, Everett could only bring himself to swallow and nod again.

Anne returned a minute later, bypassing the desk and opening the glass door. "There are already two support people in with her," she told them as they entered, confirming exactly what Brennan had just said as she handed their licences back to them, "but Gemma would prefer you both to join her instead." She sounded as though this sort of thing was a regular occurrence, and Everett supposed that it probably was.

"How is she doing?" he found himself asking as he followed the woman down the hallway, wincing as he caught muted, agonised screaming from a closed door as they passed it. His heart hammered in his chest.

Substantially shorter than him, Anne craned her neck as she turned to offer him a gentle smile. "She's definitely getting to the pointy end now. It's been a relatively quick escalation this evening." Eyes forward again, she explained, "I've had ladies in here labouring for upwards of fifteen hours."

"Christ," he muttered, the urge to turn tail and flee rising up again. He hated himself a little for it.

"And here we are," she stopped at a door that read 'Birth Suite 3' and knocked, then turned the handle and poked her head in, verbally declaring, "Knock knock!" in a voice that was far too chirpy in Everett's estimation. Then she pushed the door open and said, "I've got Uncle and Daddy here."

Daddy.

Everett choked on air. He wasn't ready for this.

A large hand landed in the middle of his back and gave him a shove forward into the room after the midwife. An older man with grey hair and a pretty brunette were sat on either side of a hospital bed, the latter looking him up and down with wide, curious eyes while the former frowned. But Everett's attention was drawn to the woman on the bed itself, her fair hair plastered to her forehead, the green in her hazel eyes more pronounced than he recalled (possibly because they were rimmed red from tears she'd no doubt shed in pain and her own panic), and her hands clutching her very gravid belly over the thin, papery material of a hospital gown.

"Gemma," he murmured, a myriad of emotions infused into the two syllables.

Her lower lip quivered, but she attempted a watery smile, "Hi."

Brennan cleared his throat, "Hey, Dad, how about I walk you and Sara out?" Though it was posed as a question, it was clearly more an instruction, and the two people on either side of the bed understood that. Thankfully, neither seemed insulted that Gemma had chosen to replace them with the two men who had been brought through into the room.

The slim brunette stood and squeezed Gemma's hand, bending to whisper something Everett couldn't catch, but that had the fair-haired woman rolling her eyes. The older gentleman on the other side of the bed waited until Sara had made her way to Brennan's side before he pressed a kiss to Gemma's forehead and told her how much he loved her and how strong she was. He also added that he couldn't wait to meet his grandchild. He then walked towards Brennan, but came to stand in front of Everett first.

Silently, Everett catalogued the similarities between the man Gemma called 'Dad' and Brennan –the same dark eyes and olive coloured skin, the same long faces and thin noses– but he waited for the man to speak, anticipating hostility.

"You and I will be having a discussion tomorrow," Marcus said in a low voice, and Everett inclined his head in acknowledgement.

"Yes, sir."

He'd never done well with fathers – not his own, and certainly not any belonging to his paramours. He was fairly certain this one was already a lost cause, given the circumstances.

With one last piercing stare, the older man turned on his heel and led the small troupe out the door, leaving Everett and Gemma alone with only a single midwife seated at a desk on the other side of the room. The midwife was at least pretending that she wasn't eavesdropping and was busying herself with a medical chart.

"Gemma–" he began, but she grimaced and clutched at her belly, breathing in deeply through her nose and then exhaling slowly through her mouth. It lasted probably half a minute, maybe more.

"*Shit*," she hissed, eyes shut, rubbing across the bump that housed their child. Opening her eyes back up, she found a point on the wall behind him to stare at, unable to meet his gaze. "Sorry. That was a strong one."

"And we're still about three minutes apart at this stage," the midwife offered without looking across at them, writing something down in the chart. When she did look up, she smiled warmly at Gemma, "but consistent, so that's great."

"Yay," Gemma responded with a liberal dose of sarcasm before she turned her attention back to Everett. "So, um, hi. Again."

He couldn't help the snort of amusement that escaped him, and it was enough to get him moving from his position in the middle of the room to her side. He had no idea what to say first. Did he apologise for how terribly things had ended for them in November? Did he try and explain about his stolen phone? How on earth was he supposed to even begin to touch on the fact that he'd gotten her pregnant and then literally become uncontactable? He swallowed roughly. "Hi."

The corners of her lips lifted, before her expression fell, guilt marring her pretty features. "I'm so sorry you had to find out like this," she whispered, finally forcing herself to meet his gaze. "I tried so many different ways to get in touch with you–"

"Let's not worry about that right now," he told her, reaching for her hand (the one not currently resting on her rounded belly.) "I've a lot to apologise for, myself. But I believe we've more important things to focus on at the minute."

"You don't have to do this," she refuted, though the way she clutched at his hand contradicted the words. Her eyes welled with tears, but she continued, "I don't expect anything from you. I'm not… I'm not going to chase you for child support or anything. I'm happy to sign something to that effect if you need me to. I just…well, I didn't think it was fair you not knowing."

"I most certainly do not want you to sign anything," he frowned and squeezed her hand. "We're both a part of this, Fox." He finally forced himself to properly look at her stomach. His own lurched. "Boy or girl?"

"I don't know – I decided to be surprised. You know, to keep the trend going." She rubbed the swell in a large, circular motion before looking back at him, still clearly uncertain, "Do you have a preference?"

"No," he answered honestly, trying not to think too hard on the fact that he'd never wanted either. "Do you?"

She shook her head, then groaned suddenly, bending forward and repeating the same breathing exercise as before. "Oh, God, they're getting worse."

"And a bit closer together," the midwife chimed in again, this time getting up and making her way to the foot of the bed. "How's about we see how dilated you are? Then maybe you can get up and try walking around again. Or try the shower? I hear it's magic for pain relief."

Everett blinked at her. "Sorry – walking around?" He tilted his head back in Gemma's direction. "They let you do that?"

She huffed a laugh, drawing her knees up so the midwife could do as she'd intended. Everett kept his eyes firmly glued to Gemma's while she responded, "They don't chain us to the beds, you know. The walking's supposed to help speed things up. I got tired out from bouncing on the exercise ball–" she gestured towards the comically large yoga ball tucked into the far corner of the room, "–and decided to take a break, but my birth plan is—*motherfucker* that *hurts.*" She yelped and flinched back from the midwife's probing.

"Sorry," the other woman said with empathy, "breathe through it for me, okay? It won't take long."

Gemma squeezed her eyes shut and whimpered through the exam, exhaling shakily in relief as the midwife finally withdrew and told her she was done. "You're at seven centimetres," she declared happily, "I think we'll have a baby before midnight." She then pressed a device to Gemma's belly, which Gemma told him was to check on the baby's heart rate, and nodded, satisfied with whatever her findings had been.

Everett glanced at the clock. It was just past seven. Five more hours seemed like a long time. "Are you alright, love?" he asked, seeing the pain still etched across Gemma's face.

"Yeah," she answered. "Just sore."

He brought her hand to his mouth and brushed a kiss across the back of her knuckles. "How can I help?"

"Keep distracting me," she answered, her eyes drawn to his lips and her hand. She gave herself a shake. "Um, maybe put on some music? I have a playlist on my phone. Just random stuff."

"I've got it," Brennan announced, re-entering the room. He crossed to her other side and kissed her forehead. "Still haven't popped my nephew out yet, Gems? What have you been doing all afternoon?"

"Could be a niece," she reminded him with a fond roll of her eyes, "and I've just been lazing around, obviously. Netflix and zero chilling."

"Pretty sure Netflix and Chilling is what landed you here," he shot back in the process of digging into her bag for her phone, emerging victorious with his prize. "PIN?"

"Not happening. Hand it over." She snatched the device from him and entered her PIN, then clicked on her music app and selected her playlist, hitting shuffle. Brennan plugged it into the stereo provided and adjusted the volume. Adele's *Hello* started up, and Everett thought it only mildly ironic.

"See, you're not completely useless," she teased her brother before clutching at her stomach and going through another contraction, cursing again at the end. She sighed heavily once it was over and flopped back against her pillow. "They're definitely getting worse."

"Try the shower," the midwife urged again. "Most women swear by the hot water on their back and belly." She offered Gemma a soft smile. "It's too late for the epi, and too early for the gas and air. Hot water is your best bet for pain relief right now."

"Okay," Gemma swallowed and swung her legs over the edge of the bed, allowing Everett to assist her off and hold her steady while she acclimated to standing again. Brennan also rounded the bed to stand at her other side and she looked between the two men. "Uh, no offence, but I'd rather my brother not see me naked." She looked back up at Everett, her cheeks colouring. "Would you mind, um, helping me in there?"

It hadn't occurred to Everett that her showering meant the robe coming off. He wondered what it said about him that he was almost afraid of seeing her pregnant form bare. He'd never considered himself shallow before, and he wasn't even certain it was an issue of not finding her attractive, because this moment was not about that at all. Instead, it was because it would affirm the situation that he'd found himself in, and he couldn't possibly ignore the reality of it any longer.

Still, he nodded, hoping his expression gave none of his panic away, and softly answered, "Of course, love. Or, rather, of course not." Because she'd asked if he'd mind, not if he would help.

His head felt full and jumbled, and he was making a fool of himself, but she smiled back at him again and squeezed the hand she was holding as he led her into the adjoining bathroom.

"I knew what you meant," she replied almost timidly, and he hated that she no longer felt the confidence to tease him that she'd had in November.

The midwife –whose name tag he finally noticed read 'Christie'– already had the two showerheads in the bathroom running. She gave Gemma a reassuring smile, "Just call out if you need me, okay?"

Gemma agreed with a bob of her head and then the two of them were left alone in the large, tiled room, the door mostly shutting behind Christie's retreating form. She'd left it open a crack for them to call out if they needed her.

"Could you untie the back of this thing?" Gemma asked quietly, turning to allow him access to the back of the gown, where it was tied at the nape of her neck and her waist.

He made short work of both knots and she thanked him before visibly steeling herself and slipping the papery garment down her arms and off. She folded it neatly and placed it down on the closed toilet seat, separated from the shower by a floor length shower curtain, keeping her gaze averted.

She was as terrified of his reaction to her pregnant body as he was. It broke him a little to realise it.

He quickly unbuttoned the sleeves of his shirt and rolled them up to his elbows, suddenly regretting wearing the white item, with its blue & grey paisley pattern. (Rowena had told him it made his eyes 'pop' and had insisted he wear it at least once to the Con for his fans' sake.) Next, he removed his watch and slipped his phone and wallet from his pockets, placing the items on top of Gemma's gown, out of the way of the spray. He also rid himself of his shoes and socks because it seemed logical.

In that time, Gemma had already moved to stand between the two shower heads and had removed one from the bracket on the wall to aim it directly over her belly. She was bracing herself against the assistance bar on the wall with her free hand and grimacing through another contraction, once again breathing out through her mouth with her eyes shut.

Everett removed the other showerhead and cleared his throat, asking where she'd like it directed.

"Uh, my lower back, please." When she finally forced herself to meet his gaze, her eyes were sad, but she attempted a smile, bitterly quipping, "Bit like hosing down a beached whale, right?"

"Stop it," he reprimanded, frowning. "You're pregnant, not a whale." Clearly, pregnancy hadn't helped her insecurities any. Another thing to add to his list of self-recriminations because he felt he was responsible for this.

"To-may-to, to-mah-to." Her lower lip quivered. "I wish you weren't seeing me like this."

"Like what? In labour with our kid?" He had no idea where his confidence was coming from, considering how uneasy he still was with the concept. "Darling, I told you – we're both a part of this."

"Except five hours ago you had no idea this was happening and now I've upended your life and–"

"And nothing. I'm an adult. If anything, I upended your life in November when I put my foot in my mouth and ruined what had potential to be something wonderful between us. And, to top that spectacular behaviour off, I apparently left you pregnant and alone." With his free hand, he scratched at the back of his neck. "I never meant that what happened between us was a mistake, or something to regret. My mistake was rushing it, especially when I had to leave the country. I tried to explain, but..." He trailed off. She'd been there: she knew how well that conversation had gone.

Fat tears began rolling down her cheeks. "I thought we weren't going to talk about it."

"Well, not with an audience," he gave a half shrug. "But, at the very least, you deserve an apology, and an explanation."

"I appreciate that," Gemma smiled through her tears. "And I *am* glad you're here."

Despite his ratcheting anxiety, he returned the smile. "I am as well." As her expression morphed back to pained, he asked, "Is the hot water helping at all?"

"It is," she hissed, not sounding at all convincing while she attempted to breathe through the contraction, which was lasting longer than the last few had. "It's actually wonderful. They're just getting a bit more intense."

Everett took the second shower head from her, and she braced both hands on the bar in front of her, stretching out under the warm spray with an almost feline grace. "I'm assuming that's a good sign?"

"I mean, I haven't done this before, so I wouldn't actually know, but...I think so?"

"My phone was stolen," he blurted awkwardly, feeling his cheeks flush at the dubious expression she wore, clearly wondering at his non-sequitur. "I had every intention of getting in touch with you, but my contacts weren't backed up, and the SIM was only a travel SIM, so I had no bills I could refer back to…" he sighed. "I regret that you've gone through all of this on your own. That I inadvertently put you in this position."

Understanding dawned and she rubbed a soothing circle over her belly. "I'll admit, when I found out I was pregnant, I…well, my reaction wasn't exactly sunshine and lollipops. And I definitely wasn't happy when I couldn't find a way to contact you." He could only imagine the despair and frustration she might have felt. "But I have amazing friends, and a great support system, and I love this baby already…though not so much right at this second," she hastened to add, doubling over and groaning.

"What do you need?" he asked, concerned at how much faster that contraction had seemed to crash over her. "How can I help?"

"I…I think I need to sit."

He set the shower heads back in their brackets and kept them aimed at her as best he could. "Are you right to hold on to the rail for a moment while I grab the shower seat?" He didn't dare step away in case she didn't feel she could continue to stand on her own, but when she nodded, he ducked back around the curtain and snagged the seat that was pushed up against the wall between the shower and the toilet. It was made of plastic and plastic-coated metal, and had a hole in the middle of the seat much like a toilet seat did. He didn't want to think too long on why that might be necessary.

Setting it down beside her under the hot water, heedless of the spray now seeping into his shirt and trousers, he guided her down into it, noting the sigh of relief that left her as she sat.

"Well, this is a glamorous look for me, I'm sure," she muttered with the same self-deprecation that had laced her whale comment. "But thankyo–*holy shit*, have you *lived* in the gym since I last saw you?" Her eyes were wide as she stared at him, and she blushed heavily as she realised that she'd spoken aloud.

Everett laughed at both the unexpected assessment (his wet, previously white shirt left nothing to the imagination at this point) and the embarrassment on her face. He hadn't given much thought to the fact that, after being cast in a role which had required him to bulk up, he'd maintained the effort, finding the gym time therapeutic. He still wasn't quite as broad or muscular as his brother, but the changes since November were quite noticeable. "You did suggest I distract you, did you not?"

"I–" she went to reply, then cried out in pain, clutching low beneath her belly, pressing down on her pubic bone and hip with splayed out palms. She looked up at him after the pain passed, terror evident in her eyes for the first time that he'd seen since he'd arrived. "I've changed my mind. Everett, I can't do this."

"I don't think that's an option at this point," He hesitated between kneeling at her side or fetching the midwife, because that hadn't been anything like any of the contractions that he'd witnessed prior. "Should I get help?"

"No. No, I think…I think I'm just, uh, dilating more? It felt like I was being torn in half. It was…kind of like pressure? But not? I can't describe it. But it sucked."

He grimaced, having tried to ignore the specifics of what giving birth was going to entail for her. Clearing his throat, he asked, "Earlier, you mentioned a birth plan?" Because plans he could work with. He didn't like uncertainty. Improvisation had never been his strong suit.

She groaned. "Yeah, back when I had no idea just how hard this was, I originally thought I wanted to give birth while squatting or remaining upright, maybe leaning over the side of the bed." At his horrified expression, she explained, "Gravity helps, apparently. Makes the whole thing go faster. That's what all the blogs say. But I'm already exhausted, and I don't think I can stay upright." He could see her hands shaking, and it took him half a moment to realise that it wasn't from the cold, given the hot water still sluicing over her.

"Hey, it's alright," he soothed, at her side within two strides. He crouched beside the chair, attempting to be as far out of the shower's reach as possible, resting one hand atop of her forearm while his other gripped the back of the chair to keep himself stable. "You're doing so well, love."

Whatever refutation she was going to shoot back at him died on the end of her tongue as another contraction built up and crashed over her like a wave, only this time she pulled his hand across her bare stomach, pushing it down against her while she whimpered.

"Christ," he uttered, feeling the tightening beneath her skin slowly easing away, though the swell of her belly remained firm.

She came back to her senses and blushed. "Shit, sorry," she picked his hand back up and moved it back to the arm of the chair. "I didn't mean to…well, I know that all of this is kind of confronting, but–"

"Breathe," he instructed, cutting off her babbling. Locking his gaze with hers, he tentatively shifted his hand back to her belly, resting it over the same spot she'd unceremoniously pushed it against. "I wouldn't be here if I didn't want to be."

He'd said something similar to her when they'd first met, and even though the circumstances weren't ideal, he wasn't walking away from the life he'd helped create. It had started as a matter of pride and good form –the right thing to do– but he was still drawn to Gemma like a moth to flame and could feel himself becoming emotionally invested in their child. He supposed that wasn't a bad thing –it was probably a good sign that he wasn't going to repeat his father's mistakes– but it only added to his terror of their rapidly impending birth.

Gemma sniffled miserably, "You haven't even asked if I'm sure it's yours."

"My solicitor might request a paternity test when I update my will, but I highly doubt you and Brennan would have gone to so much effort to track me down if there was even a chance you were unsure," he explained gently, with his hand still on her belly.

He watched as she she bit her lip, processing his words.

There was faint movement beneath his palm, and he inhaled sharply. "Was that–?"

She nodded, beginning to smile at his mystified expression.

"I'm sorry you missed the fun stuff," she eventually replied, glancing down at his hand. "The kicking, as you might have gathered just now, was actually really cool. Well, except for in the middle of the night when I wanted to sleep and he–"

"Or she."

Gemma's lips quirked again at the correction, "–*or she* thought it was a great time for a solo disco."

Opening his mouth to tease her, he could feel as the next contraction built beneath her skin, the muscle beneath his hand tightening as the rest of her body tensed. As with the last one, she moaned in pain, only this time she gripped his hand and locked terrified eyes with him, declaring, "I...I need to push."

He felt his heart drop into his stomach. He wasn't ready. Which felt ridiculous because he wasn't the one actually going through the birthing process. With wide eyes of his own, he turned his head towards the not-entirely-shut bathroom door and shouted for help.

Brennan barrelled in first, and it was testament to how scared Gemma was that she said nothing of being naked in front of him when she'd been concerned about the fact barely fifteen minutes earlier. The midwife –Christie, he reminded himself– followed at a more sedate pace.

"What's going on?" the other woman asked, making her way to Gemma's other side. She made short work of shutting off the showers so she could examine her patient.

"I really needed to push."

Christie's brown eyes widened minutely, but she remained calm (almost irritatingly chirpy) as she responded, "Well, that's happened a lot faster than we thought it would, hasn't it?" She glanced up at Brennan. "Could you pass me one of those towels from behind you?" He rushed to do that, and she turned her attention back to Gemma. "I'm just going to check and make sure you're dilated enough, alright?" Gemma nodded, her lower lip quivering with impending tears, and the midwife kept her tone soothing. "Why don't you start trying to dry off a little and I'll just fetch my mirror. Stay sitting, I'll only be a moment."

Everett helped pat her down with the second towel Brennan handed over, drying places he assumed she'd struggle to reach, like her back and her legs. She offered him a shaky, but genuinely grateful smile. "You should probably ditch the shirt," she said, gesturing to the translucent fabric plastered to his chest, "and dry off a bit as well."

"Don't think I don't see straight through your attempt to see me shirtless again, Fox," he teased, partially out of nerves of his own, but also because he wanted to keep her distracted from her own fear. Even so, he reached for the buttons with trembling fingers and did as she'd suggested, not at all surprised to find her gaze glued to his now broader chest and biceps as he pulled the clingy material off and tossed the shirt towards the sink. His trousers were also damp, but they were staying put. "My eyes are up here, darling."

She exhaled with obvious frustration. "Listen, bud, you knocked me up. I'm allowed to ogle."

That was much more like the woman he'd gotten to know all those months earlier, and the snarky response elicited a bark of laughter out of him. "Ogle away," he offered, sweeping his damp hair back off his face.

Christie returned with the promised mirror and made an amused sound, even as she casually slid the mirror under the seat. "That's one way to distract the patient, Mr Rhodes."

"Hospital approved, I'm certain," he sassed back, winking at Gemma, resolutely not looking towards the reflective surface beneath her.

"Fairly sure a lot of women would pay extra for this," she agreed, the grin on her face beginning to fade as the familiar pain began to build again. He grasped her hand and, with his free hand, rubbed at her belly the way he'd watched her do, noting that this time the contraction seemed longer again. This time she made an almost guttural sound as she squeezed her eyes shut and declared, "I *need* to push!"

"Okay, breathe for me, Gemma," the midwife attempted to calm her. "Deep breath in through the nose…that's it. Good. Now out slowly through the mouth. 'Atta girl. Again." Gemma complied shakily a second time, and the tightness under Everett's palm receded. "Alright. So, you're right – you're ready to start delivery. Guess being upright helped things along, huh?" Gemma whimpered and Everett swallowed roughly. "But we need to leave the shower to do that. Did you still want to attempt an upright birth, or–"

"No!" Gemma cried, her entire demeanour shifting to panicked and terrified. "No. I can't. I can't do this. I can't stand up. I can't. I just…*I can't.*"

"Gems," Brennan attempted –and Everett finally noticed that the other man was rubbing soothing circles on his sister's back– but she shook her head, refusing to listen.

"Alright," Everett intervened. "Gemma, darling, look at me." She did as he asked, tears sliding down her cheeks. "We need to get you into the other room. Brennan and I will support you, alright? We'll take it step by step."

It took her a moment, but she eventually nodded and allowed the two men to help her from the seat, one on either side, each with an arm around her. "Did you want your robe back?" Brennan asked her, and she sighed.

"What's the point? You've seen me naked, and things are only going to get worse from here."

Brennan shrugged. "Okay, but you're not throwing this back on me when you get retroactive embarrassment."

"*Pfft*," Gemma argued, "I retain the right to blame you anyway."

Christie chuckled at that, muttering about siblings never changing.

"How do you want to do this?" Everett asked as they neared the bed, but Gemma's knees buckled as another contraction escalated.

The midwife took charge. "Okay, hun, you're sure you don't want to try stick with your plan?" Gemma nodded, sobbing as she tried to breathe through the pain while her support people held her up. Christie was adjusting the bed, lowering it so that it would be easier to climb into and raising the back into a more seated position. "Alright. Dad, climb up on the bed and we'll get Gemma to settle in between your legs with her back to your chest."

Dad.

The casual address threw him for a moment, but Everett did exactly as he was told, and Brennan assisted Gemma in with him. Christie smiled and raised the bed up higher, directing Gemma to bring her knees up as close to her chest as she could get them, informing Gemma that she was going to make things uncomfortable again as she affixed a fetal monitor to the baby's head inside her.

"Hey, spoiler alert, from what I can see, bub is gonna' have Dad's head of hair." Christie said with cheer, obviously trying to distract Gemma before she handed over a plastic tube, connected to a point in the wall, explaining that it was the only pain relief option left to her.

Everett had stopped listening for a moment, his brain stuck on the offhand 'spoiler alert'. He'd not given any thought to what the kid might actually look like until that moment. *His* hair. Why did that suddenly fill him with pride? He swallowed and zoned back in as Christie was still discussing the pain relief.

"I know you're a nurse," she acknowledged, "but do you know how to use the Gas and Air?"

Gemma clutched at her prize as though it might be taken at any moment. "Breathe in deeply as the contraction builds, not when I'm already in the middle of it."

"That's it, good girl," the midwife praised, and Gemma's expression told him that she was biting back a snide response as another contraction seemed to rise out of nowhere. Christie used her distraction to affix the monitor, informing them, "Bub's nice and close, so I don't think that this is going to take too long."

"*Fuck,*" Gemma cursed, bending forward and groaning before remembering the pain relief. She took in a deep breath from the tube, then declared, "I've gotta–"

Christie nodded, positioned at the foot of the bed. "Go for it, hun."

Gemma tugged Everett's hands around to her belly, gripping them tightly as she bore down and cried out. This, he decided, was enough to convince him to go and get a damn vasectomy. Why did women choose to go through this more than once?

Still, the words he said aloud were of support and praise. "You've got this, Fox."

She flopped back against him, attempting to catch her breath before the next contraction. "I don't want to do this anymore," she reiterated, sounding miserable.

Unable to stop himself, he kissed her temple. "What can I do, love?"

"Keep distracting me."

Brennan cleared his throat, and Everett imagined he felt even more useless than Everett himself did. "Want the music up louder?" he asked, already reaching for the phone.

"Please," Gemma agreed, before whimpering again and sucking in from the tube as yet another contraction escalated. The opening strains of Billy Joel's '*My Life*' played while Gemma repeated the same action as earlier, only this time she groaned and growled as she pushed.

Another midwife had entered the room to assist by this stage, but neither he nor Gemma paid too much attention. Brennan was tasked with feeding Gemma ice chips and wiping sweat from her brow, offering his own soothing encouragements while she snippily told him to shut up.

The entire scenario felt surreal to Everett. When, after the twelfth contraction since they'd climbed into the bed, irritatingly familiar chords began playing out of the tinny speaker, he decided he'd reached peak Bizarro World. "Seriously?" he asked her. "Can we change this one?"

"I told you, I *like* this song," she snapped, her voice turning hoarse from all the throaty sounds she made as she pushed during each contraction. "I – *aaaaarrgghh!*"

"Keep pushing," Christie urged, excitedly. "Bub's crowning."

"*I fucking can't!*" Gemma cried back at her, collapsing against Everett's chest with tears streaming down her cheeks.

He had no idea what possessed him –perhaps the terror at the midwife's declaration, or his surprise at Gemma's sudden shift to anger– but he began singing along with his own voice as it spilled out from the stereo, feeling utterly ridiculous as he crooned the stupid sea-shanty into her ear.

"Oh my God," Gemma craned her neck to stare at him, startled, her hazel eyes filled with wonder. "Don't you *dare* stop singing," she demanded, already becoming swept up in another contraction. They were coming hard and fast now, and he hoped that was a sign she'd be lucky enough to birth their baby quickly.

This time as she bore down, her scream was horrific and guttural and louder than any others she'd issued. He stopped singing.

"Well done! Head's out!" Christie announced, beaming up at Gemma and Everett. He refused to look down, coward that he was.

"Gemma, I need you to push carefully on the next one," the other midwife instructed the labouring woman, "because the shoulders are the widest part and we're going to try and avoid tearing, okay?"

Tearing. Everett winced at just the thought. Gemma, on the other hand, demanded, "How the ever-loving fuck am I supposed to push *carefully*?"

The midwife took it in stride, just reiterating that she needed to at least try not to push too hard, and the next minutes were some of the most nerve-wracking and horrifying that Everett had ever experienced in his life. They seemed to stretch on for eternity, the midwives guiding Gemma as she screeched and swore and practically bent over double in front of him, squeezing his hands tightly. And then she gasped, with the room seeming to fall eerily silent for a split second, save for the music playing, before the lusty cry of a newborn cut through Roy Orbison's warbling during the Traveling Wilburys' *'Handle With Care'*. (And, in an instant, it became his favourite song.)

"Congratulations, Mummy and Daddy, it's a girl!" Christie announced, lifting the babe –still attached via the purple, twisting umbilical cord– and placing her directly onto Gemma's chest, pushing her to relax back against Everett.

On instinct, he brought his shaking hands up to cover Gemma's, which were already cradling the baby to her bare skin. A blanket was draped over them, and he barely paid attention as the midwives coached Gemma through delivering the placenta and whatever else that entailed.

"*Gemma*," he breathed, choked up by a bout of emotion that took him by surprise.

How was it possible to so fiercely love a person that hadn't existed until that very moment? The baby was perfect and, even if he had questioned her paternity, staring at her wrinkled but petite features, he didn't think he'd have a leg to stand on if he tried.

She was covered in a white, waxy substance (which blogs would later tell him was called vernix) and remnants of blood. But, beneath all of that, he could see that she had a generous head of dark hair, eyes the exact same shape as his, little perfectly rounded ears that also matched his own, and her mouth –even pulled into a moue of discomfort– was also a mirror image of his. He thought maybe she had Gemma's nose and chin, but the rest was all him.

Suddenly overwhelmed and completely besotted, he understood why parents chose to do this more than once.

Gemma turned her head to face him and, driven by adrenaline and endorphins, he ducked his head to capture her lips with his own, the angle awkward, but the moment too perfect to pass up. He pressed the side of his forehead against hers after he pulled away, murmuring, "You were amazing, love. She's perfect."

Gemma gave a watery laugh, peering back down at the baby who was squinting up at them from atop her heart. "You would say that – she looks *just* like you!"

What did it say about him that he could only preen in satisfaction over that? "Yeah, and she's divine." He'd been so afraid of this tiny person's existence, but now he only felt the urge to love and protect her.

Under the blanket, he carefully shifted his hand so he could gently stroke the baby's soft, pink skin with his index finger. His entire world felt as though it had shifted on its axis, and he knew he had a lot to consider now.

After a few more minutes, wherein Brennan congratulated them and teased his sister gently for not providing the nephew he'd been banking on, the cord was cut –given his position, neither midwife bothered to ask Everett if he wanted the honours (and he didn't)– and the baby was taken momentarily to be measured and weighed. Everett committed the details to memory as she was handed back to Gemma, grizzling and rooting unsteadily for food.

"Have you decided on a name?" Christie asked from the desk across the room, clearly filling out paperwork while the older midwife assisted Gemma with positioning the baby to feed.

Gemma nodded, opening her mouth to respond, then shut it. She tried to look up at Everett, quietly asking him whether he minded her choosing. "I've no ideas of my own," he confessed gently, "and you've done all the hard work to this point. All I ask, if it's alright, is that you choose an actual name and spell it correctly."

Despite snorting, she nodded. "No arbitrary replacing of 'i's and 'e's with 'y's or apostrophes, got it."

"Or 's's with 'z's, or 'c's and 'k's with 'x's."

She shuddered. "Or mashing two names together portmanteau-style."

"We get it," Brennan interrupted with obvious exasperation as Everett began to include a new rule, "you're both name snobs. Lucky you're on the same page. Now come on, Gems, I need to know what to call my niece."

Gemma gazed down lovingly at the baby who was snuffling as she suckled at her breast. "Zoe," she said with confidence, explaining, "It means 'life' – and she's my whole life now, as cheesy as that sounds." She craned her neck to smile back at him. "So, I guess, meet little Zoe Beatrice Fox Rhodes."

* * *

His mother. Gemma had named the baby –their daughter (bloody hell, he had a *daughter*)– after his mother. Well, Zoe's middle name, at least. *And* she had given her his surname, something he'd protested because he didn't feel he'd earned that right. Gemma had remained firm on the issue, though, completely mystifying him. Even hours after the fact, Everett's mind was still reeling over Gemma's choices.

They'd been relocated from the birthing suites to a private room (which Gemma told him was a perk from having fantastic health insurance and also aided by her role as a nurse in that very same hospital), and Gemma had all but passed out after the adrenaline from the evening had worn off. Brennan had brought up Everett's bag from the car and then bid them goodnight, and it had left the actor alone with his thoughts.

He was thankful that the room Gemma had been allocated had a large, squishy reclining chair by the window for him to sleep in, because he'd had no intention of leaving her side. Even if he'd had to bribe his way to sleeping on the floor, he would have done it. At Gemma's immediate bedside, a clear, plastic, rectangular tub on wheels contained their sleeping newborn, and he couldn't take his eyes off her.

It hadn't really sunk in yet that he was a father. It struck him that he really should call his mother and brother at the very least, considering they were his only family and deserved to know that they now had a beautiful little lady to dote on. Besides, it would behove him to inform them before the tabloids did, or he'd never hear the end of it.

It would be late Sunday morning in the UK, and he considered that he might even catch them together for their usual Sunday roast lunch. Decided, he located his phone and snagged his Bluetooth earphones, hoping to save Gemma from their reactions waking her. He kept one free, only inserting one of the earbuds while the other dangled over his shoulder so he could keep an ear out for signs of either of his girls waking. Then he Facetimed his mother, deciding that this was news he had to deliver as close to face-to-face as possible.

"Everett," she answered with surprise, and it took a moment for the video feed to clear up from the pixelated mess he was seeing. His mother's expression was one of concern by the time his screen focused. "It's not like you to call without notice. Not that I'm complaining. I do love to hear from my baby." He could hear his brother's amused chortle from off screen. She frowned into her phone, asking, "Are you alright, sweetheart? You look shattered."

He hadn't given much thought to his appearance besides locating a shirt, seeing as the one he'd been wearing was still drying in the ensuite bathroom. He imagined he looked as wrecked as he felt, though. He ran a hand through his hair and sighed. "I've had a day," he answered ambiguously, attempting to keep his voice low. "Can you, uh, get Charlie in the frame, too? I've got some news, and I'd rather tell you together."

Beatrice's eyebrows winged upwards (he'd inherited his expressive set from her) and she looked off screen and tilted her neck, having a silent –but obvious– conversation with his brother. Soon enough, Charlie was at their mother's side, offering a gruff, "Alright, Everett?"

"You should both sit," he suggested. He could feel his nerves escalating.

Their opinions meant the world to him, and he knew that having a surprise child with a fan he'd shared a one-night stand with wasn't the most responsible news he could be dropping on them. But, ultimately, he knew that they'd adore Zoe because she was his daughter, and he couldn't imagine ever being ashamed of her existence.

Exchanging another uneasy glance between them, they pulled up chairs and his mother readjusted her hold on her phone, setting it down on the table they were sat at and resting it against something, allowing a little extra distance between it and themselves so he could see them both properly. "What's going on?" she asked in the same measured tone she'd used when he'd get into trouble at school.

It was fitting, really. He was beginning to feel a bit like a reckless teenager instead of a successful thirty-five-year-old man. He attempted to muster a reassuring smile, but they'd always seen through him.

"I'm a father," Everett told them, swallowing roughly into the stunned silence. "I have a daughter. She was born a couple of hours ago."

"*What?*" his mother's voice was shrill. "How…when…*Everett*, what?"

On the screen, Charlie placed a calming hand over her forearm and cast a bewildered glance in Everett's direction, "You didn't think a little warning would have been nice?"

"I didn't get any," he shot back, realising his sharp tone a touch too late. He looked over towards the bed, but both Gemma and Zoe remained fast asleep. Lowering his voice again, he sighed and scrubbed his free hand tiredly over his face. "I only found out today, literally a handful of hours before she was born, and, before you ask, she's definitely mine."

His mother shook her head, visibly upset. "What do you mean you only found out today?"

Bracing himself, he launched into the whole sordid tale. He explained how he and Gemma had met, the spark he'd felt between them, how he had done everything in his power to spend as much time with her as he could in the limited window they'd had. Admitting that he'd slept with her too soon –not knowing when he'd have the chance to truly be with her again, if ever– and then put his foot in his mouth, hurting her in the process, made his heart ache. Detailing the comedy of errors where their only means of contacting one another were removed –especially knowing now that she'd been desperate to inform him of his impending fatherhood– made it worse.

Everett told them about her brother finding him in Sydney, about the phone call Brennan had taken that had shaken them both up, and about getting his sorry arse onto the first flight back to Brisbane that he could. Finally, he told them that he'd managed to make it in time. That Gemma –the goddess that she was– hadn't despised him on sight, and that he'd been there as their daughter entered the world.

To their credit, both his mother and his brother listened to his story without interruption, though he could tell from their expressions that they both had questions. He wasn't certain he had the answers that would appease them, but he'd do his best.

"She looks just like me, Mum," he finished, feeling emotional all over again. "She's perfect."

Unsurprisingly, it was Charlie who spoke first, shaking his head. "A fan, mate? Really?"

"I know," he'd been through it a thousand times in his own head, even before he'd learned there had been lasting consequences from his and Gemma's time spent together. "But she's different. I felt a connection with her."

"Christ," his older brother muttered derisively. "How can you be in your mid-thirties and still getting yourself into strife? Didn't I give you the safe sex talk when you were, what, fourteen?"

Rolling his eyes at the lecture, the actor turned just a little condescending in response. "Turns out those warnings on condom boxes about being 98% effective? An actual thing." There was no way he was admitting that he'd been momentarily careless. Not to Charlie. That was a secret he was taking straight to his grave.

"Stop being crass, both of you." His mother finally found her voice, admonishing both her sons, turning her head between them both. Her expression softened as she looked back at Everett. "I'm a grandmother."

He nodded, relief washing over him at her acceptance and the wonder in her tone. "And I'm a Dad." His lips quirked and he teased, "Making football-head there," he jutted his chin towards Charlie, "an Uncle."

"Stop riling your brother up," Beatrice admonished him, but there was little heat to it. "Is she with you? Can I see her? What's her name?"

"Zoe. Her name is Zoe," he answered, beaming back at his mother, "Zoe Beatrice Fox Rhodes." He glanced up, away from the screen, checking that Gemma and the baby were still asleep.

As he might have predicted, his mother bit back a surprised sob. "Oh, *Everett...*"

He shook his head and glanced over at the sleeping mother of his child. His tone was warm when he admitted, "That was all Gemma."

His brother grumbled something about emotional manipulation, but he wisely ignored it, smirking to himself when his mother visibly elbowed Charlie and told him to watch himself.

"I want to see my grandbaby," Beatrice repeated, and Everett nodded, more than happy to indulge her. He hadn't really had anyone to share her perfection with yet –aside from Gemma and her brother, and a quick photo texted to Sam– and was pleased to be able to do so.

"Alright. Just a tic." He got up and quietly padded over to the bedside where the baby was slumbering, just as worn out from the trauma of birth as her mother.

She was swaddled in a rainbow-coloured hospital blanket, with a little knitted beanie (gifted by the hospital for her to keep) atop her head, but wisps of her surprisingly long, fine dark hair were curling out from underneath it. Even though he'd only seen her minutes earlier, his heart still squeezed at the sight of her.

He pressed the button on his screen to switch the camera to the one at the back of the phone, aiming it towards the plastic hospital bassinet. His mother leaned forward in her seat, extending a trembling hand towards the screen as she inhaled sharply.

"Oh, sweetheart, she's beautiful."

Standing too close to the bed, he didn't want to risk answering aloud, so he gave the phone a jiggle to acknowledge the comment.

His mum continued, "You're right, she's the spitting image of you as a baby." She sighed. "Oh, I want a cuddle."

Everett hadn't understood the appeal in holding babies until he'd finally held Zoe in his arms. She'd been warm and surprisingly solid for how tiny and fragile she appeared. He hadn't wanted to put her down.

Before he knew what he was doing, he had wandered back to the window, switching the camera back and quietly declared, "I'll fly you out here to meet her. Both of you."

"Darling, you don't have to do that," his mother argued, while Charlie simultaneously asked him whether he wasn't expected back in LA.

He shook his head. "I've told Rowena to cancel my flights back for now. I've finished filming for the time being and I'm going to stay here as long as my VISA will allow."

He had to work out where, exactly, he was going to stay, and was pretty much banking on Gemma allowing him to come home with her and their daughter. The idea of being parted from the tiny person they'd made was too painful to entertain. (And that very feeling still had him reeling, because he hadn't expected to feel this way – not so soon, perhaps not even at all.)

"And what are you going to do for work?" his brother prodded. "You've a child to support now and all."

Everett was already regretting the offer to fly Charlie out. He had a feeling his first impression upon Gemma would not be a good one. He didn't want to ponder too long on why that thought upset him. "I'm sure Rowena will find me something. There are film studios on the Gold Coast. Australia has a rapidly growing entertainment industry."

"You're serious about this? About giving up everything you've worked for for some–"

"Watch your words, mate," the actor's tone turned warning, interrupting his brother before he could say something regrettable.

Charlie rolled his eyes, but mercifully kept his mouth shut. Beatrice resumed the conversation, bringing it back to lighter, happier things. They spoke for a little while longer, until Everett yawned widely, and his mother offered him a soft smile.

"Go to bed, love. Get some sleep. God knows you'll not get enough now that you've a newborn in your life."

He nodded, exchanged goodbyes and a reiteration that he'd fly them out to meet Zoe as soon as he could arrange it, and terminated the call. His girls were both still fast asleep and, soon enough, so was he.

* * *

"...I mean, *damn*, Gems," the hushed, unfamiliar voice stirred him the next morning, and it took him a few moments to get his bearings, "I totally get it now. I think my ovaries combusted just looking at him."

Grateful for his career choice, he was able to maintain the facade of sleep, smothering the smirk that threatened to undermine his act.

"Sara, shut up," came Gemma's whispered admonishment. "It's not like him being attractive is a surprise. I know you Googled him."

"Google did *not* do him justice," was the flippant response.

"You're an idiot."

The other woman –Sara– huffed dramatically. "And you're still seriously not going to give me any of the details? Not even now?"

"*Especially* not now."

"But I tell you everything about my hook-ups."

A light snort. "Yeah, and now I'll never be able to look Roger in the eye again, thanks to you."

"Meh," Everett cracked open an eye to watch the leggy brunette shrug before she turned her attention back to the baby in her arms. "Your hot friend makes cute kids."

"I had some part in that, too, just so you know."

"I don't know that I believe that. I feel like you were just incubating a tiny, female clone of Captain Abtastic."

"*Sara*," the reprimand was destroyed by the smile in Gemma's voice. "Stop it. Imagine if he heard you."

"Oh, I'll happily tell him to his face – and what a face it is, right?"

"You're enjoying this way too much."

"Come on, tell me you didn't watch *that* man pick up *this* baby and that you didn't get all hot and bothered. I mean, hot A.F. guy holding a newborn? Isn't that what we ovary-wielding types are wired to enjoy?"

Everett wished he could risk opening his eyes to see Gemma's expression, because the silence after Sara's mildly invasive question stretched on slightly too long. "I just gave birth," she eventually hedged. "There's not going to be any enjoyment of that kind for a *long* time."

"Oh, hell no. Please don't tell me you've already relegated yourself back to spinsterhood. It took, what, over two years for you to break that last dry spell?"

"And look what *that* got me."

Everett took a moment to process that. Two years. *Two years*, and then he had broken her heart and knocked her up all in one evening. *Well done, Rhodes. Idiot.*

The other woman sighed. "I'm giving Sleeping Beauty a pass for now because he's stepped up and you said he was genuinely apologetic…and if there's a chance that he's going to redeem himself, he can take it. But, if I ever see Scott or Brett again, I'm going to chop their itty, bitty–"

"Sara!" Gemma momentarily forgot to keep her voice low, and he opted to save her from the conversation by 'waking' at the sound, while she cursed. "Shit. Sorry. We didn't mean to wake you up."

"Speak for yourself," Sara's smile was wolfish as she grinned at him. "We haven't been properly introduced. I'm Sara – Gem's best friend." She lifted the crook of her arm, which was still holding the sleeping baby. "Congrats on the clone."

"Thank you," he tilted his head, accepting the congratulations and smiled softly at his daughter before turning his attention to Gemma while he adjusted his seat and sat up. "How are you feeling?"

They'd been up a few times with Zoe during the night, and also when the midwives would do their rounds and observations. He'd done his best to help where he could, quickly learning how to change a nappy and a onesie. He was tired and dying for a coffee, and he could only imagine how much worse she felt.

"Sore," she acknowledged, "and gross. I can't wait to shower."

"If you wish to do so now, I'm sure Sara and I can manage keeping one newborn in line."

Gemma chuckled. "I guess I could pee again anyway," she sighed, then moved to get up and grimaced. "Oh. *Ergh.*"

"What's wrong?" he was at her side almost instantly, putting a hand to her back and extending the other to offer her support. She grimaced.

"Just…the bleeding. Ugh. I didn't realise it was gonna be this bad. Pretty sure my maternity pad hasn't held up." She flushed, averting her gaze, "Sorry, TMI."

"I'm a grown man, and you just had a baby. *Our* baby. I'm hardly surprised that you're experiencing a natural phenomenon like postpartum bleeding." He frowned. "However, Google tells me that too much is cause for concern, so promise me you'll mention it to the next midwife, alright?"

He was not oblivious to the way Sara mouthed 'marry him' at Gemma, but he was too busy ensuring that the mother of his child take his worries seriously to acknowledge it.

Her hazel eyes were wide and startled as she looked up at him. "You Googled that?"

"I researched what to expect in the coming days and weeks, yes," he wasn't ashamed of doing so. "I might not have been here for the past nine months, love, but I'm here now and I do care." He swallowed, hating that they had an audience. "About both of you."

"Weeks?" She practically squeaked. "You're not flying back to LA?"

Grabbing her overnight bag, he began assisting her towards the ensuite bathroom, telling her what he'd told his brother the previous night. "I'll have to return eventually," he said as he set out her shampoo and conditioner in the shower and her toothbrush and toothpaste on the basin. He put the packet of maternity pads on top of the cistern of the toilet as well, "But that won't be for a little while yet."

Google had informed him that as a UK passport holder on a working VISA he could stay in Australia for 90 days. He didn't know that he'd be able to stay that long anyway, but these were all issues they'd need to discuss eventually.

She watched as he organised her belongings for her, the corners of her lips curling upwards despite whatever attempt she was making to remain neutral around him. "Where are you staying?"

Everett glanced away, nervously rubbing the back of his neck. "I was hoping that perhaps you might allow me to crash on your sofa?" His blue eyes were big and pleading when he finally looked back at her. "I don't want to put you on the spot, and I know ours is an awkward situation, but I don't want to be too far from Zoe." A short huff of self-deprecating laughter escaped him, and he shrugged, "I didn't expect to feel this way about her. Especially not so soon."

"I can't say I'm not relieved," Gemma replied quietly. "Having a kid sprung on you after a one-nighter –even if you're not famous– isn't exactly something most guys can deal with, you know?" She seemed to steel herself, planting her hands on her hips and forcing herself to stare him down. "And it's great that you're so attached now, but…" she sucked in a breath, "but I need you to really think about what this is going do to your life. To your career. And I need you to make sure you're sure about whatever you choose to do about your place in her life, because I won't have you coming in and out of it when it suits you."

He blinked, taken by surprise at the sudden vehemence of her words.

She bit her lip and continued. "I mean, obviously you'll need to work, and you live overseas, and we have to work out the finer details, but you can't just decide to be Daddy now and then disappear and reappear on a whim."

It was clear to him that this was a speech she'd been building in her head for months, possibly from the moment she'd discovered she was pregnant, but that she likely hadn't intended on delivering it in the bathroom of her hospital room. He tried not to be insulted by her implication that he would abandon his daughter, because she didn't really know him (and that was his own damn fault) and she had spent her entire pregnancy preparing to be a sole parent.

Still, the words stung, and he set his jaw. "You're right," he informed her carefully, folding his arms across his chest, "we do need to work out the finer details, and we need to get to know one another properly. My father walked out on us when I was small – believe me when I say that I will not be leaving a child of mine to the same fate, regardless of the circumstances of her conception or birth."

Gemma appeared to consider his response, her expression softening as she nodded. "Okay. I'm glad. And I really am thankful that you're here, okay?" She offered him a tentative smile, "So, yeah, you can come stay with us. But you're not sleeping on the couch."

In the relief that overcame him, he almost missed that last declaration – one which echoed words that he felt had set them on this insane path to begin with. Only this time there was no hotel room and no building sexual tension between them. *Well,* he mused as he caught her eyes drifting to his biceps, *not any that we can act upon just yet.*

"Alright, well, I'll, uh, leave you to shower," he cleared his throat, pulling her from wherever her own thoughts had gone. "You don't need help?" She seemed to be recovering from labour without any issues, but he'd gathered by now that she was also stubborn, and fiercely independent, and wouldn't ask for help unless she absolutely had to.

"I'm good, I promise," she answered, digging in her bag for clean, comfortable clothing.

Everett nodded and made his way out of the bathroom.

* * *

Gemma's father cooed over Zoe for precisely ten minutes and fifty-three seconds before he requested that Everett walk with him to collect coffee for everyone. He had arrived with Brennan and a third, stand-offish dark-haired man (introduced to him as Jeff, Brennan's boyfriend) just as Sara was leaving to begin her shift across the hospital, and Everett couldn't think of a single reason to deny him. At least he'd finally get a coffee and something to eat, he supposed.

"Dad, go easy on him," Gemma urged, Zoe once again attached to her breast.

"I'll be fine, love," Everett assured her, warmed that she was attempting to deflect some of the ire he felt he'd earned. "Are you drinking real coffee, or would you prefer your latte decaffeinated?"

"God, I miss caffeine," she sighed, then looked down at the nursing baby, "but I think I should still go decaf for now. Just in case." She smiled back up at him, "But bonus points for remembering how I take my coffee."

He smirked. "It's burned into my brain, Fox. Along with a bizarre fact about koalas."

Marcus cleared his throat and he nodded, following the older man out the door. It wasn't until they were in the relative privacy of one of the hallways that led to the elevators that the older man finally spoke.

"I've thought a lot about what I'd say to you when I finally met you," he began calmly. "I've seen Gemma heartbroken twice before, but never quite like she was after your…" he rolled his wrist, searching for the right euphemism, "affair."

Everett winced. That wasn't the word he'd have chosen, but he didn't correct the man. Instead, he waited for him to continue, knowing there was more to be said.

"You're a father now, with a daughter of your own. I hope you never have to comfort her through the situation Gemma was faced with."

Alright, ouch. The old man wasn't pulling his punches. Everett swallowed and nodded. But Marcus wasn't done.

"I appreciate that the situation is unique, and both Gemma and Brennan have assured me that you seem genuinely invested and apologetic for the way things happened. However," he stopped walking, drawing his salt and pepper eyebrows together in consternation, "if you hurt her –or my beautiful new granddaughter– by disappearing from their lives, I don't care who you are, I will find you and destroy you. Understood?"

"Perfectly," Everett answered, bobbing his head. "And I assure you, just as I've already told Gemma, I have no intention of abandoning my child. I mightn't always be physically present due to the nature of my career, but I will *always* maintain contact."

"How can you be so sure?"

Everett stared him straight in the eye, his tone steely. "Aside from how intensely I love her, I won't subject my daughter to the same childhood I had."

There was a tense moment where it was obvious that Marcus was searching his gaze, assessing the truth of his words. He seemed to find whatever it was he was looking for, because he nodded, then broke into a wide smile and clapped the actor on the back. "Good boy. Welcome to the family."

And, to Everett's surprise, that was that.

* * *

Chapter Nine

"Looks like you'll be discharged tomorrow," Frankie, the current midwife on shift, announced while completing her observations just after lunch time.

"Ah, and here I was getting used to being waited on hand and foot," Gemma replied with a cheeky grin.

Frankie arched an eyebrow beneath a mass of curly red hair, "Pretty sure your Baby Daddy's going to keep that trend going for you at home."

It was only the fact that Everett was not currently in the room to hear the epithet that kept Gemma from rolling her eyes at it. It wasn't like she could deny the situation. And, despite confidentiality agreements and The Privacy Act, she was surprised that she hadn't seen or heard anything online about him having a surprise kid yet. She'd been keeping an eye on his fan pages for that very purpose, not wanting to be caught on the back foot. (Well, not again.)

"Where is Mister Rhodes, anyhow?" Frankie asked, and she was a little too casual for Gemma to take the question at face value.

Honestly, she'd been expecting him to be harassed by a number of the hospital staff once word got around as to who he was, but she was pleased to be proven wrong. She even felt a little guilty – these were her colleagues (even if she'd never met the majority of them, what with working in completely different wards) and she shouldn't have assumed they'd be anything other than professional.

"A friend of his surprised him with a visit and I talked him into leaving for some fresh air and a proper debrief."

When Samuel Becker had knocked on her room's door, Gemma had felt awkward. Though he probably didn't recall their previous meeting at the Brisbane convention, it was seared into her brain.

She'd been desperately attempting to get in touch with Everett, feeling her time running out, and had hoped that she could convince Becker to take a message back to LA with him. He'd steadfastly followed the rules, unable to accept anything from her, and she'd had to bite her tongue to prevent herself from breaking down and telling him the whole unfortunate story.

Some part of her still felt that she should have just thrown it out there and told him while she had the chance, but he probably would have thought she was a crazy person. After all, in what reality would someone like Everett Rhodes actually sleep with a fan?

Everett had been so happy to see him, though. Even more so when Samuel wheeled in Everett's previously abandoned suitcase and explained that he'd opted to bring it himself rather than have it couriered from Sydney.

"My best friend just became a Dad," he'd declared with an almost stereotypical 'All American' smile, dimples in his cheeks and all, "I needed to meet my honorary niece in person. I've switched my flight back to LA to tomorrow."

Everett had then apologised for not automatically introducing 'Sam' to Gemma, and there was a moment where she could have sworn that the American actor recognised her. But it was gone in a blink, and they'd exchanged strained pleasantries before she'd extended Zoe towards him.

He had run a hand through his sand-coloured hair and hadn't been able to prevent the low whistle or the "Definitely yours, huh?" directed at Everett, which had mildly raised her hackles.

Swallowing back a snarky retort –because she understood that it was perfectly reasonable in their circumstances to question Zoe's paternity– Gemma had just snorted and mumbled something about cloning machines.

Becker had then soothed his gaffe by saying, "She's beautiful. Congratulations."

She'd sat back as the two men had chatted quietly, until she'd realised that Everett hadn't really had anyone to discuss the sudden changes in his life with and he certainly wasn't going to unload all of his fears and anxieties while she was present. She liked to think that maybe one day, when they knew each other better, he might be comfortable venting to her, but he needed a support system now. So, she'd cleared her throat and suggested that maybe the two actors go grab a late lunch and catch up properly.

"You haven't left this building since you got here," she'd urged Everett when he seemed as though he was going to argue with her, "and I'm sure you've been running on adrenaline alone since Brennan found you yesterday. Go. Get some fresh air, and food that isn't from a vending machine. Vent to your friend who is here for you and you alone. Trust me, okay? It'll help."

Gemma hadn't been able to read the expression he'd worn as he'd canted his head in acquiescence, but he'd promised to bring her back a sweet treat, so she didn't think he'd minded her bossing him around too much.

She was brought back to the present by the disappointed sigh from the voluptuous midwife. "It's a pity. I'm a bit of a fan myself."

Gemma knew she had no right to feel possessive, but the urge to tell Frankie to back off was strong. She forced a smile, "I'm sure he gets it a lot."

"How'd you meet?" Frankie asked, fluffing her pillow.

Gemma recognised the stalling tactic for what it was, but still found herself explaining, "We got stuck in a lift together. He talked me down from an epic anxiety attack and then asked me to dinner." She very deliberately ignored the part in between where she –a starry-eyed fangirl– had been going to a convention specifically to see him. That part still made her uncomfortable.

"And what followed," Everett's own voice supplied, picking up from where she'd opted to end the story as he entered the room, putting a little white paper bag down on the wheeled table beside her. He pressed a kiss to her temple, resting his hip against the side of her hospital bed, continuing, "if I recall correctly, was that I harassed you into becoming my tour-guide for the week and you were too nice to turn me down."

The chaste kiss –and then the flirtatious wink that followed his assessment– threw her completely. He'd kissed her passionately after Zoe was born, reminding her of exactly how she'd wound up becoming pregnant to start with, but she had written that off as the actions of an overwhelmed man riding a wave of first-time dad endorphins. This was wholly unexpected.

Frankie made an 'aww' sound that pulled Gemma back into the moment.

"Yeah, well, you gave me the puppy-dog eyes," she argued lightly, "which wasn't exactly fair."

He grinned back at her and shrugged, "I never said I played fair, love."

"Okay, well, I can see you're in good hands," Frankie beamed at them, finishing up her observations on Zoe, who hadn't squirmed or cried while she was poked and prodded, "and this little lady is doing perfectly, too."

At her side, Gemma could feel the tension leave Everett's body at the declaration, and Sara's words from earlier that morning rattled around in her brain. *Yes,* she admitted to herself, *seeing him all paternal is a damn turn on.*

Clearly, Frankie felt the same way, because instead of placing Zoe back in the bassinet like all the midwives before her had done, she extended the baby towards her father. "Wanna go to Daddy?" she asked Zoe while batting big, blue eyes at Everett.

With eyes only for his daughter, he leaned forward and took the baby, settling her into the crook of his left arm and stroking her cheek with his right index finger. Gemma was torn between committing the besotted expression on his face to memory or arching her brow at the almost irritatingly beautiful midwife who still hadn't moved on to her next patient. (And, alright, objectively, she knew that she was just projecting how frumpy and gross she felt next to this very attractive woman who hadn't just given birth, but she felt she could blame her hormones for her irrational dislike at this point.)

Frankie caught Gemma's eye and mouthed 'You're so lucky', and Gemma could only bite her lip and nod.

This was all so surreal to her.

Did Everett think she expected him to be interested in her? Because she didn't. She was under absolutely no illusions as to their relationship. Did she still think he was gorgeous? Absolutely. But she still didn't really know him.

Sure, she'd fallen head over heels in love with him over the course of that five days, but he'd broken her in the short-term car park at Brisbane International Airport, and she'd spent the following nine and a half months rebuilding her walls and cursing his name.

Then there was the fact that they lived in completely separate worlds, and on different continents to boot. Just working out how to co-parent was going to be hard enough on its own. Neither of them needed the additional pressure of making a romance between them work.

She wondered how often she'd need to remind herself of these things before they stuck.

* * *

"Here we are, home sweet home," Gemma spoke to Zoe as she carried her across the threshold of her townhouse. Everett had insisted on carrying their bags and was returning to Brennan's car (because her brother had also had a baby seat fitted, despite her telling him he didn't have to) for the insane amount of flowers and gifts that her friends, colleagues and family had brought. "You're probably going to really impress the neighbours with your multiple middle-of-the-night wake up calls."

Big, blue eyes stared up at her with their unfocused newborn gaze, and she smiled, "Maybe we'll give them some earplugs and bourbon to ease the pain, huh?"

"I'm more a gin man, myself," Everett declared, bypassing her to drop the haul of gifts onto the small dining table in front of the kitchen. He turned and made his way back, shutting the front door before informing Gemma that Brennan was heading out to buy her groceries. He guided her to the couch and turned back towards the kitchen, asking, "Want a tea or coffee?"

"Actually...a Milo, please? Made on hot milk, not water." She'd complained bitterly about the midwives making the malted, chocolatey beverage with hot water during her short hospital stay and was dying to drink it the way it should be made.

He'd only been to her place the once, way back in November, but Everett navigated her kitchen as though he lived there. He pulled the tin of Milo from the pantry and plucked a teabag from the decorative container on the same shelf, before locating two mugs on his first try opening a cupboard. Then he filled and set the kettle to boil before he focused on her drink.

She watched as he heated the milk in a mug in the microwave, then added a few heaped teaspoons of the chocolate granules after having read the tin. He stirred it and brought it to his lips for a taste test as he made his way back towards the couch.

"Not bad," he mused, setting it down on the coffee table in front of her and reaching for Zoe so that she could drink it while it was warm, "but I'll stick with tea."

Gemma handed over the baby, the butterflies in her stomach starting up again at the way he seemed to melt any time he held her. Despite the way things had ended between them, she was back to beginning to think he was as close to perfect as any man could get. These thoughts were dangerous –the same kind that had led her into the situation she was in now– and she tried to stamp down on them before she could get attached again.

She picked up her mug and took a sip, humming happily. It was much better than the watered-down swill the hospital served up. Everett smiled down at her, rocking Zoe, and she found her thoughts drifting again.

It was good that he loved their daughter. It was good that, even though he had not been expecting it, he seemed to enjoy being a father. It was great that he wanted to stick around for a while and work out where to go from there. But that didn't mean that anything should develop between the two of them. Gemma didn't want to put herself in a position where she could be hurt again, and especially not by him.

Oblivious to the spiralling, circular nature of her thoughts, Everett cleared his throat. "I, uh, I've arranged for my Mum and brother to come meet her."

The sloshing of the liquid in her mug gave away her sudden burst of nerves and she set it down quickly, wiping her hands on her pyjama pants. "Oh. Huh. Okay. Yeah. That...that makes sense. I mean, of course they'd want to meet your daughter."

God, they were going to hate her. She was just some fan, and she'd ruined his life, and she just knew their visit was going to be uncomfortable. Gemma shifted in her seat, realising she was about to make it even worse, but she'd set rules for her family and friends, and she needed to make it clear that she expected the same of his family. People she'd never met. People who would already be judging her for the whole 'knocked up one-night stand' thing.

"They need to get their whooping cough vaccinations if they want to hold her. And, um, no kissing her either. I know that sounds really unfair –because you and I can kiss her– but...*oh*, you have had your whooping cough vaccination, too, right?"

"Breathe, love," Everett sighed and sat down beside her. "Firstly, yes, I'm up to date with all my vaccinations, mostly because I travel so much." She relaxed a little at that. "Secondly, I've already been through those rules and added a few of my own. Mum'll be fine, but Charlie can be a bit of a tosser, so I wanted to cut off any of his drama while I could." He switched Zoe into the crook of his other arm so he could reach out and rub soothing circles on Gemma's back, the warmth of his thigh pressing into hers providing an unexpected comfort on its own – proof that she wasn't alone in this. "And finally, why don't you tell me exactly what you're most worried about?"

She hated that he could still read her so well. Averting her gaze, she fiddled with a loose thread on her pants. "It's stupid," she told him quietly, "but...they're going to hate me."

"Why would you think that?"

Her expression turned incredulous. "Oh, I don't know – because one minute you're a carefree bachelor in Hollywood's top 100, the next you're being thrust into Daddydom by some random you slept with once?" She all but cried, throwing her hands in the air. "I've ruined–"

"Stop it." His tone was firm, his gaze hardened. "Nobody has ruined anything. Zoe is...Gemma, she's amazing. You're right; it's all been a bit of a shock. But even so, I've never been happier than I felt the first time I held her. Do you understand that? And Mum is so excited to be a Nan, and she's so looking forward to meeting you..."

He trailed off, and it didn't escape her notice that he hadn't mentioned his brother.

"But Charlie sees it all a bit differently, right?"

"I couldn't give a rat's arse what Charlie thinks," his tone went back to hard and unforgiving. "And if he says one word to you that upsets you–"

"So, he *is* going to hate me."

Exhaling, Everett shook his head. "He can't possibly hate you, Fox. He may, perhaps, question your motivations, much like Brennan and Jeff have questioned mine, though."

She cringed, recalling Jeff's meeting with Everett in the hospital. To say her usually affable brother-practically-in-law had been unfriendly was an understatement. "Yeah, sorry about them. They're just–"

"Being protective of you and Zoe," he brushed her apology off, understanding colouring his tone. "It's what older siblings do." He pressed a kiss to her temple, then added, "However, Charlie's aware that I did wrong by you, not the other way around. If I hadn't put my foot in my mouth, things might have developed a bit differently."

Gemma nodded. "I don't like hypotheticals. What's done is done and we can't change anything. But, yeah, I did spend a lot of time thinking about how, if I'd just listened…if I'd given you the chance to explain…" Her lower lip began to quiver, and her sinuses stung with impending tears. "Sorry, hormones," she cursed, wiping her eyes. All the blogs and books she'd read talked about the Baby Blues hitting around day three, and she was beginning to understand what they meant.

His gaze was apologetic. "If I hadn't said–"

"Don't. It's okay. It's in the past. It's done." They'd discussed it a few times now, and while she understood that he hadn't meant he regretted being with her, the words still haunted her, still hurt, and she didn't want to go over it again.

The silence between them was still a little awkward, so she picked her mug back up and sipped at the drink he'd made her. She set it back down once it was finished and decided to try and salvage the situation between them. "So, um, wanna see Zoe's room?"

Everett brightened considerably and pushed himself to his feet, offering her a hand up. "Lead the way," he declared, the baby now asleep in his arms, his tea forgotten.

She led him upstairs –aware that he'd never been to this part of her home before– and walked through the small living area at the top of the stairs, past the bathroom and to the door at the far end of the short hallway. She was proud of the room she'd put together for her baby, and was excited to share it, even though he probably wouldn't appreciate the small touches she'd made.

Being a rental, she couldn't paint the walls, but she had changed the curtains and put down a rug to match the fairy-tale theme she'd chosen. She'd gone with a white sleigh style cot and dresser set, the dresser being the right height to also work as a change table once she'd added the padded change mat to the top. She'd found a light grey gliding chair which she had set up next to the window with matching foot stool, and had a low-lying bookshelf complete with a selection of books to read to her baby under the window itself.

The wall above the cot was bare, as she'd been waiting to meet her baby before she ordered the artwork that she planned to hang there, as it would feature the baby's name. She made a mental note to order it from the artist she'd found on Etsy now that she had a name to match the theme.

"This is lovely, Gemma," Everett said as he stepped into the middle of the space. The rug under his feet depicted a version of Disney's Neverland, with fairies and pirates and the lost boys, while the curtains had a more generic 'Enchanted Forest' sort of landscape, also with fairies and woodland creatures. His eyes landed on a teddy bear dressed in full pirate regalia. "Is that supposed to be a teddy version of me?"

She wondered if the question was intended to come out teasing, because he seemed oddly choked up. "I mean, they don't make teddy versions of the non-canonical, long-lost son of Long John Silver, but…yeah. I…I wanted our kid to have some sort of connection to you. Even if they never got a chance to meet you."

And just like that, the tension was back. His face fell, and he swallowed.

"You wouldn't have continued trying? Maybe brought her to the next convention I attended nearby?"

"Well, that was kind of going to be my final plan, yeah," she acknowledged. "I'm glad it didn't come to that. Pretty sure giving you a heart attack in front of all your adoring fans would have sucked for both of us."

He snorted, and she could see him imagining how he might have reacted if he'd looked up from the signing desk to find Gemma holding Zoe. "You would have at least done it at Photo Ops," he argued, starting to become playful again as the fear in his eyes receded.

She leaned her hip against the cot, rolling her eyes, even though he was right on the money with his assessment. "Oh, *sure*. And then I would have been responsible for all the people behind me missing out on their photos because you can't tell me that you would have let me just walk back out when my 30 seconds of 'Hey, long time no see, by the way, surprise! We made a kid, now smile for the camera!' were up."

Everett snickered, "I highly doubt you'd have been that blunt."

"Like you wouldn't have taken one look at her and worked it out anyway."

He glanced back down at their daughter, his smile turning soft again. "Yeah, well, I like to think I'd have been just as infatuated the instant I saw her, though the few hours' warning was probably helpful."

"I'll bet," Gemma bit her lip, then moved past him to the dresser, opening one of the top drawers to pull out the rainbow notebook she'd purchased at the Gold Coast convention. She'd found a use for it after all. Extending it towards him, she found herself mildly nervous for his reaction. "I started writing you letters after I found out I was pregnant," she explained quietly. "When I couldn't immediately get a hold of you, it became…cathartic, I guess. Sharing it with you even though you weren't there. It's stupid, but–"

"It's not," he refuted, reaching out with his free hand to take the notebook from her. "It means a lot that you still wanted to share it with me, even after…" he sighed, hanging his head. "You must have hated me."

Gemma nodded. "Some of that might come through in the first few entries." She twirled a loose tendril of hair around her index finger. "The, um, the letters became more like a journal, I guess, after a while. And then I figured I might remove the first few letters and give it to our kid -to Zoe- if I never got a chance to give it to you." She'd even included some of the ultrasound print outs along the way, and believed he'd likely appreciate that.

"Well, perhaps we can still do that once I've read it?" His suggestion was a peace offering and an apology all rolled into one.

Her throat tightened with emotion. "Yeah. Yeah, that might be nice."

* * *

"I've been thinking I should probably get Rowena to organise some posts on my official socials," Everett told her later that evening as they awkwardly readied themselves for bed.

Gemma had insisted that he might as well stay with her, because the two-seater couches in her house (both the upstairs and downstairs) were not big enough or comfortable enough to sleep on and she had no guest room to speak of. Zoe was asleep in a bassinet on her side of the bed, though they both knew she'd wake up within the next couple of hours searching for food.

Propped up against the headboard, Gemma offered him a small smile of encouragement. "That's probably a good idea. But...I don't love the idea of her face being out there, you know?"

Nobody would really expect that his child -or her mother- weren't in LA, and she assumed that he was hoping to play on that for as long as he could. Eventually, someone would recognise him here, but it was nice to feel like a normal -if slightly dysfunctional- family unit for the time being.

He nodded and fluffed his pillow. "Yeah, I was thinking perhaps an artistic photo of just her little hand around my finger, or her tiny feet in my hand, or a photo of me holding her, but where you can only see the back of her head? What are your thoughts?"

"Well, the money shot is definitely hot man holding tiny baby," Gemma considered, but she felt oddly possessive about it and didn't want to share that image with the entire world. "But I actually really like the idea of her hand holding your finger."

There was a glint in his eyes, like he could tell exactly why she'd voted for the ambiguous photo over the one that would likely send his fans into a bigger frenzy, but he nodded. "Then I'll snap one –or have you snap one– when she next wakes. Gives me time to think of an appropriate message to send with it."

"I say 'Now you can really call me 'Daddy'' works," she offered up, trying to cover her momentary slip of jealousy with humour, and he let out a startled bark of laughter, rolling onto his side to face her as he grinned.

"I'm not old enough for the Daddy fetishists, am I?"

"I mean, there's fanfic…" she mused, before her eyes went wide, and her cheeks flushed. "Which I swear I don't read." *Anymore.* Not since November. That would have made it even weirder. Plus, she had firsthand experience with him naked, and fanfiction just didn't compare.

Not that she'd looked.

(Okay, she'd totally lied. She had, because even though she'd hated him, old habits were hard to break, and *Happily Never After* fanfiction was her escapism and comfort mechanism. And, *boy*, had she needed both comfort and an escape from reality in spades.)

The expression on his face was somewhere between amused and fond. "I'm sure you don't," he responded, but he didn't sound convinced.

"Oh, shut up," she swatted at him before she yawned.

"Get some sleep while you can, love," he urged gently, his amusement shifting to warmth and concern. "Little Miss will be awake again before you know it."

The sound she made was noncommittal, but still she rolled over to face the bassinet, putting her back to him. Her bed was only queen sized, putting them in much closer quarters than the bed they'd shared in November. She drifted asleep to the sound of him turning the pages of the notebook she'd given him.

* * *

Gemma's phone lit up with the matching Instagram and Facebook notifications the next day.

'Welcome to the world, my darling Zoe. Daddy loves you.' was the simple caption to the photo she'd taken for him in the middle of the night, with a couple of hashtags about new babies and new parenthood thrown in for fun. Someone had filtered it to black and white, and Zoe's fingers looked impossibly small wrapped around his index finger, and even tinier against his large, masculine hand as a whole.

Gemma knew she shouldn't do it, but she read the comments that were already streaming in –fans responding in states of shock and surprise and 'Is this why you left the convention in Sydney early?'– and bit her lip. There were so many 'I didn't realise he was dating anyone's and comments speculating about who he might have had the baby with, and a whole heap of nosy bitches who were demanding he share how cute his baby was and not just tease them with a glimpse. Just who did they think they were, demanding that of him?

"Don't read the comments, love. That's always the first rule of social media." Everett said, peeking at her phone as he sat beside her on the couch and set their lunch of simple salad sandwiches on the coffee table. Zoe was again sleeping (all the blogs said it was normal for newborns to sleep more than they were awake) and they were enjoying the silence.

"It just shits me that these people think they're entitled to the private details of your life," she complained, reaching for her sandwich. "You give an inch, and they want a mile."

He shrugged, biting into his own, chewing and swallowing as he contemplated his reply. "Haven't we had this discussion before?"

The lettuce inside her sandwich crunched as she took an agitated bite of her own. "Yeah," she acknowledged, "but that was when it was just your personal life I was defending. Now there's Zoe to worry about."

"I'll do my best to keep her from the public eye, Gemma. You have my word."

What else could she do but nod?

* * *

"Are you sure you want me to come with you?" Gemma called the question from the bathroom while she attempted to do her makeup for the first time in what felt like months. Everett had been living with her for a little under two weeks (and she marvelled over the fact that Zoe was already 2 weeks old) and his family had finally flown in the previous day.

He'd put them up in a hotel in the city and had made plans to bring Gemma and Zoe to their hotel, to the downstairs restaurant, for their initial meeting. Naturally, Gemma was having second thoughts.

"You could just take Zoe and go without me," she added, swearing as the shaking of her hand left her eyeliner lopsided. "You can take some expressed milk and have a Daddy-daughter day."

Admittedly, she hated the thought of being separated from her baby like that, but her fear of confronting his family was worse.

"Or," he drawled, leaning against the doorway, "you can come with me as planned, negating the need to sterilise bottles and pack extra crap into her overflowing nappy bag."

Gemma was not unaware of the fact that they'd essentially fallen into some semblance of a relationship again. It was unfair how well they seemed to just fit into each other's lives, treating one another like an old married couple might, instead of the relative strangers they were. They traded off baby duties without having to discuss it, took turns at the household chores and meal prep (though, more often than not, it was Everett who cooked because he was just naturally better at it).

He was still as tactile and demonstrative as ever, pressing chaste kisses to her temple and the top of her head with easy affection. In turn, she'd found herself loosening up around him again. To be honest, it was hard to fully have her walls up after how amazing he'd been while she'd given birth. He'd seen her at her absolute worst and most vulnerable, and he'd been nothing but supportive and helpful, even while he must have been panicked and terrified at the sudden change to his circumstances.

But even after that, he'd surpassed her wildest dreams with how easily he took to fatherhood and not once had he complained that he hadn't asked for this, or that it was too hard. She couldn't quite understand it because she had voiced those thoughts herself. A lot. Babies were hard work, and she often felt like she was drowning. If he hadn't been there…well, she didn't like to dwell on that.

"That's all I am to you, isn't it?" she responded playfully, carefully fixing her eyeliner. "I'm the cow who provides the milk on tap. That's the only reason you and Zoe need me around."

"Now, darling, you know you're more to me than *just* a cow," he snarked, and she poked her tongue out at him. His expression and tone sobered, and he stepped up beside her, staring her down via their reflections in the mirror. "Seriously though, Gemma, you've nothing to worry about today. They're going to adore you."

She eyed her makeup critically and decided that it would have to do before she turned to peer up at him. "You can't know that."

"I can," he insisted. "They'll love you because I love you."

Her eyes widened. They hadn't spoken about feelings. It had taken her five days to fall in love with him and almost nine months to convince herself that she was over him. In the past two weeks, she'd done her best to ignore any resurgence of those original feelings.

Backing up, she felt literally cornered in the small bathroom. "Everett…"

He seemed to finally realise the declaration he'd made, and he cringed and held his hands up in surrender. "Alright, so I could have possibly timed that better," he began, "and, obviously, I don't expect you to…to reciprocate or…or…anything." He concluded lamely.

"It's been two weeks," she refuted. "You can't possibly–"

Everett arched an eyebrow. "Is there really a rule on how long it takes to love someone? Because I loved Zoe instantly."

She didn't bother arguing that a parental love was different to romantic feelings. Besides, she'd fallen head over heels for him in the first five days of knowing him, so it wasn't like she had much of a leg to stand on with that argument.

Still, she attempted to rationalise his declaration. "Well, no, but…look, is it possible these are just misplaced feelings? Like, you love Zoe, and I'm just…I don't know…just the vessel that made her, or whatever? Plus, outside of my family, I think I've been your only human contact for the last couple of weeks, so there's also Stockholm Syndrome to consider."

There was a hint of irritation in his reply. "I don't have Stockholm Syndrome, Fox."

"But–"

"I had feelings for you in November," he blurted, and there was a slight flush to his cheeks that told her he hadn't intended on doing so, "and I'm aware that I fucked things up back then, but this time with you has only made those feelings stronger. And, yes, I'm sure some part of it is because you're the mother of my child and I watched you bring her into this world, but it's more than that." He reached out and tilted her head up with his index finger, looking her in the eye. "Being with you is effortless, Gemma. You understand me –and challenge me– in ways nobody else has. You mightn't have noticed, but I've essentially moved in with you and, aside from the baby, the transition has been seamless. That doesn't ordinarily happen. We just *work*, love."

The fact that he was putting voice to thoughts she'd only had minutes earlier had her heart beating hard in her chest. "Things are complicated right now," she reasoned, "and we're both still in that honeymoon phase with Zoe. And you haven't moved in permanently – your home is still in LA and what happens when you have to go back? Do you change your mind again and tell me you regret everything?"

That was a low blow, and she knew it. The pained look on his face made her instantly wish she hadn't said it, but it was too late.

He glanced at the ceiling and set his jaw, the tic in his cheek telling her that she may have pushed him too far, but he was perfectly calm and composed when he met her gaze again. "You can attempt to push me away, but it won't work." He checked his watch, then ran his hand through his hair. "And we're going to be late if we keep debating this."

Her nerves fired back up again, but he smiled gently and took her hand, squeezing it. "They're going to love you."

∗ ∗ ∗

Charlie most certainly did not love her. He'd made that abundantly clear, and Gemma had felt on the defensive from the second she'd shaken his hand before they'd all walked into the hotel restaurant. Beatrice, though, was lovely. She was tall and prim and proper but exuded the same charisma and warmth that Everett did, instantly setting her at ease.

Watching Everett interacting with his mother was also a revelation. She could tell instantly that they were close –but thankfully, he wasn't a sickeningly cloying Mummy's boy like Scott had been– and that he wanted so badly for her and Gemma to get along. She could also see that Beatrice was where he'd inherited his mannerisms and insightful nature from, though the elegant blonde woman informed her that "Everett is the spitting image of his father."

Everett didn't enjoy the comparison, and the way Charlie smirked –having inherited their mother's fair colouring– made her want to comfort the younger of the men. She squeezed Everett's thigh under the table they were sat around and offered him a reassuring smile when he turned his head towards her in askance. He seemed to understand and responded with a short, grateful nod.

"So, how is fatherhood treating you, little brother? Looking forward to returning to your real life yet?"

Everett's expression darkened further, and the reassuring squeeze Gemma had given him morphed into a tight grip. Charlie was fishing for a reaction from either of them, and she refused to give him the satisfaction. She hoped Everett would hold his temper and do the same.

"Zoe's wonderful," he replied with the same gushing tone he always seemed to fall into any time he spoke about their daughter, "and I'll be devastated when I have to go back to LA."

Charlie made an exaggerated sound of sympathy, "Pity that's where your livelihood comes from, then, isn't it?"

This time, Beatrice shot her eldest a sideways glance that clearly read 'Behave', but she was too busy cuddling and talking nonsense to her granddaughter to really get involved.

Gemma decided to intervene. "Does she look much like Everett did as a baby?" she asked the woman seated across from her, effectively changing the conversation.

Beatrice gazed down at the baby in her arms, beaming. "Oh, most definitely. Maybe a bit pudgier, but chubby babies are healthy babies and, oh, I could just eat those little thigh rolls." She smiled across at Gemma. "And her head of hair! You must have suffered with dreadful heartburn."

With Everett's gaze now on her, she nodded. "Yeah. It was pretty constant. Looks like the old wives' tale is true."

"Was it a terribly difficult pregnancy?" Beatrice asked, genuinely curious. "I had no issues with Charlie, but Everett was a nightmare."

"Nothing's changed there, then, eh?" Charlie couldn't help the dig and Gemma rolled her eyes at him.

"Clever," she praised in a tone that said she thought he was anything but. Cursing herself for allowing him to get under her skin, she doubled down on her resolve and smiled sweetly at Beatrice. "It wasn't too bad. Minimal morning sickness, unless anyone came near me with bananas, but I was exhausted all the time, and I got lightheaded a lot, so had to make sure I always had water and something to snack on on hand."

That had been what had clued her on to her pregnancy. She'd fainted at work and had come to on a spare hospital bed, Sara having called her on-again-off-again doctor boyfriend to come and check her over. Gemma had argued that she was likely just dehydrated (she hadn't been taking care of herself in the weeks following her heartbreak) and exhausted from her depressive state and back-to-back shifts spent on her feet. When Roger had very cautiously handed her the little, yellow-lidded sample cup, a pipette and a hospital-issued hCG strip, she'd felt the world collapsing under her feet. Re-emerging from the bathroom, tear-streaked and broken all over again, Brennan had been waiting for her. (It turned out that they'd called him, as her nominated emergency contact, when she'd fainted.) The resulting conversation hadn't been fun.

"Oh, you poor dear," Everett's mother responded with genuine empathy, "The exhaustion is a killer. And you don't even get to recover once the baby is born, because then it's multiple night wake-ups and very little time to rest during the day. And anyone who tells you to sleep when the baby sleeps has no concept of the fact that the rest of your life doesn't stop just because you've got a child now."

"Well, I've been really lucky to have Everett with me," Gemma acknowledged, beaming in his direction. Despite their earlier awkward exchange, she truly was grateful that he'd stuck around and that he had been so heavily involved. "He's been my equal in everything and has made sure that we both rest when we can…" she trailed off, her own words shaking up feelings she was trying to deny. She cleared her throat and smiled at his mother. "You've raised *such* a good man, Beatrice. I don't know what he's told you about me, but I…I pretty much grew up without parents, and I was so afraid of being alone in this." A tear slid down her cheek, but she continued, "I know you raised your boys on your own, and, with how wonderful Everett is, I can only hope to be half the mother you are."

While Beatrice offered her a watery smile in response, Charlie scoffed. "Laying it on a bit thick, aren't you?"

"Alright, that's it," Everett stood up, practically growling, "walk with me, Charlie."

"Everett, it's fine," Gemma reached for his hand, but he remained standing and glowering at his brother.

"No," he gritted out, "my brother and I need to get some air."

Sighing, Charlie rose from his seat and bowed with condescension. "Lead the way, little brother."

The younger man gave the women remaining at the table a tight smile. "We'll return before our meals arrive."

Gemma watched them go with sad eyes.

"They've always been like chalk and cheese," Beatrice told her, following her gaze. "Everett might take after Michael in appearance, but Charlie's got their father's temperament." Gemma turned her attention back to her daughter's grandmother, and the woman's tone turned apologetic. "He's always been fairly hard on Everett. There's only seven years between them, but I think he fancies himself a father figure rather than an older brother."

"It's because he cares," Gemma nodded. "My older brother…well, adoptive," and she wasn't going into the whole foster thing, "he's a bit the same. Gave Everett hell for a few days, until I threatened to revoke his Uncle privileges." She sighed. "I think Everett thought he deserved it, but he had no idea about Zoe. He had no reason to even think he might have left me with, uh, a *souvenir*, and he's really been–"

"Wonderful," Beatrice supplied, smirking Everett's smirk at her, "so you've said."

Gemma blushed.

The older woman chuckled. "He's always been a sensitive boy, our Everett." She paused. "I'll admit, I was a little concerned when he called and sprang the news of his daughter's arrival on us." She ran her finger around the rim of her water glass as she mused, "Who was this strange woman who had suddenly entered into his life in such a big, permanent way? However, I trust his judgement. He's always worn his heart on his sleeve, but rarely ever given it away." She sighed and looked down at Zoe, stroking her downy soft hair as the baby's arms flailed a little jerkily. "Oh, listen to me, mixing my metaphors. I'm becoming terribly maudlin in my old age. And now I'm a Nan!"

"I…" Gemma wasn't quite sure how to respond. "You have to know, I never intended on turning his life upside down."

"Oh, sweetheart, I know," Beatrice was quick to reassure her. "I like to think that I'm fairly good at reading people, and you don't strike me as the gold-digging, fame-seeking type. And, if anything, it's your life that will have been turned topsy-turvy more than his."

"You can say that again," Gemma agreed, sighing. "I really don't know how you raised two little boys on your own. One of her –and I'm not even on my own right now– is hard enough."

"I won't tell you it gets easier," the older woman shifted the baby to her other arm so she could reach across the table and squeeze Gemma's forearm, "because every age has its own challenges, but you adapt, and you just make it work. Take it day by day. And some are better than others."

She'd never had a mother, and the maternal affection rolling off the woman in waves had her sniffling back tears. "Sorry," she wiped at her eyes, feeling silly. "Hormones."

Despite the knowing glint in her eyes, Beatrice allowed the excuse. "Ah, I remember those days. Thankfully, that does get easier as your hormones settle out."

Gemma smiled and they made small talk for a little while longer before Zoe began to whine, rooting around for food. Beatrice carefully passed her back to her mother, and Gemma unbuttoned her blouse and assisted the baby to latch on for feeding. She felt a little awkward breastfeeding in such a public setting for the first time, but she'd discovered the previous week (when she had decided to start going for small walks in her local park, nothing too strenuous) that Zoe hated being covered while she ate. Gemma couldn't say she blamed her – having something draped over her head during a meal would be irritating.

Thankfully, the restaurant wasn't very busy, and the table they'd chosen was tucked into a quiet corner, so she didn't feel too exposed. Besides, there was absolutely nothing shameful in what she was doing, and if her baby needed food, she was going to provide it.

Everett and Charlie returned just as the waiter was placing their meals down on the table, and Zoe was drifting off, now milk drunk and satiated. Everett pressed a kiss to the top of Gemma's head, taking the baby while she tucked herself away and did her blouse back up. He'd already snagged the burping cloth she'd had on her shoulder and put it to his own, patting Zoe's back until she belched, and he chuckled.

"That never gets old for you, does it?" Gemma shook her head fondly, before gesturing in Charlie's direction with her eyes and silently asking Everett if he was okay.

Before he could answer, Beatrice asked her sons aloud, "Now, have the two of you sorted yourselves out?" She picked up her cutlery and glanced between them, then landed a firm stare on her eldest, "Because I do believe Gemma's owed an apology."

"Oh, no," that just made the younger woman uncomfortable, "it's fine." She reached for her glass of water and took a sip, placing the glass back down and aiming a small smile in Charlie's direction. "You're just looking out for your brother. I get it."

"And yet, he could have been less of an arse about it," Everett shrugged at her side, Zoe fast asleep against his shoulder.

Charlie rolled his eyes, picking up his own knife and fork, but sighed and offered Gemma a half-hearted, "I apologise, Fox."

It seemed so very much like the reaction of a chastened little boy –and not a man in his early forties– that it took everything in her power to smother her amusement. "Okay," she accepted gracefully, swirling her pasta around on her fork and taking her first bite of her lunch.

* * *

Chapter Ten

"So, your brother is only barely being civil to me, and you think it's a good idea to get our families together?" Gemma asked Everett the next day in response to his announcement that, with Brennan's help, he had arranged a meeting of the two families for that evening. "You're a crazy person."

He shrugged, leaning against the door frame to the nursery. "He'll be on his best behaviour because he'll be well and truly outnumbered."

Brennan and Jeff had graciously offered to host a barbeque at their home, and that seemed to be a much more private, casual way for Gemma to get to know his family better, and vice versa, without having them invade her private space.

"Well, as long as he's only being nice because he's threatened into it," she scoffed back with a liberal dose of sarcasm. Caught in the middle of changing Zoe (because he'd thought it best to spring his news on her while she was distracted), she finished up fixing the tabs on the baby's nappy and zipped up the onesie from foot to chin. She sighed, lifted Zoe up against her shoulder and pinned him with a glare. "You couldn't have asked me first?"

No, he couldn't have, because she would have refused and he knew it. He much preferred asking for forgiveness than permission. With a sheepish smile, he aimed for his most innocent expression. "I'm sorry?"

He watched as she fought back an amused smile. "One of these days, I'll be immune to your tricks, bud."

"Ah, but today is not that day," Everett crowed, sweeping forward to kiss her forehead. He smiled genuinely as he pulled away. "Thank you, Gemma."

Her expression softened. "Yeah, well, I guess it's not actually the worst idea in the world. They're all going to be connected through Zoe for...well, forever. They might as well start getting to know each other now."

He'd thought the same thing, which was why he'd reached out to Brennan to begin with. The fact that Marcus, Brennan and Jeff (and Sara, though she technically wasn't Gemma's family) would be more than willing to put Charlie in his place if he stepped out of line again was a bonus that Everett revelled in.

Despite her obvious growing unease over the course of the day, Everett was surprised that Gemma seemed in high spirits when it came time to leave for her brother's house. He supposed that, unlike the previous day, she was bolstered by the knowledge that her family would be there. Similarly, she'd seemed comfortable enough with his mother by the end of lunch, so it was only Charlie they needed to worry about.

Damn Charlie. He'd barely been able to get through to him during their brief one-on-one talk the previous day. Oh, he understood that Charlie was trying, in his misguided way, to protect Everett's best interests, but he couldn't quite grasp that those included Zoe now, and –because she was Zoe's mother– Gemma herself.

"I wish I could drink," she muttered to him as they climbed out of the car. He swung Zoe's nappy bag over his shoulder without complaint while she grabbed the baby herself. Zoe whined at the interruption to her car-induced nap, and Gemma hushed her softly.

Feeling mildly guilty, Everett frowned. "Should we go back and get some of your frozen milk?" He checked his watch. "Or we could pop into the local shops for some formula?"

Gemma shook her head. "No, it's fine. I'm just being whiny."

"No," he refuted as they made their way down the cobbled path that led to Brennan and Jeff's front door, "you're sacrificing a great deal to breastfeed, and my family being here isn't making you any more comfortable. I'd be surprised if you weren't somewhat resentful." He bit his lip. "But if you choose not to breastfeed any longer–"

The look she shot him was somewhere between exasperated and fond. "You'd support whatever decision I make; yeah, I know." She rolled her eyes. "You're just *perfect.*"

He couldn't help but find her irritation amusing. "I do try," he responded lightly.

She muttered something under her breath that he couldn't quite catch and pressed the doorbell. Jeff greeted them enthusiastically. (Well, technically he greeted Gemma and Zoe with enthusiasm, and offered a lukewarm 'Hey' to Everett, but he saw it as progress.)

"Hand over my niece," he playfully demanded of Gemma, beaming and dissolving into baby-talk as she complied. "Bren's out back," he offered mid-babble, gesturing with a jerk of his head.

Gemma kissed Jeff's cheek and led the way through the house, past the kitchen and dining area and out onto the patio. There they found Brennan and Marcus milling about a large barbeque, beers in hand.

"Sweetheart," Marcus said, moving towards them to embrace Gemma, asking, "how are you feeling?"

As he waited for his daughter's response, he took Everett by surprise, also greeting him with a quick hug and strong clap on the back.

Gemma reassured her father that she was doing well, and they fell into a short conversation about Zoe, with Brennan interrupting to offer his own salutations before returning to his spot at the barbeque.

"You'll have to go fight Jeff if you want baby cuddles," Gemma eventually informed her father, jutting her chin towards the sliding door that led back into the house. "Assert your privilege as Grandpa or whatever."

The older man nodded, beaming at the title, and wandered off to do just that. Everett set the nappy bag down by the end seat at the table, noting with a smile that it was already set and overflowing with bowls of salads and bread rolls and a steaming casserole dish full of creamy potato bake.

"I thought you said this was a casual affair," he teased Brennan lightly, and grinned as the other man rolled his eyes at him.

"This is casual, mate. We've got the paper plates out."

"Ah, yes; that definitely detracts from the abundance of effort you've gone to."

Brennan smirked and shrugged. "Let's be real – Jeff did most of that. I'm just in charge of not overcooking the steak."

Gemma cleared her throat, distracting Everett from the witty retort he'd been formulating. "Your family's here."

Sure enough, he could hear his mother effusively thanking Jeff for hosting dinner as she was led through the house towards them. Charlie's baritone followed with his own thanks, and Everett imagined that their Mum had given him a good old-fashioned talking to about the expectations on his behaviour. That thought amused Everett to no end, especially given that Charlie was forty-two.

Serves the tosser right, too, he thought to himself as the man in question appeared in the doorway.

"Alright, Charlie?" Everett greeted, shaking his brother's hand before turning to their mother, "Hi, Mum."

She hugged Gemma first, then him. "This was a lovely idea, darling," she told him, before turning to Gemma, "I'm so looking forward to getting to know your family."

At his side, Gemma nodded, but he could feel how tense she was now that his brother was standing across from her again. Thankfully, Brennan swooped in, wiping his hands on his jeans before offering one to Beatrice and introducing himself as Gemma's brother.

"And you must be Everett's brother," Brennan turned to Charlie, hand extended. "I won't lie – I was expecting shorter and brunette."

"Brennan," Gemma chastised, "you can't just–"

Charlie chuckled, and the tension was broken. "It's alright," he shook Brennan's hand, "I like to say Everett's the runt of the family."

"There are only two of us," Everett played along with a put-upon sigh.

"Yeah," Charlie's green eyes glinted with mirth. "And you're the runt."

Brennan turned to Gemma with a sly smile of his own, but she snorted and waggled a finger at him. "Say the words, Bren, I dare you."

He wisely shut up. Off to the side of the outdoor area, Marcus and Beatrice were already bonding over mutual grandparenthood, Zoe now cradled in her Nan's arms. Jeff had made his way over to the barbeque in Brennan's absence, and the sound and smell of sizzling meat was intoxicating.

"Anyone for a beer? Or wine? Or something else?" Jeff asked, tongs in hand as he gestured at the fridge tucked into the corner beside the barbeque.

Brennan seemed to snap back into 'host mode', and assisted with everyone's requests, and Sara arrived, letting herself in via the gate around the side of the house. She announced her presence with a kiss to Gemma's cheek, a flirty wink in Everett's direction, and finished her rounds by snagging Jeff's wine glass directly from his hand. Taking a prim sip, she sauntered back over to Gemma's side and eyed Charlie up and down.

"The brother?" she asked Gemma, but her narrowed gaze never left the tall blond man.

Everett smothered a snort at the affronted look on Charlie's face. Gemma sounded somewhere between amused and annoyed when she scolded her friend. "Yes. Behave."

Sara shook her head. "Not a chance." She bared her teeth towards Charlie in what Everett could only call a predatory smile and extended her manicured hand. "Sara."

"Charlie," Everett watched his brother reply, taking the proffered hand in his, "a pleasure."

Gemma's best friend gave him another visible once-over and sniffed, "We'll see about that."

Charlie snorted and she scowled, but the stiff interaction only served to make Gemma laugh. She tugged Sara away to meet Beatrice, and Everett watched as all the women were soon giggling and fawning over Zoe.

"How are you holding up?" Charlie's quiet question startled Everett from his silent observations.

"Uh…sorry, what?"

Charlie pointed the neck of his beer bottle towards the gaggle of women and Marcus. "How are you doing with all this? I mean really?"

Everett regarded his brother with contemplation, surprised by the sudden change in the man's attitude from the previous day. He opted to give him the benefit of the doubt.

"I'm surprised by how alright I am, to be honest," he answered, a small smile tugging at the corners of his lips as his gaze drifted back over to where his daughter was being playfully fought over. "I didn't expect I'd enjoy being a dad, but I couldn't just walk away, you know?"

"Mmhmm," Charlie nodded as he swallowed another mouthful of his drink. "You did the responsible thing, stepping up and all."

Considering the harsh words they'd shot at each other the previous day, when Everett had all but dragged his brother from the restaurant, Everett wasn't quite sure how to respond. Thankfully, he was rescued from the awkward conversation by Jeff's announcement that their meals were cooked.

"Everyone grab a plate, help yourselves and find a seat," Brennan added, gesturing for Everett and Charlie to comply with the gentle order. "Guests first!"

It wasn't long before everyone was seated around the overflowing outdoor table, chatting with an ease that Everett hadn't anticipated. Charlie continued to surprise him, smiling genuinely and asking Everett and Gemma questions about Zoe that the pair were more than happy to answer.

The steak was cooked to medium-rare perfection, and Everett couldn't help but joke with Brennan about the fact that, not only had he cooked the steak, he'd also barbequed large field mushrooms smothered in garlic butter, haloumi, and some chicken skewers. It was a veritable feast. "Casual my arse, mate."

"This is all Dad's fault," Gemma explained before Brennan could snark back. With her fork hovering above her plate, she cast a beaming smile in Marcus' direction, where he was seated towards the far end of the table to her right. "He always over-caters when he's entertaining, and it's a habit Bren and I have sort of inherited."

"Better to have too much food than too little, I reckon," Marcus shrugged, reaching for his beer.

"Here here!" Charlie agreed, raising his own bottle in salute.

Sara leaned over from his other side and clinked her wine glass against it.

"Cheers to that!"

"Hold up," Charlie pulled his bottle back, smirking, "did you just agree with me, princess?"

"Ugh, it'll be the last time," Sara snarked back, scowling. "And call me 'princess' again and I'll be using this big, sharp knife here-" she waggled her steak knife for emphasis "-to demonstrate why it's a bad idea."

Everett watched as his brother gave her a quick salute, clearly more amused than intimidated by the feisty brunette. Sara rolled her eyes and turned to join the conversation Jeff was having with Beatrice on her other side.

Zoe had drifted off after a quick feed and was sleeping in the crook of Everett's arm as he ate one-handed. Gemma moved to cut his food for him, and Charlie quipped that his brother was essentially still a toddler, making her laugh.

"I was *just* about to say that!" she responded.

Everett shook his head and groaned. "I think I liked it better when you didn't get along. Having the both of you plotting against me doesn't bode well at all."

The smile on his face completely undermined his words.

Under the table, Gemma squeezed his thigh. He bent to press a kiss to the top of her head.

"Thank you," he murmured while Charlie was distracted, once again bickering with Sara.

Gemma merely shrugged and smiled before turning her attention back to Jeff on her other side and, for a moment, Everett could imagine spending future events (Christmases, birthdays, and the like) just like this. It was a little chaotic, but it felt good.

It wasn't until they were driving home that he realised that this was how he'd always imagined a family should feel.

* * *

"Oh, I don't want to leave the little lamb," Beatrice lamented, tearing up as she smoothed her hand through Zoe's dark hair for the final time. She gave the baby in her arms a longing look as she handed her back to her father.

"You'll miss your flight if you leave it any longer," Everett responded, giving her a one-armed hug, mindful of the baby in his other arm. "But I'm glad you came." He looked at his brother as he pulled back and stretched his arm out wide to also hug him goodbye, "both of you."

"Well, we couldn't not meet the newest member of our family, eh?" Charlie responded, thumping him on the back before running his finger down Zoe's arm. "She *is* wonderful, Everett."

They'd only stayed the week and, despite the rough start between Charlie and Gemma, Everett had really enjoyed having his family around. He smiled back at his older brother and nodded. "I'm aware."

Gemma returned to his side from hugging his mother goodbye, their whispered exchange too quiet for him to understand, but both women were teary-eyed as they parted. It warmed him to know that they'd become quite close (his mother had actually been a bit of a godsend, soothing them both through the sudden onset of what she referred to as 'The Witching Hour' – sudden bouts of Zoe's inconsolable screaming that lasted hours every evening), but made his heart ache to see them both upset.

"Oh, go on, then," Charlie sighed with exaggeration, stepping in front of Gemma, his arms outstretched. "I'll miss you, too, you firecracker."

She laughed as she hugged him, pressing a kiss to his cheek that did not make Everett jealous (nope, not in the least) and straightening his jacket. "Yeah, well, you're always welcome back, okay? Both of you. You're family."

How she could make such sweeping declarations like that, but completely ignore any feelings that she might share with him, Everett had no clue.

Alright, he had a clue – she didn't want to get hurt again, which was fair. He had to earn back her trust. It had only been a week since he'd accidentally blurted out his feelings for her, and they'd spent most of that week surrounded by their families. At night, when they were finally alone, they were both too exhausted to discuss anything serious, and he suspected she preferred things that way.

But with his mother and brother returning to the UK, he hoped that they could finally steal some quiet time alone to properly discuss where they stood.

"Make sure to send us photos and updates," his mother insisted as Charlie began to lead her away through the bright yellow archway that led downstairs to Customs.

"We will!" Gemma called after them, waving.

Everett slung his free arm around Gemma's shoulder as they meandered back to the car park. He was particularly pleased to see how well she and his mum had taken to one another. Not only because it would make things easier as they navigated their way through raising Zoe, but because he knew that Gemma had never really had a maternal influence in her life, so perhaps having his mum to talk to might benefit her. Besides, they were similar in many ways, both fiercely independent women with fiery tempers and wits. He couldn't wait to see Zoe grow up in the same fashion.

Of course, if she happened to be a Daddy's girl, he wouldn't mind that, either.

Gemma climbed into the passenger seat of her car while Everett buckled Zoe into her car seat. He'd insisted on getting used to driving in Brisbane, arguing that he was going to be around for years and he'd have to familiarise himself with her environment. She'd double checked that her insurance would cover him as a visitor with an international licence and had then agreed that it made sense.

He'd been driving in LA for a few years, so it took a little getting used to being back on the right side of the car and driving on the left side of the road, but after a few short drives around her neighbourhood –and with a crash course on the differences in road rules– he had his bearings again. It felt oddly domestic, and he supposed it was, this life he'd settled into. He knew that at some point the bubble would have to burst, and he'd have to return to LA and to his career.

Everett didn't want to think about that, though. The concept of walking away from his daughter –of missing any of her milestones– hurt. It would have to happen, and he and Gemma had to discuss the logistics of it all, but he continued to put it off.

Gemma, it seemed, was thinking along the same wavelength, because once he had navigated his way out of the airport and northbound onto the Gateway Motorway, she quietly spoke. "It's weird to think that you'll be heading through that departures gate in, what, a handful of weeks?"

"I've tried not to think too much on that," he admitted, flicking her a sideways glance before concentrating on the road again.

"Me either," she surprised him by reaching across the centre console to squeeze his thigh. "I've gotten used to having you around." The word 'again' lingered between them after her statement, unspoken but understood nonetheless. She retracted her hand and fiddled with it in her lap, staring out the passenger side window. "You've got about two months left on your VISA?"

The past three weeks had flown by, so two months sounded like no time at all. He swallowed, his Adam's apple bobbing with the effort. "Yeah," he replied softly.

"We're going to need to talk about it."

Some part of him wanted to snark, to tell her that that was exactly what they were doing in that moment, but the fact that she seemed just as reluctant for him to leave tempered his defensiveness. A week earlier he'd declared his feelings for her and she'd all but shot him down, and yet she clearly didn't want him to leave. Did he dare get his hopes up that she would return his affection if given a little more time and reassurance that, even if he had to leave, he would always return?

"I know," Everett answered with a nod, "and we will. But I have no idea where to start…or how we're going to make this work, only that we have to. Somehow." He chanced another quick look in her direction. "And I'd much rather discuss it when I can face you properly."

Out of the corner of his eye, he watched her lips twist upwards. He was onto her: she tended to try and weasel out of emotionally charged conversations by having them at inopportune times, and this was no exception.

"Well," she mused, "at least you're being honest. And I wish I knew how we're going to make it work, too."

He spared one more glance in her direction, hoping he was able to convey his conviction properly. "We'll sort it out together, love, I promise."

* * *

They'd stopped pretending that they didn't snuggle together during the night, given that they always gravitated to one another once they were asleep and always woke wrapped up together. Now, when they went to bed once Zoe was out (after once again screaming for the better part of three hours), he'd extend his arm and she'd use his shoulder as a pillow, her arm draped across his stomach or chest. They never discussed it, even though it seemed to go against her 'just friends' motto, and he wondered whether she craved the chaste intimacy as badly as he did.

"What are we going to do when you have to leave?" Gemma asked him, whispering into the darkness as her fingers tightened their hold on the fabric of the t-shirt he'd worn to bed.

"We'll set up a Facetime schedule," he began with the easy stuff. "I'll want to see her every other day if possible. More frequently would be preferable, but you've a life to lead, too, and the time difference is a bitch."

A bit of tension left her shoulders and he rubbed at the one he could reach. "I'll send you updates as well," she told him. "I know you don't want to miss anything, but...I mean...it's inevitable, right?"

It was, but acknowledging that seemed defeatist somehow, so he moved on with his thoughts, "I'll attempt to come back regularly. Every few months at the absolute worst case–"

"Depending on filming schedules," she interrupted firmly, shifting to stare at his profile. "Everett, you know better than I do that, depending on what role you land next, you mightn't be able to come back for at least six months. Maybe more. And...well, it mightn't be what either of us want, but we'll deal with it when it happens, okay? But don't go putting pressure on yourself to stick to a visiting schedule that might not be achievable."

"What if..." he licked his lips. "Obviously, not anytime soon, but...what if you and Zoe flew out to me?"

"You want me to take a baby on a, what, twelve hour flight? Are you insane?"

He frowned. "People do it all the time."

"When they've got no other choice. And other passengers curse them for it."

"Screw the other passengers," he snapped. "If I'm filming for six months or more, then we don't have any other choice."

"And if I'm working?"

He hadn't thought of that. He supposed her maternity leave would only last so long, especially if she wanted to keep paying for rent and food. (They hadn't discussed his portion of the financial burden of raising a child yet, either, and she skirted the issue any time he raised it.)

Not wanting to argue, he exhaled. "We'll cross that bridge when it comes to it, then."

"Okay," she backed off, her tone also softening from the defensive one it had crept into. "I guess that's all we can do for any of it, right?"

He wanted to bring up the concept of sending her payments for Zoe's ongoing needs but decided it could wait a little longer.

* * *

Everett started thinking about real estate later that week when he visited Brennan and Jeff's place to make use of their home gym. It was good of them to let him use their equipment, but he wondered if maybe he should invest in a house here where he could have his own home gym and perhaps a pool, given the temperate climate in South East Queensland.

The exchange rate was strong against the Australian dollar, and a quick search online showed him that he could get a spacious, modern, four-bedroom, two-bathroom home near to Gemma's brother's place at a fraction of the cost of something similar in his (admittedly upscale) neighbourhood in LA.

He already knew that the neighbourhood in which Brennan and Jeff lived was somewhat more affluent than Gemma's –given the comparative proximity to the city centre and the altogether more manicured feel of the area– and he guessed it might be a safer environment as well. It wasn't that Gemma's suburb felt at all unsafe, but there was an obvious socio-economic divide between the two.

If Everett purchased a home here –and could convince her to live in it– she wouldn't need to concern herself with paying rent, and he could feel as though he was finally contributing to their daughter's needs. He was already considering selling his house in LA and downsizing to an apartment, particularly because any extended spare time he'd have would be spent here watching Zoe grow up, and he barely spent any time in his home whenever he was filming. It just made sense to him.

He hoped it would also make sense to Gemma.

Still, he kept his thoughts to himself for a few more days, deciding to arm himself with a bit more knowledge on the local real estate market before he broached the subject with her. She caught him in the middle of one such attempt to research a few days later.

"Whatcha' looking at?" Gemma peered over at his laptop screen as she dropped into the couch seat beside him.

The coffee table between the couch and TV had long since been moved, and Zoe was currently on her belly on a brightly coloured mat in front of them, grizzling her way through mandated 'tummy time', essential for her development.

Gemma's brow furrowed before he could answer. "Real estate? In Brisbane?"

"Yeah," he licked his lips anxiously, suspecting that this conversation was not going to go smoothly. "I was thinking, with your lease coming up for renewal–"

"That I would renew it as planned."

It was his turn to frown. "Actually, I was hoping you might consider moving somewhere with a bit more space." He chanced a small, hopeful smile. "Maybe a bit closer to Brennan and Jeff's, even."

Expression shuttered, she folded her arms and jutted her chin. "I can't afford a bigger place, and I certainly can't afford to live closer to the city."

"Perhaps not on your own, but–"

"Absolutely not."

"Gemma…" He smothered a sigh and closed the lid of his laptop, setting the whole thing aside so he could shift in his seat to face her. "I need to contribute. You're raising my daughter."

"She's mine, too," her reply was somewhat petulant, but she met his gaze with her own determined one. "And I don't need your money."

"No, you don't *want* my money," he couldn't help the frustration that bled into his tone, "there's a difference."

She was silent for a moment, contemplating the implications of what he'd just said. Even he knew how it sounded, and he braced himself for the reaction. She didn't disappoint. "Excuse me?" she'd taken (understandable) offence. "Do you not think I can provide for her on my own? Because, buddy, I was going to be just fine without you. And I will be once you're gone."

He'd earned that, but it stung. "You were going to survive, yes," he attempted to explain, "but you deserve more than that. Our daughter deserves more than that."

"Wow," Gemma was decidedly unimpressed, "guilt. That's a new one. Fuck you, too."

It amazed him sometimes that they could get along so effortlessly and then walk right into a minefield of an argument without any warning. Though he did concede that he'd known this one would be a difficult conversation, and he hadn't exactly been tactful. But, even so, he was beginning to become frustrated with how stubborn she was. Did she not understand that he wanted to contribute?

With a groan of frustration, he reached for her and she pulled away. "Gemma, I'm not *trying* to guilt you."

"Are we adding gaslighting to your list of sins, too, then?"

"For fuck's sake," he snapped, and her eyes widened because it was the first time that he'd truly stood his ground with her, or that he'd come close to losing his temper at all. He paused and took a breath. "You're a wonderful mother, and I'm sure that –regardless of whether I'm here or not– Zoe will want for nothing. But I don't just want to help provide for her, love, I *need* to."

She contemplated his words, her shoulders dropping with defeat. "I understand that, I do, but...what exactly are you proposing here? Because it looked like you were looking to buy a place and I don't have enough for a deposit saved up, or–"

"Well, it would make more sense to buy a permanent home, wouldn't it? Your rental money is paying off someone else's mortgage." He shrugged. "I have the funds for a deposit –to be honest, I have the funds to purchase a home completely– and it would save you on rent."

Gemma shook her head. "I'm not living rent-free in a house that you've bought."

"Why not?"

"What do you mean 'why not'? How can you not see how that's a bad idea for me?"

Trying to remain patient, he asked, "Can you explain it to me?"

"I...well, I don't like the idea of being in your debt or beholden to you or whatever," her hazel eyes stared imploringly into his. "If you own the roof over my head and don't expect me to pay my way, that's exactly how it will feel. Like I'm a kept woman." She looked away. "And then...you know...what happens if I started dating or whatever? That would just feel weird, living in your house but bringing another man home."

Everett felt like he'd taken a punch to the gut. "Dating?" he echoed flatly. Hadn't he made his feelings perfectly clear? Weren't they already essentially in a relationship? Zoe was whining at their feet, but for the first time since her birth he paid her no mind. "Gemma...I...I hoped that you and I..."

"I know," she wouldn't look at him. "But that's ridiculous. You live in LA. You've dated –or slept with, or *whatever*– some of the most gorgeous women in the world, and when you get back over there–"

"Hang on, what?" He cut her off, incredulous. "Firstly, rumours of my sexual exploits have been greatly exaggerated by the tabloids, and I thought you'd realise that. Secondly, I'm not the sort of man who would cheat on my partner simply because I'm in another country. Finally, I think *you* are gorgeous, and I don't have eyes for anyone else."

"Oh, please," she rolled her eyes, "I'm even frumpier now than I was in November."

He finally gave in and bent forward to pick Zoe up, because her whines were escalating to cries. Tummy time was not her favourite activity. "Gemma," he rolled his own eyes right back at her, "you had a baby less than a month ago." And she'd been pushing herself to exercise and diet far more than he thought was healthy, but he'd not thought it his place to comment.

"Exactly!" She flung her hands into the air. "I've got a whole bunch of new stretch marks, and my boobs will never be the same again, and I'm just...*blergh*."

Everett sighed. What was he supposed to say to that? "You're being too critical of yourself, darling."

She shrugged silently, and he realised that she had once again managed to derail the conversation to avoid resolving the issue.

Steeling his jaw, he decided to put it back on track. "But, even if you're not interested in pursuing a relationship with me, that shouldn't prevent you from living in a more spacious home, closer to your family. If you really wanted to, we could organise it so that I pay for half the house, covering the deposit, and we can arrange a loan for the other half, the payments for which should be less than the rent you're paying now, given the current interest rates."

Gemma blinked at him, conflict clouding her expression. Cocking her head thoughtfully, she slumped back against the arm of the couch. "That... isn't a bad suggestion."

Shifting Zoe to his shoulder where she seemed content to drool against him, Everett's lips quirked. "I've been known to use logic occasionally."

* * *

They found a house a couple of weeks later. It was a low-set brick and tile home less than five minutes' drive from Brennan and Jeff's house and twenty minutes' drive from Gemma's work, even in traffic. It had four bedrooms plus a study, a media room and an open plan kitchen-dining-lounge area that led out to a large patio area and an inground lap pool. There was also enough yard space for a small playground, or a trampoline – something Gemma wanted to be able to get Zoe when she was old enough.

The realtor, a portly man who appeared to be in his sixties, led them through the house, pointing out all the 'selling points' while asking them borderline inappropriate questions. Gemma hadn't been able to prevent the giggles from escaping her when he'd asked Everett what he did for a living, and then offered him the advice: "If the acting thing doesn't pan out, you should think about a 'real' job."

Everett had smirked and nodded and said he'd keep that in mind.

The master suite of the house was almost the size of the entire downstairs area of her current home. It had a huge ensuite bathroom, a massive walk-in wardrobe, and enough space for both a king size bed and a full sitting area or 'parents retreat' (according to the agent.)

Everett liked that it was bright and airy, but he was particularly impressed by how private the home felt. The block of land was generous, and the house was set back from the street, surrounded by six-foot-high fencing (and an electric security gate), with plenty of space between the house and either of the neighbours. The pool was also blocked from prying eyes, courtesy of the shrubbery planted high up on retaining walls.

Wandering away from the realtor, he asked Gemma for her thoughts. He knew the price was a little higher than she had wanted to pay, but this was a home that he could see her and Zoe staying in for the foreseeable future. He was wearing Zoe against his chest in a baby carrier and bounced lightly as he waited for her response.

"It ticks all the boxes," she told him, "but I don't think I'll qualify for a loan for half of the asking price."

"What if–"

"You're not buying the whole thing outright."

"–I was guarantor on your application?" he finished, arching his brow at her.

Her cheeks flushed.

"I don't love that, but…" she glanced around, likely already imagining a future in the house, "okay."

He'd expected more of an argument and schooled his features to hide his surprise. Offering her a soft smile, he reached for her hand and pulled it to his lips, ghosting a kiss over the back of her knuckles. "Thank you, love."

Her eyes watched his lips for just a moment too long before she shook herself and turned back towards the realtor.

"Let's talk price," she declared, suddenly channelling a version of herself that Everett hadn't seen before. Everett stood back and watched as she became a stoic, cut-throat negotiator, making demands and bartering with the man who –up until that point– had clearly assumed Everett would be handling the negotiating.

She was firm, unruffled, and had the realtor on the back foot, and Everett swore that he had never been more turned on.

"Gemma," he murmured as they signed the final offer to be delivered to the vendor, his voice low and a little rough with arousal, "where the hell did you learn to do that?"

Her hazel eyes glinted with mischief, and it was clear to him that she had thoroughly enjoyed herself. "I learned to barter on the playground," she shrugged, "and I've always just had a knack for it."

"I'll say – that was amazing."

The blush on her cheeks only made him want her more.

* * *

She'd argued with him about paying for professional removalists until he reminded her that –come moving day– Zoe would be ten weeks old and it would make more sense for them to devote their energy to unpacking than attempting to lug everything around themselves. In the end, she convinced him to allow her to pay for half of the costs involved. (He was quickly learning to pick his battles.)

The move itself went off without a hitch, something they were both eternally grateful for. Their first night in their new home (a thought that still sent a little thrill through him, even though they'd not discussed or labelled their relationship) was spent eating pizza while sprawled across the new king-sized bed he'd insisted on buying for the master suite. Gemma's old queen bed now was in place in the guest bedroom at the far end of the hall. Because of the size of the master suite, Zoe's crib fit comfortably at the foot of the bed.

All the literature he'd read had suggested that it was best practice to keep the baby in your bedroom for at least the first six months, if not a year of its life, but that would not have been achievable in Gemma's townhouse. Especially not once Zoe outgrew her bassinet.

"I'm sorry I fought you on this," Gemma spoke quietly, shaking him from his musings. Her gaze had followed his to the crib, where Zoe was sleeping fitfully (thankfully the episodes of colicky screaming prior to bedtime were becoming shorter, but she seemed to take longer to settle into sleep.) "Moving, I mean." She sighed and looked at him, offering a tentative smile. "It was definitely the right thing to do."

He considered teasing her to lighten the mood, but it wasn't often that she opened up to him and he didn't want to miss out on an opportunity to get closer. Wiping his palms on his jeans, which were already somewhat dirty from the move, he reached for her hand. "You're fiercely independent, Fox. I understand why you were resistant at first." His thumb moved over her knuckles. "But I am glad you changed your mind."

"Me too," he almost missed the admission with how softly it was spoken. She licked her lips, and his eyes were drawn to the action, and he found himself leaning towards her.

"Gemma, I–"

Zoe chose that moment to squawk, and they both jumped, with Everett silently cursing their daughter's shocking timing as Gemma pulled back and climbed off the bed to tend to her.

He sighed and collected the pizza box, taking it out to the kitchen while he willed his heart rate to calm down. Rowena had called earlier that week to confirm his return flight to LA in another week's time, and he felt as though he had a countdown clock hanging over his head.

At least this time when he left, he'd (obviously) remain in contact, and he knew where she lived (because he co-owned the house). He had just hoped that by the time he did leave, their relationship would be on stronger ground. However, time was running out.

When he returned to the bedroom, Gemma was already placing Zoe back down in her crib again.

"She just wanted some comfort, I think," she mused, carefully stroking the baby's fine, dark hair. "She wasn't hungry."

"It's been a big day," he acknowledged, coming to stand beside her. Unable to help himself, he wrapped his arm around her waist and kissed the top of her head. He peered down at their daughter –who had seemingly doubled in size from the tiny, squalling creature that had seized his heart so unexpectedly– and wondered, not for the first time, how he would survive getting onto a plane and leaving her behind.

Gemma yawned and he swallowed. They'd not discussed sleeping arrangements, but with a perfectly good guest room down the hall, there was no longer any reason to continue to share a bed. Coward that he was, he merely pulled away from her and said, "I'll let you get to bed, love."

She startled and stared up at Everett with obvious confusion. "And where are you going?"

He gestured over his shoulder. "To the guest room?"

It took her a moment of blinking before something akin to understanding settled into her expression, followed by regret. She grasped for his hand. "Really?" she asked, "Whose benefit is that for?"

"I just assumed you'd like your space back." She had emotional walls a mile high, and he didn't want to argue with her over it anymore. "At your place, there wasn't really a choice, but here…" he shrugged, trailing off. "Darling, you know how I feel, but I won't force anything between us."

Biting her lip, she glanced down at their entwined hands. He wished he could read her thoughts. "I don't want to date anyone else."

The seeming non-sequitur threw him for a loop, though the words lifted his hopes. "Pardon?"

"When you first suggested buying a house," she exhaled shakily, "I only said it to piss you off. Y'know, to try and talk you out of what I thought was an act of obligation." She made the confession while still looking down, refusing to meet his gaze, and he recalled the argument with clarity.

Despite himself, he couldn't help but snicker gently. "It might surprise you, love, but I consider myself well versed in your diversionary tactics." When that failed to get a rise out of her, he brought his free hand up to tilt her chin, forcing her to look him in the eye. "But I am glad to hear that you don't have plans to see anyone else. And none of this–" he gestured around them vaguely, "–is an obligation."

"I know," her lips pulled into a small, but genuine smile. "It's been ten weeks and I've been waiting for the other shoe to drop, you know? Waiting for you to stop acting and admit that this isn't the life you want, but…I mean, ten weeks without a crack in the facade? You're a good actor, but you're not *that* good."

"I should take offence to that," he jibed lightly, "but I've not been acting."

"I know," she reiterated. "It's just taken me a while to realise it."

They'd never really spoken of her former lovers –it wasn't a subject he wanted to entertain at all– but he could only imagine the type of people they had been for her to just assume she was being lied to and manipulated.

"So, where does that leave us, then?"

It was disheartening when she shrugged and averted her gaze again, settling her sights back on Zoe. "I don't know," she admitted sadly. "I don't want to date anyone else –and I don't want you to date anyone else, which is selfish of me– but…"

"You're afraid." The words escaped him before he could stop them, but he had hit the nail on the head because she huffed out a breath and nodded.

"You're leaving in less than a week. It feels like *déjà vu.*"

"Things are quite a bit different to last time," Everett responded softly. "Neither one of us is going to vanish from the other's life. We have multiple ways to contact each other. We share a home. More importantly, we share a daughter." He ran his hand through his hair before scratching behind his ear. "I'm content to take things slowly, love. We're essentially in a relationship as it is. Besides, being separated by half the world is going to pump the breaks on rushing things anyway."

Gemma remained silent, and he hoped she was giving thought to what he'd said. After a few more moments, the ghost of a smile flitted over her face, and she brought her gaze back up to meet his. "Okay."

His eyes lit up, a wide, surprised grin spreading across his features. "Yeah?"

"Yeah."

Everett closed the space between them, slanting his lips over hers. The last time he'd kissed her like this had been in the moments after Zoe's birth. Then, he'd been an overwhelmed, surprisingly overjoyed new father, thanking her for the gift she'd given him. This time reminded him of their first kisses, practically sparking with passion and chemistry, but tempered by emotions that he hadn't dared to feel during that first night together.

One of her hands threaded into the hair at the back of his head, the other curling into the cotton of his t-shirt.

"Taking it slow, huh?" she teased as they separated for air.

"What?" he asked, unable to hide his mirth, gripping her waist possessively now that he was allowed the privilege, "I can't kiss my girlfriend, the mother of my child?"

"Oh, God, you're going to be insufferable about this, aren't you?" Though she was rolling her eyes, the fondness with which she spoke belied her words.

He chuckled. "Most definitely."

* * *

Chapter Eleven

"I'll be back for Christmas," Everett promised, bending to press his forehead against Gemma's as he hovered outside the stupid bright yellow 'Departures' archway. It had no business being such a bright, cheerful colour. They were ignorant of the people bustling past them, too concerned with having to part ways.

Rowena had attempted to book him for the annual Gold Coast Pop!Con convention, but his VISA wouldn't quite cover the stay. The fact that it had been almost a year since their first meeting made parting now even more painful.

Gemma swallowed, willing herself not to cry. "You can't promise that," she told him, feeling her lower lip quiver involuntarily as he ran the palm of his hand up and down her arm in a soothing gesture. "What happens if you land a role?"

"They'll shut down production over the holidays," his response was calm and logical, and she hated that he could be so rational while she felt bereft in a sea of unwelcome emotions, "and I'm not missing her first Christmas." He punctuated the statement by running his fingers through the soft, inky-dark hair poking out of the carrier strapped to her chest.

Gemma's heart ached at the sadness in his gaze as he looked down at their daughter, and she knew he didn't want to leave her.

The last week had been spent in a haze of unpacking the new house, organising new furniture to fill the extra space, stealing kisses, and trying to avoid the fact that he had to leave again.

She regretted that now. Regretted not properly discussing it. Regretted that they'd resolved to progress slowly. Regretted that she'd gone and gotten attached again and there was every chance that he might return to his old life and realise how much easier and better it was without her and a clingy baby in it.

Yes, these were contradictory regrets, but she felt them all the same.

But she kept those words in, knowing from experience how destructive such a confession could be.

"Christmas it is, then," Gemma eventually acknowledged, her voice tight. Christmas was almost six weeks away. They'd spoken about him being gone for longer periods at a time than that, but now that it wasn't just a hypothetical situation, it sucked.

"God, I'm going to miss you both," he lamented, ducking to kiss the top of Zoe's head before landing a brief, chaste kiss to Gemma's lips. "I'll call when I land." He cupped her face with his hand. "I love you."

"Damn it," she cursed as tears slid down her cheeks, "Everett…"

She hadn't said the words yet, too afraid that things would still go terribly wrong –that it was still too soon– and she didn't want the moment where she did acknowledge her feelings to be in such a public setting, or when he was leaving the country.

"I know, darling," he brushed her tears away with his thumbs. "There's no rush."

She really hated his stupid calm, rational, supportive vibe. It made it that much harder to let him go.

Glancing at her watch, she felt her stomach drop. They'd pushed it until the last few minutes for check-in, and she knew that it could take ages to get through customs, so loitering any longer might prove to be a mistake. "You'd better go," she murmured, tilting her head for one last kiss.

Despite his earlier propriety, Everett slanted his lips over hers and kissed her deeply, as though he was trying to memorise every detail of her mouth and the way they moved together. She supposed he might have been – it would be over a month before they'd next have the chance to indulge like this again.

He pulled away with obvious reluctance before shifting his stance so he could press his lips to their daughter's forehead one last time. "I love you, too," he told the baby softly, and Gemma bit back a sob, even while he stroked Zoe's head and added, "be good for Mum, alright?"

Then he forced himself to turn and walk through the archway for departing passengers only. He stepped onto the descending escalator and turned back, waving goodbye until they could no longer see one another.

Gemma managed to hold the tears at bay until she was in the car.

* * *

"How are you holding up?" Jeff asked her later that evening, having popped around under the guise of 'wanting to see his niece'. (He wasn't fooling anyone.)

Gemma had to admit, it was nice being less than five minutes' drive from her brother and brother-out-of-law. She and Jeff were now seated at the dining table, each nursing a cold glass of wine (she'd already fed Zoe and put her down for the first leg of her night's sleep).

Running her finger around the rim of her glass, she shrugged. "I'm fine."

Jeff scoffed, shaking his head, causing the black hair of his fringe to fall into his eyes. He brushed it away. "Gems, come on. It's okay to admit you miss him."

She hadn't told anyone about the fact that she and Everett had gone from simply co-parenting to attempting a relationship, but she suspected that they'd been able to predict it happening anyway. Why else would she have bought a house with the man? Platonic co-parents didn't do that.

Still, she was stubborn, and she didn't need another lecture from Brennan about how she was only setting herself (and Zoe) up for future pain and disappointment. Hoping to deflect Jeff's underlying probing, she shrugged, "Well, yeah, I'll definitely miss having the help around here."

194

Her brother's boyfriend set his wine down and pinned her with a hard stare. "Gemma."

"I'm okay," she assured him, "I promise."

He leaned back in his seat, assessing her. "We've known each other for how long?"

She did the mental maths. "Eight years?" He'd been the experienced nurse she'd been assigned to work alongside during the final months of her practical training, and they'd quickly become friends. She'd accidentally introduced him to Brennan a few months later, and both men had been smitten with each other. The rest was history.

Nodding, he agreed, "Eight years. And you're basically my sister now, even if your brother's too lame to put a ring on my damn finger already."

She snorted, because it was an ongoing joke, the stalemate between the two men. (Both expected the other to propose, and neither was backing down.)

He ignored her and continued to bludgeon her with his point. "So, I know you, Gems: whether you want to admit it or not, you love this guy, and it's going to suck not seeing him every day when you've literally been living together for months." His smile was warm, without a hint of judgement. "Yeah, I'll admit that I wanted to strangle him at first. But…I've also seen how happy you've been these last few months –happier than you ever were with Scott– so I think Everett might actually be good for you. And, you know, if you want to cry it out or whatever, I'm here, okay?"

"Alright," she backed down, acknowledging the fact that he was being genuinely supportive. She lifted her glass and took a sip, buying herself a few more moments to get her thoughts in order. Jeff waited patiently, sipping his own wine, and eventually she stared into the bottom of her glass and admitted, "We're together. We're taking things slow, trying to do things right, I guess. Well, as right as we can when we've already got a kid together. But…yeah, I already miss him." She bit her lip and glanced up into Jeff's sympathetic gaze. "He said he loves me."

"And you think it's too soon."

Her friend hadn't phrased it as a question because he knew her well enough to know that a declaration made so soon would make her uncomfortable, whether the words were true or not.

"Isn't it?" she asked, sounding plaintive even to her own ears. "He doesn't really know me."

She wasn't expecting Jeff to chuckle. "He's lived with you for almost three months, babe. And he saw you in labour. Trust me, he knows you." His expression softened out and he leaned forward to squeeze her hand. "And I'd bet you know him pretty well by now, too."

Do I? She wondered. When they were together, things seemed too easy. Sure, Everett had some frustrating habits (he was an even neater neat-freak than she was, so she'd often find that he'd moved something she'd set aside for future use, and he tended to use the last of things like milk, or cheese, or toilet paper and would forget to add it to the shopping list) but they just *clicked*.

She knew how he took his tea and coffee, that he had an insane sweet tooth and could sniff out a hidden stash of chocolate with the same accuracy as a police sniffer dog, that he actually disliked both the Beatles and the Rolling Stones, and that he was mildly allergic to cats. She knew his favourite food was his mum's roast pork, that he secretly listened to Lady Gaga when he worked out, and that his biggest dream was to write and direct his own feature film.

She also knew that he'd spent time cataloguing her own habits and likes and dislikes, and that he seemed more genuinely interested in her happiness than anyone she'd dated before.

With an internal sigh, she conceded that Jeff might actually have a point.

"I guess," she found herself replying, swirling the remaining liquid in her glass. "But...don't you think it's too good to be true?"

This was her main concern. Everett seemed too perfect. He had from the beginning. When he'd put his foot in his mouth and broken her heart, there had been a part of her that had been relieved. Vindicated, even. Because he'd been flawed, and human, and not the almost impossible specimen of perfection that had existed in the days preceding their whirlwind relationship's inevitable implosion.

Then he'd walked through her birth suite door and thrown her for yet another loop.

Once again, he seemed almost too sweet, too supportive, too helpful, too…*everything*. So of course she was waiting for things to go wrong again, for him to buckle under the pressure of two different worlds pulling him in opposite directions. The fact that he hadn't yet was encouraging, but his return to LA was going to be the true test of his commitment to their daughter, and to her.

Jeff shook his head in response to her question. "Maybe if I hadn't seen how much he loves Zoe, or how he looks at you…but, Gemma, I think he's the real deal."

She wanted Jeff's words to reassure her, but she wasn't convinced. Not yet.

* * *

"How are my girls?" Everett sounded utterly exhausted. Once the pixellation on her screen cleared, Gemma didn't think he looked much better than he sounded.

He'd done as he'd promised, calling her as soon as he was safely ensconced in the back of an Uber. It didn't bother her that it was almost 3 a.m. in Brisbane when he called. She'd been up with Zoe anyway, only just having put her back down in her cot, and was glad to know that he'd landed and was on his way home.

"Better than you, I'm betting," she responded with empathy. "How was the flight?"

Running his free hand through his hair, he sighed. "Long."

"Yeah, well, at least you didn't travel cattle class."

That elicited an amused snort, but his words came out bitterly. "One of the few perks of my job."

Eyebrows drawing down, Gemma shook her head. "You love your job." He'd defended it passionately at one point. "This is just something we've both got to get used to."

"Easy for you to say: you're not separated from your daughter."

Everett's bitter retort kind of stung, but she reminded herself that he was exhausted, and that this was the first time he was separated from Zoe by more than half an hour's drive since her birth. In fact, though it seemed almost wrong to think it, she was somewhat relieved that he was hurting – it was proof that he genuinely cared.

I'm an awful person, she mused, even while she sympathetically replied, "I wish things could be different."

He scrubbed his hand over his face, groaning. "I'm sorry, love. I didn't mean to imply that this isn't going to be difficult for you."

"I know," and she did, truly. "It's just a different sort of difficult." Determined to lift his mood, she turned playfully petulant. "My live-in slave has gone. I have to cook my own meals now. It's unheard of," she teased, reclining against her pile of pillows. His scent lingered in the sheets, and she hated to think it would be gone once she washed them.

Thankfully, her words had the desired effect, and he leered, "Surely you're going to miss me for more than my culinary skills."

"Well, I'll miss your help keeping this place clean, too, I guess." The bed felt too large and empty without him, too, but she was trying to keep things light and playful.

"Hmm," he said, affecting a thoughtful expression, but his eyes glinted with mischief as his voice dropped sinfully, "anything else about me you'll miss, Fox?"

"You're in the back of an Uber," she reminded him with a laugh, shaking her head before yawning involuntarily. "Behave."

His gaze softened. "I should let you get back to sleep."

Gemma felt a pang of longing and regret, but she nodded, "I'll call you later, when Zoe's awake again."

His smile didn't quite reach his gorgeous blue eyes, but he was genuine when he said, "I look forward to it, darling. Love you."

Swallowing hard, she blew him a kiss and terminated the call.

* * *

'Rowena's booked me for some interviews about fatherhood' read the text that Gemma woke up to. She felt like her stomach dropped while her heart leapt into her throat. A quick Google told her that it was almost 2 p.m. in LA, so she called him immediately, even though the baby was still asleep and he might have also been attempting to sleep off his jet lag.

Everett answered on the third ring.

She barely let him finish his 'Hello'. "I hope you told Rowena that you won't be divulging any more information about Zoe than what's been posted online."

She hadn't spoken to his agent directly, but there was already no love lost between them. The other woman had made it very clear that getting Everett's career back on track was her priority, and that she saw Gemma and Zoe as an inconvenience at best.

"Breathe, Gemma," he attempted to soothe her, and she was glad she'd opted for a standard phone call instead of Facetime, because it allowed her to roll her eyes and make faces in her displeasure.

"Don't 'breathe' me! I have a right to be anxious about this."

There was a brief moment of silence before he calmly acknowledged, "Of course you do." Frustration bled into his tone, though, as he continued, "And I made you a promise when she was all of a few days old that I have no intention of breaking."

Well, now she felt guilty for snapping at him. "Sorry," she tried to sound as though she really meant it, but she was still annoyed at Rowena for springing this on him. "I just...I wasn't expecting you to be thrown into it so soon."

She supposed she should have been – he'd told her that his agent had been fielding interview requests ever since he'd publicly announced Zoe's birth. He'd put them off, telling Rowena that he was taking a few months of paternity leave. He'd even had his social media updated with a note thanking his fans for their supportive messages (and there had been a tonne of them) but that he was stepping back for a while to enjoy being a new dad.

"I know, love," he exhaled heavily, "but we both knew that something like this would happen eventually. To be honest, I'm surprised nobody's photographed us out and about back home yet." As the weather in Brisbane had warmed with the oncoming summer, they'd spent a lot more time visiting local parks and beaches, indulging in the weather that 'Sunny Queensland' was known for.

She'd thought the same thing with every outing, but most people tended to keep to themselves. Plus, nobody would have expected Everett Rhodes to be living in suburban Brisbane, of all places. Byron Bay, perhaps. Sydney even. But Brisbane? If any of his fans had spotted him, they might have just thought he was a lookalike.

"Yeah," Gemma agreed defeatedly. "I just freaked out a bit. I'm sorry." She sounded much more genuine this time. "And, okay, as a fan, I kinda do want to hear you babbling excitedly about your baby."

His laugh was rich and warm as it came down the line. "As a fan, you say?"

"Uh huh," her own smile began to stretch her lips, "I wouldn't be surprised if this changes the roles you're offered going forward, either."

"So now that I have a kid, you expect I'll be cast in more family friendly roles?" He sounded equal parts amused and curious, "Or are you hinting that the daddy fetishists are going to be out in droves?"

"A bit of both, really," she answered honestly, just as Zoe started to whine and grizzle.

On the other end of the call, Everett made his own sound of distress. "Oh, God, I miss her." His tone had shifted to morose almost immediately, "Can we switch to Facetime? I need to see her."

"I'll change and feed her first, alright? That way she'll be all smiles for you."

"Alright," he answered with obvious reluctance, "I'll talk to you soon."

She tried not to be too upset that he hung up without his customary 'love you' at the end.

* * *

Everett emailed her copies of the completed interviews a couple of days later. In each one, he'd gushed about his daughter in a way that made her fall a little bit more in love with him with every word, but he'd remained careful not to give any private details away.

The first two interviews had stuck to surface topics, asking him about changing diapers and middle-of-the-night feedings. They really played into the old, misogynistic view that men weren't good at that sort of thing, but he'd shut them down skilfully with his usual deflective charm.

"I'm a parent," he'd said during the first one, shrugging at the interviewer across the desk from him, "it doesn't matter if you're a mum or a dad – changing a nappy isn't fun for anyone." The host had twittered ridiculously and moved on to other mundane questions.

It was the final interview, though, that had Gemma's hackles rising. Some breakfast TV show with godawful bright orange couches and a host and hostess with matching plastic smiles. They rubbed her the wrong way as soon as they grinned at the camera, and their questions went from light-hearted to intrusive quickly.

"Our sources say that this has all been quite a surprise for you," the woman on the couch across from him began, her plastic smile turning almost predatory.

Everett could obviously sense where she was going with the topic, because there was a minute flash of irritation across his own face before his expression smoothed out and he interrupted with: "Is anyone ever truly prepared for parenthood? Talk about a shock to the system!" He cast a charming smile up into the studio audience, encouraging them to laugh and agree.

The bitch on the couch pressed on, though, ignoring his attempt to derail her probing. She leaned forward towards him, affecting a conspiratorial air, "What I mean to say is that you didn't know you were going to be a father until the baby was born." There was an obvious ripple of surprise through the audience before the camera panned back to the hosts. Gemma wanted to slap both of their smug expressions away. "Is that true?"

"I was actually present at her birth, but I would ask you whether it makes a difference when I learned about my –at the time– impending fatherhood," Everett responded coolly, his own smile changing, becoming more aggressive despite his tone remaining perfectly pleasant. "Nine hours, nine days, nine weeks, nine months – does it actually change anything? At the end of the day, I still have a beautiful daughter who I love more than words can properly express." As the audience reacted enthusiastically to his answer, he leaned forward in his own seat, and his gaze was unforgiving, even though he sounded confused and apologetic, "So, forgive me, but I'm not sure what your question just now was trying to achieve, other than to stir up drama for drama's sake."

She didn't think she'd ever been more turned on by him than in that moment. It was such a pity that he was on the other side of the world.

'I tore Rowena a new one for the last interview,' the text came through a couple of hours later, after she'd responded to his email with a rant about the audacity of the TV hosts.

'So you should have.' She texted back, still fuming. Her thumbs flew over the keyboard on the phone screen. *'I'm willing to put money on her having tipped them off about the surprise thing.'* It made him quite the sympathetic figure, after all.

His response seemed to take forever, the ellipses that denoted his typing popping up and disappearing a few times as he clearly rethought his response. His eventual reply (*'The thought had occurred to me, too.'*) was disappointing.

Gemma sighed and set her phone aside, unsure where to go from there.

It lit up with another text a few minutes later. *'Either way, she knows that I'll walk out if it happens again. You & Zoe are my everything. Love you.'*

She sent a love heart emoji back, resolved that the first time she admitted her feelings would not be via text message.

It would be to his face.

Preferably in person.

* * *

It really only took a week of Everett being gone for Gemma to realise just how much more difficult parenting a three-month-old was without a partner. She'd known it would be harder, of course, but not having someone to pass Zoe off to when the screaming became too much, or to leave the baby with when she needed to go to the toilet or have a shower was rough. She'd always acknowledged the fact that Everett shared the parenting duties with her equally, but she'd thought that she'd be able to manage.

She was starting to think that she'd been wrong.

Or was that just the sleep deprivation talking?

It also sucked not having someone to share the emotional load with, never mind the physical one. It felt like she never got a break, never a moment's peace. Even when Zoe drifted into a nap, Gemma remained alert, one ear waiting for the inevitable wails of a hungry or wet baby waking up.

She was Mummy one hundred percent of the time, and she was beginning to feel as though she didn't remember the person she'd been before. Then she felt guilty for feeling resentful, and it became a painful, vicious cycle.

How had she ever thought that she'd be able to do this on her own?

Before Everett had stepped back into her life, she'd been set on doing just that. But now? Now she was terrified that he'd choose to stay in LA, that he'd realise how much easier life was on the other side, and she'd be left quite literally holding the baby.

She loved Zoe. There was no doubt about that. But sometimes –usually at the end of a long day of tending to the baby's every need– Gemma resented the fact that Everett was somewhere else, free to do his own thing.

It took a lot of effort to remind herself that he would much prefer being home with her and Zoe.

For the most part, Gemma was able to keep her resentment bubbling away beneath the surface. Her calls with Everett were Zoe-centric, though she could tell he was concerned that their own relationship seemed to have stalled. *What the hell did he expect?* she wondered. What could they really achieve, seventeen hours' time difference apart, literally half a world away from each other?

Her family had noticed her mood slipping, but she wasn't quite sure how to verbalise what was wrong when they asked. Having Zoe had been her choice, so she really had no right to complain now (or, at least, that was how she felt.)

Both her brother and his boyfriend had attempted to convince her to talk to them, to let it all out, but she couldn't bring herself to do so. Not even when they roped Sara in to try and talk to her.

How was Gemma supposed to explain it to them? She felt guilty for resenting her baby, for not being able to handle the pressure of parenting and loving a tiny, helpless kid of only a few months old.

Unfortunately, it was Everett who got her to admit what was going on during one of their scheduled Facetime calls.

"Gemma, love, are you alright?" he frowned in concern, and she focused on the background behind him. He was in a trailer, filming a guest star spot in a random sitcom.

As his girlfriend, she thought she should have paid more attention, but her interest levels had plummeted. (The former fangirl inside her cringed at that.) Some part of her also knew it wasn't fair on him, but her mood was low, and she was jealous that he was out working –seemingly enjoying himself– while she was trapped with the baby.

"I'm fine." An actress she was not, and he'd always had the uncanny ability to read her, even through a little smartphone screen.

With a shake of his head, he lightly said, "It's my experience that when a woman says she's fine, that's rarely the case." Then he tilted his head and gave her the full puppy-dog expression. "Talk to me. Please."

"There's nothing to talk about. I'm *fine*."

He studied her for a moment in silence, then tentatively offered, "It's okay to want –to need– a break and some time for yourself." His voice and expression turned soft and empathetic. "You look shattered."

Damn him for reading all those blogs and parenting books! Feeling her eyes well with tears, Gemma shrugged. She didn't trust herself to speak.

"Have you considered asking Brennan and Jeff to take her for a bit? Maybe even overnight so you can recharge?"

She hadn't, because that would involve admitting to them that she wasn't coping, and she just couldn't do it. What sort of mother couldn't look after her own baby?

Everett frowned, as if he could read her self-recriminating thoughts. "Love, there's no shame in needing a break."

Gemma bit her lip, trying to will her tears away, but failed. As the first few slipped down her cheeks, she clenched her eyes shut and heard him sigh.

"Oh, darling…"

Whatever vestiges of control she'd had finally evaporated at the murmured epithet, and she found herself sobbing. Through ugly tears and heaving breaths, she blurted it all out. Her resentment. Her guilt. Her fear. Her jealousy that he had escaped this madness.

She couldn't look at him (in fact, she'd put the phone down away from her, so he had a view of the ceiling while she ranted) and she only felt mounting embarrassment and self-recrimination once her sobs began to subside.

"Love, perhaps…perhaps you should speak to your doctor," he said with obvious caution as her crying tapered off.

"Ugh," she groaned, scrubbing at her face with her hands. Her eyes stung, and she knew that if she looked in a mirror they'd be puffy and red, the rest of her face blotchy. She hated crying. She definitely couldn't face him again like this. "I'm just tired," she responded, and even her voice betrayed her by coming out hoarse and scratchy, "I'm fine."

"Damn it, Gemma, you're not fine!" he argued back, and she could imagine that his expression was as hard and dark as his tone (but she still wasn't getting close enough to the phone to face him). "I'm worried about you."

"I've gotta go," she mumbled.

Everett protested, but she grabbed the phone and terminated the call without so much as a goodbye.

She ignored her phone for the rest of the afternoon, feeling guilty that she'd taken his time with Zoe from him, but unable to face him after her meltdown.

It shouldn't have surprised her that he'd call Brennan, but when she opened her front door to her brother's concerned face, she blinked in surprise anyway.

"I'm packing Zoe a bag and taking her for the night," Brennan informed her, his frown seemingly permanently etched onto his face, "and tomorrow we'll talk."

Gemma followed her brother down the hall towards Zoe's room, muttering, "I'm going to kill him."

"Why? Because he cares? Because he's worried about you?" Brennan objected, throwing onesies and nappies and toys haphazardly into a black duffle bag. "You're too stubborn for your own good."

She scowled, folding her arms. "I told him that I'm fine. Just tired."

Pausing midway through sorting through more baby clothes, Brennan sighed and lamented, "I just don't understand why you never said anything to us. Or Sara. Or even Dad. We're here for you, Gems."

Another lump lodged itself in her throat. Closing her eyes, she shrugged. "I didn't want you to think I couldn't handle it. That…that I'm failing."

Brennan blinked back at her, dumbfounded. "I would never think that."

Unable to look at him, she fiddled with one of Zoe's toys. A cute little rainbow-coloured koala that Everett had bought in a fit of whimsy. Even in absentia, he was perfect. (Bastard.) *He* could probably cope looking after Zoe on his own.

"Why not?" she asked quietly. "I think it."

"I don't know what to say here, Gems," her brother dropped the bag and pulled her into a hug, "but you're probably feeling a bit raw right now, so we'll talk about it tomorrow, okay? Get some rest. Read. Write. Watch your crappy TV shows." She snorted, then bit back another sob because her favourite go-to comfort show was *Happily Never After* and watching it now felt weird. "And don't worry about Zoe. Jeff and I have got it sorted, alright?"

She nodded, feeling even guiltier a few minutes later when all she felt was relief as he carried Zoe out the front door.

* * *

Chapter Twelve

Everett had never realised how much he disliked Los Angeles before. The constant cover of smog was depressing, and the city itself was unremarkable. Hollywood was a tourist trap, and Beverley Hills was the height of affectation and snobbery. Traffic was always consistently awful, and it all culminated into an oppressive environment.

In the first few days after returning from his unexpectedly extended stay in Australia, he organised to put his house on the market and simultaneously began searching for a studio apartment that would house him whenever he returned to LA for work. His solicitor had updated his will (he and Zoe had attended a discrete clinic in Brisbane to have their blood taken to confirm their relationship and, in no surprise to anyone, his paternity had been confirmed) and had documents prepared for him to sign.

After the stint Rowena had pulled with the interviews, he'd told her in no uncertain terms that he would find another agent if she leaked anything else to the media in order to boost his public appeal. Things with Gemma were tentative enough without his agent meddling in his private affairs.

The days were long, the weeks leading up to Christmas dragging. He picked up guest spots on various TV shows, auditioned for roles he had very little interest in, and attempted to be friendly and social with his friends at various events as they popped up, all while he pined for the comparatively mundane life he'd begun to build halfway around the world.

To be fair, his friends and former cast members had been incredibly supportive. Many had reached out to him after he'd initially announced Zoe's birth (all subtly wanting to know why he hadn't said anything about his impending parenthood), but this was the first time he'd seen them in person. And, despite his confidence in interviews, it was awkward.

These people *knew* him. Confessing the story to Sam –his best mate– had been one thing, but trying to navigate the minefield that was the tale of 'How Everett Rhodes Became A Doting Daddy' with everyone else was almost painful.

It wasn't that he was ashamed of Gemma or Zoe, because he wasn't. However, he knew it was the sort of train-wreck drama that tabloids salivated over, and he didn't want that for his makeshift family. Gemma had already expressed her extreme displeasure over the very vague hints of their story being leaked; the last thing he needed was for the entire world to be privy to the finer details because he'd been too honest with the wrong people.

So, at a casual networking event a few weeks into his return to LA, when Everett found himself being embraced by Christina Belle, his former co-star (amongst other things), he pasted on a confident smile and braced himself for her questions.

"You're a dad!" she cried as they separated from their reunion hug, though she gripped him by the biceps and held him in place. "You kept that one very close to the chest, didn't you?"

"Yeah, well, you know what this town's like," he hedged, shrugging. "How have you been?"

She shook her mane of dark hair and laughed, "You are not sidestepping this conversation that easily, buster."

"I don't know what you want me to say, Chris," he scratched behind his ear, "it's all still new to me."

His former co-star's expression softened. "I'll bet," she mused, giving his arms a sympathetic squeeze. "The last time I saw you, you weren't exactly in a serious relationship…or, shit, at least I hope you weren't." Her eyes widened and she released his arms and smacked his chest with her open palm. "That was only, what, maybe six or so months ago? Which means–"

His cheeks coloured. In the intervening months between meeting Gemma and returning to Australia, he hadn't exactly been a monk (something he was beginning to regret) and he and Chris had instigated a friends-with-benefits relationship early on in their *Happily Never After* careers. Every so often, one would call the other with an itch to scratch, knowing that there weren't any feelings involved, and they'd then go on their merry ways until the next time.

Everett hadn't been in a happy place when he'd returned from the Gold Coast convention, and he'd called upon their agreement a couple of times in a bid to distract himself. It hadn't ever worked.

"I didn't know, alright?" he hissed, ducking his head as his cheeks burned. He whispered his confession, "It's a long story, but, believe me, if I'd known, I wouldn't have–" he gestured between them "–you know."

Chris snorted. "Slept with me," she corrected his fumbled euphemism, clearly amused and thankfully not offended by the implication that he'd have chosen another woman over her. (That he was choosing another woman over her now.) "You're a big boy, Rhett, and if you can't talk about sex, you shouldn't be having it."

"Oh, fuck off," he rolled his eyes, relieved that she was happy enough to tease him. "I was trying to spare your feelings."

"Part of our whole deal is that there aren't any feelings," she shrugged, snagging herself a cocktail from a passing waiter carrying a tray of drinks. "Don't get me wrong, I love you as a friend, and I miss working with you… and, yes, the sex is fantastic, but I'm not in danger of falling in love with you, Rhodes. You're safe."

Chuckling, he nodded, reminded as to how they'd come to their arrangement to begin with. She was pragmatic, career driven, and had very little interest in relationships. He'd been the same. They'd struck an accord to relieve each other's sexual frustrations when need be. Neither of them had ever seemed interested in anything other than the sex, and their friendship and working relationships had remained unchanged.

"You're a wonder, Belle," he acknowledged, raising his own glass in toast to her. "I appreciate that you've been there for me."

"Fatherhood's made you sappy," she teased back after clinking their glasses together. She took a sip of her drink, "Tell me about her. Your daughter."

He didn't need to be asked twice. Zoe was his favourite topic of conversation, and he ached to hold her again, to breathe in her baby scent and hear her gurgling, babbling noises in person. He pulled his phone from his pocket and brought up the latest video Gemma had sent him. (Zoe had finally started rolling over, and he hated that he'd missed personally witnessing the milestone.)

"Your girl's accent's Australian," Chris observed with mild surprise. "How long has she been in LA?"

"She's not." Everett sighed. "They're back in Australia."

"Oh, Rhett," he found himself wrapped in her sympathetic hug almost instantly, "that must suck."

His throat was tight, and he could only nod until he regained control of his emotions. After a moment, he cleared his throat and pulled back from the embrace. "I'll be going back for Christmas. That's less than a month away now."

His relationship with Gemma had become strained. They'd had a huge argument after he'd called Brennan to discuss his concerns about her emotional and mental wellbeing, and she'd been cold and prickly with him ever since. Even so, he didn't regret reaching out to her brother and his partner, not when they'd then stepped in to take care of his girls in his absence.

Jeff had even managed to convince Gemma to discuss her emotional state with her doctor, and while she hadn't shared the doctor's thoughts with any of them, Jeff and Brennan informed Everett that she had willingly requested more assistance from them whenever she felt overwhelmed. And, despite the walls she'd built between Everett and herself, Brennan had assured him that she didn't seem as tense or volatile as she previously had.

Everett could only hope that she'd forgive him by the time he returned for Christmas. He'd have less than a week before he'd have to return to LA again, and he didn't want to spend it arguing with her. (In fact, he could think of much more pleasurable activities he wished to partake in with her instead.)

Christina's empathetic sigh brought him back out of his musings. "I'm sure it'll get easier," she told him, and he couldn't help but smirk.

"Empty platitudes from Christina Belle? Has hell frozen over?"

Instead of laughing, she reached for his free hand and squeezed it, observing him seriously, "I mean it. It'll get easier."

God, he hoped so.

* * *

"Are you ever going to forgive me?" the words bubbled up and out through his lips before Everett could help himself.

He was having a shit day with a director from hell (and he was thankful that this would be his final day shooting with the man) and was desperate for the camaraderie and support he'd shared with Gemma prior to his return to LA.

Their scheduled call had currently been progressing like any other from the last few weeks, focused solely on Zoe and without any of the warmth or banter that had underpinned their interactions from the day they'd met. He'd reached his own breaking point, it seemed.

Gemma blinked at him, taken aback by the bite in his tone, "I wasn't aware I was pissed at you."

Everett knew he should remain calm and wait to discuss it at a time when he was prepared to be more rational, but a bitter snort escaped him before he could rein it in. "Please," he said sarcastically, "you've been punishing me for weeks. All because I was worried about you. I wasn't aware caring was a crime, love."

"Wow, okay, what crawled up your arse today?" Her face contorted in displeasure and her defensive tone was the most animated he'd heard her in weeks.

"I'm surprised you even care to ask," he needled further, even though a little voice in his head told him that nothing good would come of it. But he was too far gone, too frustrated by the situation he'd gotten himself into and compounded by the bad day he'd been having, and he was going to push her into having it out once and for all.

Gemma scowled back at him, "Are you kidding me right now?"

"Do I look like I am?"

He felt like a dick as the hurt flickered in her expression before she covered it with an eye-roll and declared, "You're clearly in a mood and I don't want to deal with you while you're like this."

"Well, that's bloody typical, isn't it?" At this point, there were alarms blaring *'Danger! Go back!'* in his head, but he wanted to fight with her: he wanted some sort of interaction that wasn't aloof and stilted and strange. His upper lip curled, "You don't want to deal with it, so you'll just ignore it, right?"

"What the actual fuck has gotten into you?"

They'd never fought before, he realised. Not like this. They'd had arguments and gotten a little snippy, but he'd always backed off or calmed himself, and she wasn't used to him baiting her or actually losing his temper.

Perhaps the honeymoon period was well and truly over.

It was his turn to roll his eyes. "What? You're the only one allowed to have a bad day, or week, or months?"

She bit her lip, clearly feeling the sting of that barb. He watched as she rallied and took a deep breath, her expression turning sad, "Everett, honestly, this isn't like you."

This would have been an opportune time for him to also take a breath and soften his tone. Unfortunately, he was being driven by the adrenaline in his blood and his resentment that she got to watch their daughter grow while he was half a world away. "Because you know me so well, eh? After, what, four days a year ago, and three months playing house? Or perhaps you think you know me because you were a little fangirl. Did you do a lot of Googling, love?"

He knew he'd gone too far as the bright red flush spread up from her neck and over her cheeks and ears at record speed. "You know I didn't," she murmured, averting her gaze from the camera. "Please, stop."

"Perhaps," worked up and finally seeing emotions from her, the next words spilled out with the intention to inflict pain, "you should never have bothered tracking me down again. Would have saved us both a lot of heartache. Christ, Gemma, I never wanted kids in the first place."

The regret was instantaneous, his heart hammering in his chest. The implication that he wished he didn't know about his daughter made him feel as though he wasn't any better than his father after all. He didn't mean it, either. But it was too late. The damage was done. Gemma's eyes widened and welled with tears, her irises turning bright green against the red tint to her cheeks.

Her voice was tremulous as she responded, "I think we're done here." But she didn't spill a tear, not even as she leaned forward to reach for the screen. "Goodbye, Everett."

"Damn it, Gemma, wait," he protested, now keenly feeling the contrition he should have felt from his first snide remark. But the screen on his phone was back to the generic Facetime screen, the call terminated. "Fuck!" he yelled, now frustrated with himself, throwing his phone across the room, uncaring in the moment if it broke or not. He knew better than to attempt to call her back – she'd ignore his attempts and it would only irritate him more.

He sat in the uncomfortable kitchen booth seat of his trailer with his head in his hands for a while longer, wondering how he was going to make up for his hurtful, nasty comments, and startled when his phone began to ring. Forcing himself out of the seat, he located his phone on the floor and –aside from being relieved to find it unharmed– was surprised to see his brother's name on the screen.

"Charlie?" he answered after a moment's hesitation. "Is everything alright? Is Mum–"

"Mum's fine," his brother responded, sounding curt. That also took him by surprise, because their relationship had improved significantly since Charlie and their mother had visited Brisbane to meet Zoe.

Resting his hip on the kitchen bench, Everett sighed. "Not that I don't appreciate the call, then, but to what do I owe the pleasure?"

"Gemma just called," his brother explained, and he closed his eyes and pinched the bridge of his nose as the other man continued, "and she was quite upset and expressed her concern for you, Everett."

"Of course she bloody did." Turnabout was fair play and all. Everett fought back a resurgence of frustration. Of all the people to have contacted, she'd chosen his brother. A tactical move, if ever he saw one.

Charlie made a *'tsk'*ing sound. "She cares about you, you git."

Biting back a snide 'Could have fooled me', because he knew it was unfair and uncalled for, Everett exhaled. "I know. I'm just having a particularly shitty day."

"And you took it out on the mother of your child, who you already know has her own struggles. And you basically told her you didn't want your kid. Nice, little brother. Real nice." The older man scoffed down the line. "What were you thinking?"

"I wasn't, alright? Is that what you want to hear?" Perhaps Gemma had been right to sic his brother on him, knowing he was raring for a fight. If there was anyone in the world guaranteed to get his ire going, it was Charlie Rhodes.

"Everett…" Instead of biting back, Charlie sounded empathetic, derailing Everett's plan, "This is rough on you both, and you're also allowed to admit when you're struggling."

Slumping down on the small couch beside the kitchenette, Everett felt the fight leave him as quickly as it had risen. He scrubbed his hand over his face, suddenly exhausted. "I hate this," he said, finding it easier to confide in his brother when he didn't have to face him. He tilted his head back, closing his eyes as the words continued to spill over. "I hate being so far away from them. I hate knowing that Gemma's unhappy and finding it all difficult. I hate being limited to short video calls instead of being able to hold my daughter. I hate that the relationship I'd started to build with Gemma seems to have gone backwards. I hate knowing that I'll only have a week with them when I do go back…but what other options have I got? Gemma's made it clear that she'd not going to uproot her life and move Zoe over here – and why should she, when Australia is arguably a far safer, all-around better place to raise a child?" Besides, he travelled all over the world for work, so they'd still remain separated for great chunks of time even if she did move to LA.

Charlie was silent as Everett vented, waiting until the younger man paused before he offered, "Perhaps you need to start dealing with one issue at a time. You can't do anything about the separation at the moment –you need to work, and there's certainly no point taking Gemma away from her support network– however, you both need to learn to communicate better. If the calls aren't working because they're too short, or you feel as though she's being distant, why not put into writing everything you're feeling? God knows you owe the poor girl an apology at the very least. It'll be cathartic, and she might find writing out her own feelings easier than being confronted and expected to respond immediately."

Stunned by the lengthy, and surprisingly thoughtful advice, Everett blinked up at the ceiling of his trailer. "Who are you and what have you done with my brother?"

That earned him a hearty chuckle. "I'll admit, I may have Googled a bit before I called you."

Everett was overwhelmed by a wave of affection for his older brother. "Thank you," he managed to choke out, his voice gruff.

If Charlie noticed, he was kind enough to not mention it. "Anytime, little brother."

Clearing his throat, Everett asked, "You're still coming for Christmas?" It was one thing he and Gemma had agreed on – wanting Zoe's family to celebrate together, especially for her first Christmas (even if she'd never remember it herself). They'd even agreed that, if it was successful, they'd attempt to make a tradition of it.

"I wouldn't miss it."

Feeling lighter than he had all day, he smiled. "Good."

* * *

215

Everett wrote a lengthy email to Gemma later that night. Bolstered by a few bottles of beer, he expressed everything he'd been feeling since he'd stepped away from her at the airport. He apologised for being a tosser and for trying to goad her into an argument, for being an ass about their beautiful daughter (who he truly adored), and even explained that he missed the way they used to interact and that he'd wanted to confront their issues so they could return to the way things had always been.

He then had to acknowledge that, yes, he knew it was stupid –and that Charlie had also called to ram that fact home– and that he was genuinely sorry for saying hurtful things. He told her all the things that he'd told Charlie as well, expounding on how much he missed being able to hold his girls. Reiterating that he loved them, Everett apologised again.

By the time he'd finished writing, he sent the email without reading it over, afraid that he'd chicken out of sending it if he gave it too much thought.

She didn't reply.

* * *

A week after his disastrous phone call and the emotional email that had followed it, Everett was beyond frustrated and upset. Gemma still hadn't responded to his email, but she'd also skipped all of their scheduled Facetime calls, depriving him of the only chance he got to interact with Zoe. He'd even reached out to Brennan and Jeff, but wasn't surprised when they tersely asked him what he expected considering how the last call had gone.

'I just need to see Zoe,' he eventually texted Gemma, *'You don't need to speak to me. Just allow me some time with my daughter.'*

It stung that he'd poured his feelings out to her and that she hadn't even acknowledged his words with so much as an 'Okay'.

When she didn't respond, he growled and slammed his phone down on the bench in front of him, staring blindly into the little kitchenette of his new apartment. He'd moved in a few days earlier, having sold his house within a week of listing it. He'd purchased the apartment around the same time, not bothering to wait until the house sale settled, moving out earlier than his contract dictated.

It was a small studio apartment in North Hollywood. There wasn't anything overly notable about it. The building was modern and well kept, and the street below was lined with an eclectic mix of art galleries, indie theatres, offbeat restaurants and cocktail lounges. He actually quite liked the neighbourhood, even if it wasn't as upscale or manicured as his home in Studio City had been.

But now it felt oppressive, the walls of the tiny space bearing down on him. For the first time since he'd come back to LA, he wondered if maybe he'd made a mistake.

Everett sighed and pulled his phone back across the counter, sending another message before sliding it into his hip pocket and striding to the door. He grabbed his jacket from the coat hook on the wall, checked for his keys and wallet, and locked the door in his wake.

As soon as his feet hit the pavement outside the building, he took in a deep breath of the cool winter air and immediately felt a bit better. He jogged across the street, raising his hand in apology to an oncoming car. He let his feet take him in the familiar direction of one of his favourite local watering holes, and he slid into his usual booth with a relieved sigh.

"Haven't seen you around here in forever," Jen, the waitress, observed on approach, her notepad and pen at the ready, "Your usual?"

Gin and tonic on the rocks. He nodded. "Please."

He watched as she bobbed her grey-streaked hair and headed towards the bar. It was mid-afternoon, and a weekday to boot, so there were only a couple of other patrons seated around the room. It was dim, but cosy, and it reminded him more of a pub interior from home, with its polished timber counter tops and worn leather booths, than of a hole-in-the-wall bar in the middle of Los Angeles.

"Going for the hard stuff, I see," Sam observed, taking the seat across from Everett not long after he took his first sip of his drink, relishing the familiar taste. The American actor surveyed him with a concerned stare. "What's happening?"

Everett had been trying to make the best of his situation and had previously assured his best friend that things were alright. In a way, he realised that he'd done the same thing that Gemma had, hiding his struggles so as not to upset anyone else. But now he was unravelling, and he couldn't keep it bottled up any longer.

"I haven't seen Zoe in over a week," he admitted, and his throat constricted painfully. He attempted to swallow a mouthful of gin over the lump that had formed.

Sam frowned. "What? Why?" He caught Jen's eye and raised his hand, indicating that he'd like another round of drinks while Everett gathered his thoughts.

Because he'd been doing his best to pretend that things were working as planned, the Englishman knew he needed to start at the beginning. So, he did. He told his friend about how difficult he'd been finding the separation, and about the growing divide between himself and Gemma. He went on to talk about the way she'd broken down, confessing her own struggles, and how he'd felt he had no other option than to recruit her family's assistance. Explaining her resentment from there was easy.

Over the next couple of drinks, his tongue loosened, and he admitted his own growing resentment and frustration, and described the argument he'd started with her, shamefully recounting the words he'd spoken in anger.

"I'm as bad as my own dad, right?" he lamented, now well into his third G&T. He'd never been a morose drunk, and could usually hold his liquor better than this, but figured with everything going on, and Jen's drinks becoming suspiciously stronger over the course of the evening, he had every reason to let loose this way. He set his glass down heavily and glared at the circle of condensation leaving a mark on the old wooden tabletop. "What kind of man says he doesn't want his own kid?"

Sam had listened patiently to the whole sordid tale, nodding and making sounds of commiseration as appropriate. He eyed Everett with blatant sympathy and sighed. "You didn't say that, though, did you?"

"I might as well have."

"Rhett. Come on. You just said what we've all been thinking." Here, Everett glanced up from staring into the bottom of his glass, narrowing his blue eyes, but Sam continued, "You never wanted kids. This wasn't planned. Bud, if she hadn't told you–"

"Stop."

"No," the other man shook his head, vehemently arguing, "You've supported her and have done everything right, and why? Because you don't want to be your dad? Is that a good enough reason to stick by your kid? Or is this resentment only going to fester?"

Everett swallowed and looked away, quietly admitting, "I've thought about not going back."

The confession pained him. But it would be easier, wouldn't it? To cut ties now? It was clear that Gemma had zero interest in reconciling following their argument. Hell, it seemed she didn't want him to have contact with Zoe.

The other actor nodded without censure. "Understandable. Your life is here."

Everett scowled at that. "Zoe is my life, too. And she's *there*." And even if he was currently pissed with Gemma, and hurting, he still loved her, too.

He didn't know whether Sam was deliberately playing devil's advocate, or whether he genuinely believed in the suggestions he was making, especially when the fair-haired man shrugged, polished off the last of his own drink, and said, "What about seeking custody of your kid, then?"

"I've thought about it." That admission made him feel ill, too. He scratched the back of his neck. "But, honestly, I love Gemma. I couldn't do that to her. It would kill her."

He wouldn't ever dare threaten to pursue custody, but in his current mood, the temptation to put the fear of the possibility out there was strong. But he just couldn't do it. There would be no coming back from that at all, and as frustrated as he was, he wasn't that much of an arse. He was just hurting. A lot.

Sam's expression softened. "Then you've gotta keep trying. I'm sure that what you said hurt her, but she's gotta realise that she's got all the power right now, and that she's hurting you, too."

Everett snorted cynically. "So, I'm back at square one, then."

"No-one ever said this was going to be easy, man."

He didn't think truer words had ever been spoken.

* * *

After his drinks with Sam, Everett meandered home. He had to admit that he did feel a little lighter for having aired his innermost thoughts, and pulled his phone from his pocket, surprised to see a reply from Gemma had come through. Idly, he wondered if she knew that he'd been bitching about her.

His face fell as he read it.

'You made your feelings on fatherhood perfectly clear.'

"God damn it," he seethed, pinching the bridge of his nose. She had every right to be hurt by his words, but how was he supposed to make amends for them and clear the air if she refused to give him a chance to do so?

'Can we talk? Please?' Begging was definitely not beneath him.

There was no response. With Sam's words ringing in his ears, he knew only one thing.

He had to fix this.

* * *

<h1 style="text-align:center">Chapter Thirteen</h1>

"Are you sure you want to take her overnight again?" Gemma frowned at her brother as they stood at the threshold of his front door. He had Zoe cuddled against his chest, her overflowing nappy bag at his feet. "She wakes up at least twice a night and–"

"Gems, it's fine," Brennan's smile was reassuring and warm. "Take the night off. Swim. Soak in the bath. Read a book, or fanfic, or whatever it is that relaxes you. Jeff and I have got this. Besides, Micah's coming over later for beers and a catch up and I've told him to bring Rosie along – she's apparently hit a bit of a rough patch lately."

"I'm sorry to hear that." Micah was an old friend of Brennan's from university, and Rosie was his younger sister, a couple of years younger than Gemma. They'd never been close, but she liked the other woman well enough. Still, she frowned. "Isn't she a gossip columnist?"

"She's a blogger, Gem. And you know she's great with kids."

"A blogger." Gemma sighed. "You don't see a problem there?" The tabloid media still hadn't been an issue for her and Zoe, and she thought inviting one of their type directly into Zoe's life was tempting fate.

"It's not like the kid has 'Spawn of Everett Rhodes' tattooed on her forehead."

It was difficult to remain annoyed with Brennan when he amused her

221

so easily. Attempting to keep a straight face, Gemma folded her arms and echoed, "Spawn, huh? That's what you think of your niece?"

"The very cutest of spawn," he nodded, unrepentant. When he could sense her resolve wavering, he added, "You live, like, three minutes away. If there's a problem or we can't hack it for the whole night, we'll call."

Gemma considered this for a moment before she eventually nodded. "Alright." She leaned forward and kissed the top of Zoe's head before looking her brother in the eye with gratitude, "Thanks, Bren."

He shooed her away and shut the door behind her before she could change her mind.

* * *

Gemma poured herself a generous glass of wine and stared unseeingly into the backyard through the kitchen window, contemplating how to best spend her evening. She felt bereft. Sure, her family and friends had offered to take Zoe for her a number of times now, but (aside from that very first time) never overnight, and she wondered what had prompted the unexpected offer.

She supposed that her mood had backslid in the last week or so, but between the online support group she'd joined and the check-in visits to her doctor, she wasn't feeling as though she was spiralling, or out of control. Just sad.

Everett's words had cut deeply. He'd all but told her that he resented their daughter. Even though he'd sent her a long, rambling email containing heartfelt apologies and explanations, the words he'd spoken rang in her ears and tore at her heart.

And she still loved him.

She hadn't told him —wanting to wait until they were reunited— but it didn't make the feeling any less real. But now she was once again hurt and conflicted.

Everett regretted it, but that didn't change the fact that he had said the words. He'd put voice to Gemma's greatest fear. Ever since she'd seen the positive lines form on the hCG strip in that tiny hospital bathroom, she'd worried for their child. Having grown up knowing that her biological parents were out there but unattainable, she'd wanted to spare her own kid the same pain.

It would have been better if he'd taken the out that she had offered him. Because now if he walked away, there were still social media posts and interviews that Zoe would one day see. Proof that she'd had a father who knew about her and loved her…until he didn't want to try anymore.

Gemma wiped a tear away as it slipped down her cheek.

She knew she was getting ahead of herself. Everett was clearly desperate to apologise, and she did feel a little guilty for keeping Zoe from him while she attempted to clear her head. But she was wary now. Just how long would it be before he decided it really was all too hard? Were they deluding themselves to think this could actually work out for them in the long run?

She was pulled from her musings by a throat clearing behind her and she jumped, the wine in her glass sloshing over the rim with the sudden movement. She spun around, her heart hammering wildly at the thought of an intruder sneaking up on her. Blinking, she felt her jaw drop.

"Everett," she breathed, stunned. "Why…how…what…?"

He offered her a small, sheepish smile. "We need to talk, love."

He wasn't due back for another two weeks. But there he stood, his hair dishevelled and his beard scruffier than usual. He had dark circles beneath his eyes, and even the sparkling blue colour seemed to have dulled.

Feeling her eyes well with tears at the phrase that preceded all breakups, Gemma swallowed and nodded. "Wine?" she asked, holding up her glass.

"No, thank you." He shook his head and regarded her for a moment, his expression softening as he seemed to sense where her thoughts had gone. He tentatively stepped forward, quietly confessing, "I've missed you." He took a steadying breath. "And I'm so very sorry."

She could have argued. Could have told him that she had read his email, and his empty apologies, and that it was too little too late. He'd done the *one thing* that he had to have known would push her away and apologies just wouldn't cut it.

But...

He'd tried to talk to her in person and she'd gone to ground. She'd refused his calls and had taken away his only means of seeing his daughter. Was it any wonder that he'd obviously rearranged his filming schedule and flown halfway across the world to discuss the issue in person?

There was a defeated set to his shoulders. Gemma felt a pang of guilt. She knew that she wasn't entirely blameless in what had happened between them. She'd already been building a wall between them, her pride still hurting from the fact that he'd told her family about her breakdown. He'd finally called her out on it, and she'd pushed back again.

From the moment she'd met Everett Rhodes, she'd assessed him as tactile and affectionate. Being cold and aloof –especially when she knew that he loved her– had pushed him to the edge of his own emotional control.

Did that excuse what he'd said? No. But she understood now that he'd been hurting, too.

They were both human, and some of what he'd said had been true – they didn't know each other well enough yet. That sort of relationship took time and hard work. Pulling away from him hadn't helped that, either.

"I'm sorry, too," her reply was emphatic. "What you said scared me and I–"

"Wanted to protect Zoe," Everett finished for her, somehow sounding broken and understanding all at once. "I promise, Gemma, I'll never leave her."

"But you didn't want her."

His handsome face contorted into a wince, and he rubbed the back of his neck. "I never planned on having children, no. But," he hastened to continue, "I adore her. I couldn't imagine a life without her in it now. I..." he swallowed roughly. "I don't want to."

Gemma reminded herself that she hadn't been happy to discover she was pregnant, either. She'd had the better part of nine months to wrap her head around the concept of her life changing dramatically. Everett hadn't. He'd had barely a few hours between learning about her pregnancy to seeing Zoe born. But he hadn't walked away when she'd told him that he could, and he had genuinely fallen in love with their kid.

In a moment of clarity, she realised that the other shoe had finally dropped. And he was still there.

Regardless of his stress and his fear and his frustration –and regardless of her efforts to push him away– he was still there. He wasn't going anywhere. He didn't want to.

"I love you," Gemma blurted, setting her glass down on the marble bench top at her side. He blinked back at her, clearly confused by the abrupt declaration. "I know we've got a lot to talk about, and that we're kind of still fighting, and we really need to work on communicating better, but…I just…I needed you to know. I'm not…" she swallowed, shaking her head, "You can't leave again without knowing." She bit her lip and shrugged, suddenly awkward. "So, now you know."

Everett closed the space between them with a couple of long, determined strides and kissed her like she'd never been kissed before. It was a kiss of desperation and passion and pent-up longing, his arms tightening around her as his mouth moved over hers, the scruff of his beard tickling her skin. "I love you, too," he murmured as they parted for air. "Never doubt that."

Unable to formulate a reply, she kissed him again, attempting to convey her own emotions with the action. Her hands gripped at his biceps and shoulder blades, squeezing him as she reassured herself that this was real and not just a convincing dream.

When his hands travelled down her back and came to rest beneath her backside, Gemma forced herself to pull back.

"We really should talk," she told him, cursing herself a little for it.

She could see the reluctance in his gaze as he nodded.

"Come on," she took him by the hand, leading him out of the kitchen and down the short hallway that led to the master suite, "you look exhausted."

He didn't refute her assessment and followed without argument. He toed off his shoes and sat on his usual side of the bed, propping himself up against the headboard and watching her mirror his position on the bed's other side.

"I don't know where to start," she admitted, shaking her head. "I'm sorry I didn't give you any other option than to come back."

He scrubbed a hand over his face. "I said something I knew would hurt you, but I didn't think of the implications, or how awful the words truly were." He tilted his head back, staring up at the ceiling and swallowing roughly. "Of all the people to say such a thing to…I understand why you didn't want to talk to me."

"How'd you convince Brennan to take Zoe overnight?" She was surprised that he'd done that at all, really. Wouldn't seeing Zoe be his priority over her?

Still leaning back against the headboard, Everett turned his head to face her, the corners of his lips pulling into a smile. "He loves his niece. It wasn't as though I had to twist his arm. And he's done it before."

"I'm surprised you didn't want to see her first."

He reached out and took her hand in his, thumb grazing her knuckles. "I needed to set things right."

"I'd say you've managed that," Gemma informed him, feeling another pang of guilt that they could have had this conversation via Facetime if she hadn't ignored him completely.

Then again, had seeing him in person been the impetus for her change of heart? And, if so, what did that say about her? That all it took was to look at his handsome face and she forgot the hurtful words he'd said?

But that hadn't happened. Not really. He'd apologised and explained, and she'd had time to cool down. Additionally, his grand gesture of dropping everything to correct the issue in person said more about how much he cared than any words he could have written or spoken. Even if she thought it was crazy and potentially damaging to his career, she still appreciated that he'd done so.

"We need to work on our communication," he cut into her musings, squeezing her hand. "I realise that our actual relationship is fairly new, but we need to be completely honest with each other. When our only means of contact are electronic and governed by time zones and work schedules–"

"We both need to work on expressing concerns before frustrations turn into fights." She finished for him, and he nodded. "And," she continued, "I'll work on not closing you out when I'm not happy with what's been said."

"You know that we're not going to sort it all out with one conversation?"

He made a valid point, but Gemma couldn't help but feel the pressure to make sure that things between them were okay. That their relationship would be okay.

Able to read her as always, Everett tugged at her arm, drawing her closer to him. Kissing her lips, he stretched out at her side. He shifted and pressed gentle kisses over her shoulder and into the juncture where it met her neck, then another at the corner of her lips. She turned her head into him, and they kissed languidly, his hand resting on her hip.

Taking control of the kiss, Gemma reached down and cupped him over his jeans. He swore and bucked into her hand, and she grinned against his lips.

"Fox, you'll be the death of me," he told her, inhaling sharply as she wormed her hand inside his pants. "Allow me," he said, priding himself on keeping his voice steady while she continued to tease him. He unzipped his jeans and, with her assistance, shimmied out of them. They were kicked off the bed and landed in a heap that, at any other time, would offend his usual need for order and neatness.

Gemma pulled her nightie over her head and then assisted him in removing his shirt. Their lips reconnected as they attempted to assist each other out of their underwear, laughing at the awkward manoeuvring.

"Well," she declared, eyes drawn to his sizeable erection as it bobbed out of a thatch of dark curls, "I think it's time we get reacquainted." She guided him onto his back and, with mischief glinting in her eyes, used her lips to trace a trail down his body to her prize.

He kept his gaze locked on hers the entire time, his eyes fluttering shut only when she took him into her mouth, then opening them again as she licked and sucked, using her hand to stroke and pump at the base of him when she couldn't fit him all into her mouth.

"Oh *God*," he muttered as she swirled her tongue and fondled his balls.

After a time of losing himself to the exquisite pleasure of her attentions, he threaded his hand into her hair and gently urged her to stop. She looked far too proud of herself when he informed her that he had no intention of finishing so soon.

"Spoilsport," she teased, prowling over him with an almost feline grace. She kissed him before he could snark back, and he inhaled sharply as she removed herself from the kiss, sat back on her haunches, straddling him, and then sank down onto his cock after briefly lining herself up, thankful that she was on the pill and that she knew they were both free of STIs.

"Gemma," he said her name like a prayer, his hands at her hips, fingers flexing as she began to ride him, her light brown hair a halo around her face, "God...*fuck...*"

She brought her hand down to rub at her clit, but he batted it away and replaced it with his own, watching the rapture sweep across her features as she picked up her pace and chased down her orgasm, her head thrown back as it crashed over her. Gemma cried out quietly, her inner walls fluttering and clenching around him, and it took everything in his power to not follow her directly over the edge. He fucked her through it, his jaw tight with his resolve, and chuckled when she collapsed back over his chest, spent and panting.

Everett kissed her forehead, then the tip of her nose, then her lips as she basked in the afterglow, and it took a moment for her to realise that he was still gently rocking his hips up against hers, still moving inside her. She'd assumed he'd have come with her, but he was a stubborn one, her actor.

Lost in thought, and still feeling somewhat boneless, she was distracted as he rolled her onto her back. He braced himself with his forearms on either side of her head and began to slowly slide back inside her.

His eyes were locked onto her face, his expression tender and full of all the emotions and thoughts of commitment that had once scared her. But before she could open her mouth to say something –to ruin the sudden intimacy that had fallen around them– he ducked his head and kissed her.

Despite the exuberance of their previous fucking, it was a sweet kiss; gentle and loving to match his current pace. Tears sprang unbidden to her eyes as she felt him shift so that he could grasp her hand, weaving their fingers together above her head on the pillow while he gently made love to her.

And that was what he was doing. This wasn't just sex. It was most certainly making love.

It was overwhelming. She'd never –not *ever*– in her thirty years of age experienced sex this way. Brett had always been a selfish lover (always in a rush to get his rocks off, never all that interested in pleasuring her) but at seventeen she hadn't known any better. In the few instances she'd attempted to date, she'd been closed off and had usually guided the sex towards fun, rough-and-tumble encounters. Then there had been Scott, and being with him had always felt awkward.

None of her woeful sexual history was emotional. Never tender. Never loving.

Everett said nothing of the rogue tears that escaped her, probably because he knew that she would panic and close herself off again if he did. Instead, he mouthed at her neck, at her jawline, and at the corners of her lips, and whispered into her ear words of adoration and praise as he worshipped her.

And, God, he felt *amazing*. His toned body –even more muscular than the first (only) night they'd slept together– seemed to complement her body's curves and softness. And the way he felt inside her? It probably didn't hurt that he was well-endowed, but she was certain that she'd never enjoyed the stretch and glide of a cock inside her quite as much as this.

Her orgasm built slowly, the coil of tension in her belly tightening with every measured, slow thrust and with every twist of his hips, his body putting just enough pressure on her clit that she didn't feel compelled to reach between them and help herself along. Still, she gasped as the coil finally snapped, surprising her with just how intense the wave of pleasure was, considering how languid –almost lazy– their lovemaking was.

This time she felt him tense and his hips stutter, her orgasm finally pulling his from him, and he murmured a warning before he came, a quiet curse and a grunt on his lips.

Neither of them said anything. Instead, Everett slid from inside her and she felt immediately bereft, but he merely rolled aside onto his back and pulled her into his arms, pressing a lingering kiss to her temple.

She felt sticky and suddenly a little self-conscious, but her concerns were overridden as he spoke.

"Sleep, love," he told her, his voice betraying his own tenuous hold on his emotions. And, though some part of her was still a little wary of it, she was glad that he, too, had been just as moved by their reconnection.

* * *

In the morning, after a quick shower and breakfast, they drove directly to Brennan and Jeff's. It was obvious that they still had plenty to talk about but, seeing the way Everett's eyes glistened as he held his daughter for the first time in weeks, Gemma knew that they were both motivated enough now to make it work.

"You alright, love?" he asked, startling her from her thoughts. She blinked, noticing the way he had Zoe against his chest, her little ear pressed over his heart while he rubbed circles on her onesie clad back.

Even in her wildest fangirl fantasies, Gemma never would have imagined this moment of domesticity. Back when they'd met, she'd thought about rom-coms and chick flicks, but what they'd gone through to get here eclipsed that by far.

Who would have thought that a spur of the moment decision to hold a lift door would set off such a chain of events?

Offering him a reassuring smile, she nodded. "I'm great."

And she was.

They were.

He seemed to understand the path her thoughts had taken because he grinned back. "Shall we go out for dinner tonight?" he suggested with a playful glint in his eyes. "I'm suddenly craving Vietnamese."

Her heart felt fit to burst from her chest, but she played it cool, "It's a good thing I like Vietnamese food then, huh?"

"It most definitely is."

* * *

Epilogue

"Have I mentioned how ravishing you look in that dress, love?" Everett practically purred as he pulled Gemma against him on the dance floor.

She grinned up at him, bringing her hands to the lapels of his suit jacket. "You clean up pretty nicely yourself, Rhodes."

"Oi, you two, get a room already," Charlie taunted as he spun in a circle, four-year-old Zoe giggling madly in his arms. Her long, dark hair –which had been styled so carefully for the wedding, where she'd been excited to perform as flower girl– was wild from her own dancing of the last hour. Gemma silently lamented the tantrum and effort it would take to detangle in the morning. "Sara and I will take this little princess for the evening."

Everett shot his brother a thankful look over the top of Gemma's head.

"Are you sure?" Gemma asked, "She's going to be a nightmare with how much cake she's eaten."

Their usual babysitters –Brennan and Jeff– had just gotten married ("Finally," they'd both joked during the ceremony, and again during the reception speeches) and, though Sara and Charlie were both well acquainted with Zoe, they were a relatively new couple themselves. (A relationship which had completely blindsided Everett, along with his brother's declaration that he was moving to Australia to give it a shot.) Surely they might want to enjoy their night in a swanky Gold Coast hotel room without the added presence of an over-sugared four-year-old?

"Gemma, darling, I haven't seen you in weeks – let them spoil her rotten for an evening while I spoil you, eh?" Everett murmured against the shell of her ear as they continued their slow dance.

He'd only flown back home the day prior to the wedding, and Gemma and Zoe had already been sequestered away with Jeff and the rest of his wedding party, leaving Everett alone in his hotel room for the night. He'd met up with Brennan and taken his place as best man beside him the next day, tearing up when Zoe –in a much smaller version of her mother's emerald green, rockabilly-style dress– flounced down the aisle, tossing petals almost viciously at the wedding guests. Gemma had followed soon after, much more demurely, taking his breath away.

She didn't need any further convincing than that, for which he was glad. As much as he adored his daughter, he had plans for the evening which he didn't need curtailed by their precocious little girl.

"What are you waiting for?" Charlie pressed, ignoring the warning glance Everett sent him, "Get going, then."

"Anxious to see us leave?" Gemma teased him with a cheeky grin.

Thankfully, Charlie played along without giving away the sense that there was anything else afoot. "Rhett's been a right nuisance since he got back. You'll be doing us all a favour if you take one for the team."

She laughed while Everett rolled his eyes and bantered back, though he couldn't tell you what he'd said, because Gemma was finally agreeing to leave, pressing kisses to their daughter's cheeks and telling her to be good for her Uncle and Aunt. She followed that by kissing Charlie's cheeks, then located her brothers and congratulated them one last time before finally allowing Everett to pull her out of the reception to an Uber waiting for them just outside the front door of the restaurant.

Charlie hadn't been exaggerating, really. After not having seen her since he'd left for LA, Everett hadn't even been able to speak to his girlfriend until after the ceremony. (He felt marginally guilty for having made googly eyes at her for the entire event, barely paying attention as his friends tied the knot.)

Even during the meal, he'd been seated at Brennan's side at the Wedding Party table, with Gemma on Jeff's other side, too far away from him. Being able to dance with her had given him an excuse to wrap his arms around her and pull her flush against him, but Zoe had then demanded that he dance with her instead, so they'd been separated yet again. Though, that said, the heat in Gemma's gaze as she'd watched him with their daughter had him preening.

He held her hand in the backseat of the Uber, rubbing his thumb over the inside of her wrist, delighting in the way she stared back at him with hooded eyes. Even after four years together, there were still sparks of passion and life in their relationship. Despite occasional hiccups, their love was strong and true. They had outlasted the struggles of his having to live in two separate worlds, and it was that knowledge that settled any anxieties he had over the proposal plan he was putting into action.

Gemma's sharp intake of breath as they pulled up at the very hotel in which they'd met had his lips curling into a smirk. The rest of her family and friends were booked at another hotel a few minutes' walk away, and, until that moment, she'd been under the impression that they were staying in the same place.

He took her hand in his as they walked through the familiar lobby –unchanged, save for a fresh coat of white paint to the walls and a few new decorative plants– towards the trio of lifts. When he'd hatched this scheme, he'd almost considered bribing the staff to stop the lift midway to their floor, but Gemma's claustrophobia would have ruined the romance he wanted to achieve, so he'd talked himself out of that.

Instead, he'd requested the same room he'd had five years earlier, and already had their belongings from the other hotel brought over and left inside. A bottle of bubbly, sweet white wine had been delivered in an ice bucket half an hour earlier (he'd ducked into the bathroom during the wedding reception to confirm) along with two champagne flutes and some chocolate-dipped strawberries. (Despite the cliché, he knew Gemma was partial to them.) Charlie had managed to talk him out of scattered rose petals, though, and he was thankful for that.

She was blinking back tears as they rode the lift in silence due to the unfortunate luck of having to share it with another couple.

"Um, sorry," said the woman, breaking the silence that had descended, "you look really familiar."

"I get that a lot," he answered cheekily while Gemma snorted and hit his arm.

"Be nice," she demanded, though there was a glint of humour in her glistening hazel eyes.

He offered their lift-riding companions a conciliatory smile, though he was still a little unhappy that they'd inadvertently ruined the mood that had been building between he and his girlfriend. "Everett Rhodes," he greeted, "I'm an actor, though it's doubtful I've been in anything–"

"Oh! You were in *Happily Never After*!" The woman beamed. "I loved that show!"

"I'm glad to hear it," he responded, trying not to sag with relief as the elevator pinged and the doors opened. "Your floor?" he asked.

"Unfortunately," she answered, stepping out and taking her clearly awkward companion with her. "It was nice meeting you!"

The doors shut before he could respond. There was a moment's silence before Gemma started to giggle, eliciting a chuckle from him as well before he ducked his head to kiss her lips tenderly.

"Not quite how I imagined tonight beginning," he informed her, stealing another quick, chaste kiss.

She'd brought her hand up behind his head, toying with the hair at the nape of his neck as she stared into his eyes and smiled. "I'm used to that happening nowadays."

"And you've not gotten sick of me yet," he teased.

The news of his relocation to Brisbane had leaked not long after their first Christmas together, but –aside from a few incidents where photos of Zoe and Gemma had made it into the tabloids and blogs– there hadn't been many issues. He wasn't exactly an A-Lister, so the media didn't tend to follow him or make his life hell, and the local fans were generally relaxed and respectful of his space. He knew he was lucky that he was able to live a fairly "normal" existence under the radar with his little family.

She made a show of being exaggeratedly thoughtful. "Hmm, I think I'll keep you around a bit longer."

"That's what I'm counting on," he responded playfully, just as the lift stopped at their floor. With his hand at the small of her back, he guided her to their room and opened the door, gesturing for her to go in ahead of him. "Ladies first."

She toed off her heels at the door, kicking them aside as always. (It was a habit he realised he'd never break her from.) Then she strode across the room to stare out at the darkened ocean view. The moonlight caught on the foam of the small waves as they crashed at the shoreline, but it was otherwise still a disappointing view at night.

While she was distracted, he paused in the kitchenette to retrieve the ring he'd hidden away earlier, slipping the box and his hand into his trouser pocket before he approached her. She smiled up at his reflection as he stepped up behind her, then frowned as he seemed to disappear. Turning, she inhaled in surprise to find him down on one knee, a glittering ring extended towards her, still nestled in its box.

Despite the rakish grin on his face, she could tell he was nervous. He'd told her –years earlier– that he'd proposed to an ex once before, prior to his fame, and that the entire relationship had ended badly, traumatising him away from commitment for life. Or, at least until Zoe had been born, when he'd had to cowboy up and face an entire lifetime of commitment to his kid. Still, despite being forever tied to him through their daughter, and four years successfully maintaining their relationship through its ups and downs, Gemma hadn't expected a proposal.

"I don't have a speech planned," he told her, "but five years ago, we met in this hotel, and we changed each other's lives in this very room, and I'd very much like to keep that tradition going."

Despite her shock, she managed a watery chuckle at his earnest declaration. Was it weird he was proposing in the very room they'd conceived their daughter? A little. But it was also insanely sentimental, and she loved him even more for it.

Everett cleared his throat. "So, Gemma Fox, would you do me the honour of becoming my wife? Will you marry me?"

Her heart was beating rapidly. "Everett," she breathed, instinctively extending her hand, "*yes. Of course!*"

It wasn't a traditional engagement ring. The central stone was a round cut peridot, surrounded by a halo of smaller diamonds, and set in a platinum band. He'd known it was perfect the moment he found it, and the expression she wore as he slid it onto her left hand told him that he'd chosen wisely.

"Oh," she sniffled against an onslaught of happy tears, "It's beautiful."

"It reminds me of the green in your eyes."

She snorted, shaking her head with obvious affection. "There you go getting cheesy again, Rhodes."

Instead of answering, he rose to his feet and kissed her, even more desperate to reconnect with her than he had been prior to proposing. He'd been away for six weeks –only a short trip this time– but he'd missed her as terribly as always.

"You know, the last time we were here –the day we were leaving– you wore that little sundress," his breath tickled the shell of her ear while his hands fruitlessly searched for the zip of her dress, "and I imagined spinning you around, hiking up your skirt and fucking you right up against this very window."

She tilted her head, giving his mouth access to her neck. "I can't see why we can't do that right now."

"God, I love you," he praised, giving her one more lingering kiss before guiding her to turn around as promised. He reached beneath the skirt of her dress, pulling her voluminous petticoat down over her hips, catching the waistband of her underwear and removing them in the same motion. She kicked the offending garments away, and he hastily unbuckled his belt, then made short work of removing his trousers and own underwear.

He grabbed handfuls of material and hitched the skirt of her dress up, and she braced the palms of her hands against the glass, bending forward to allow him better access to her core from behind. He smothered an appreciative groan, the head of his cock finding her wet and ready for him as he shifted his hips forward. He released one of his fistfuls of fabric to line himself up before he slowly slid inside her.

"Fuck, I've missed this," she breathed, rocking back into him, silently encouraging him to move.

He nipped at the back of her neck, pulling almost all the way out before roughly thrusting back inside her, delighting in the way she clenched around him and whimpered with need.

With her hands splayed on the glass, and both of his gripping her waist, her clit was untouched, and she rotated her hips unconsciously attempting to find relief.

"Please," she panted as he set a hard and fast pace, "I need…"

Barely pausing to readjust their position, he gave her exactly what she wanted, slipping a hand around to rub at her clit just the way he knew she liked.

Rewarding him with a moan, she warned him that she was close.

"Come for me, darling," he instructed, amused that −even after five years− she still reacted enthusiastically to his accent and that particular epithet.

She came with a quiet cry, squeezing and fluttering around his cock, drawing his own release from him.

"Was that everything you imagined it would be?" she teased, scrunching her nose as he withdrew.

He smirked and took her by the hand, leading her into the bathroom and towards the shower −though they both gave the familiar giant tub matching glances of reminiscence. "Better than the fantasy, love," he responded, finally removing his shirt and tie while she unzipped the dress (another blasted hidden zip!) and allowed it to pool at her feet.

"Oh really?" She reached into the shower recess and adjusted the taps until the temperature and pressure was to her liking.

Under the spray, he wrapped his arms around her and nodded. "In the original fantasy, you hadn't just agreed to become my wife."

In fact, the original fantasy had been a goodbye, or a 'proper' farewell. He'd imagined one spectacular last hurrah and the likelihood of never seeing the beautiful woman again. Back then, he never could have anticipated the events that had already been set in motion.

She shook him from his maudlin thoughts, her hands lathering soap over his broad chest. "Well, back then, if you'd proposed, I would have accused you of being the crazy one."

He snorted and shook his head, sending droplets of water flying. "Fox, you'll always be my crazy fangirl."

Gemma beamed back up at him, nodding. "But only because Bomer was already taken."

Laughter erupted from him before he leaned down and claimed her lips. "Minx."

Her lips curled into a sultry smile and her soapy hands drifted lower to claim their prize. "Reckon we could re-enact that night?"

The thought had crossed his mind, but he shook his head. "I'd much rather create some new memories in this room."

Her smile gentled, and she nodded. "Me too."

And in the morning when they woke snuggled together, sated and still besotted, Everett Rhodes knew only one truth: he was an idiot for not having proposed sooner.

* * *

Thank you so much for reading *Handle With Care*. I really hope that you enjoyed it!

I'd love to hear what you thought of it at:

Goodreads or your preferred online retailer

(https://books2read.com/HandleWithCareVerebes)

On the fence about leaving a review?

It's okay to leave a star rating and say nothing at all.

Thank you in advance for helping me out!

And, if you'd like to read an alternate scene (where Gemma springs her surprise on Everett in person), you can claim one by subscribing to my newsletter via this link (via ebook), by emailing me at anverebes@outlook.com.

(PS - Keep turning pages for a sneak peak of *You Can't Hurry Love*)

Happy Reading!

You Can't Hurry Love (preview)

The first time Sara Carlisle heard the name 'Charlie Rhodes' it was as her best friend tearfully recounted her unpleasant meeting with the man in question.

"Who the fuck does he think he is?" Sara seethed into the phone. "Tell me your boy toy put him in his damn place, Gems, *please*." She stretched her long legs out in front of her on her grey linen couch. "What a dick."

Down the line, Gemma snorted. It made Sara smile to know that she'd cheered her friend up a measure.

Things had been a bit rough for Gemma, what with the unplanned pregnancy and the baby's somewhat famous father making his sudden reappearance in her life just in time to watch their gorgeous daughter enter the world. But Everett –or, as Sara liked to think of him, Gemma's Baby Daddy– was now also responsible for introducing Gemma to Charlie, his older brother, who was apparently a disapproving, grumpy, arrogant twit, from what Sara had gathered from the brief phone call so far.

"He's not my boy toy…or toy boy…or whatever," Gemma argued, sounding fondly exasperated as she cut off Sara's trail of thought, "but, yeah, Everett took him outside and they had a chat. And Beatrice –their mum– made him apologise when they came back, which was ten different kinds of awkward."

In Sara's opinion, Gemma was far too sweet and too concerned about what other people thought of her. Had she planned to get pregnant? No.

Had she planned for her one-night stand to go AWOL? Also no. If *anyone* had the right to be sanctimonious about their situation, it was Gemma and not the dillweed brother of the guy who had knocked her up and shattered her confidence all in one sitting.

But Sara kept that to herself, knowing that it wasn't what her bestie needed from her right then. Instead, she made a sound of agreement. "I can imagine," she offered gently before asking, "did you need me to come over?"

"Nah, it's fine," Gemma assured her, then yawned. "Everett's gonna take Zoe and I'm going to nap for a bit." She paused. "But thank you. I know you've got my back."

"Damn straight. Now go snuggle that gorgeous honorary niece of mine for me and then get yourself some rest."

They ended the call and Sara tossed her phone aside. It bounced lightly on the couch beside her. Alone in her little brick and tile home -the same one she'd lived in since birth, though she had renovated and repainted over the years, preferring a sleek, modern pallet of greys and whites over her mother's terracotta shades- she had time to muse over her best friend's situation.

Sara was genuinely concerned for her sister from another mister. She had been for months, really. Ever since Gemma had dropped the 'I-had-a-one-night-stand-with-my-favourite-actor-and-now-I'm-pregnant' bomb. If Sara had been fiercely protective of her bestie before it was nothing compared to now. Gemma was the only family she had.

They had met at university studying nursing and had clicked instantly.

Well, that wasn't entirely true. Sara was far more extroverted than Gemma, and she wasn't ashamed to admit that she'd sort of strongarmed her way into becoming the other girl's friend. They'd both been lost souls in their respective ways. And, despite their differences, it turned out that they genuinely understood each other. Over a decade later found them as close as actual sisters, if not closer.

They were deeply protective of one another, and Gemma's adoptive family had also taken Sara under their wing once her tragic story was out in the open. For a girl who had grown up with only her mum, having a large, loving family claim her as their own was something she truly cherished.

The sudden change in Gemma's circumstances, and therefore in her family's entire dynamic, was unsettling. None of them had anticipated that Everett Rhodes would react the way he had to becoming a parent so unexpectedly. While Sara was happy for her best friend, she was also afraid it would all fall apart.

Who wouldn't be?

Added to that was the conversation she and Gemma had just shared. Everett had brought his family over from the UK to introduce them to his daughter and, while his mother sounded supportive, his brother Charlie had undermined Gemma's confidence in herself and in whatever co-parenting relationship she was developing with Everett. Charlie Rhodes had all but called Gemma a gold digger!

If I ever meet the bastard, Sara thought to herself with a scowl, *I'll castrate him with the nearest sharp object.*

Fortuitously (*Though, potentially not for old Charlie boy,* she mused wickedly), Brennan rang to invite her to an extended family barbecue for the next evening. Everett apparently wanted their families to get to know one another, given that they'd be connected through Zoe forever. It was a sweet sentiment, but Sara suspected it was all going to end in tears.

At least, if she had it her way, those tears would belong to Everett's dick of a brother.

* * *

Unsurprisingly, Sara despised Charlie on sight. Oh, sure, he was tall and broad shouldered and insanely muscular with captivating green eyes, sandy-blond coloured hair, and an English accent to swoon over…but he was an arrogant arse.

He had pushed all her buttons during that first barbecue. Gemma had asked her to behave, and she truly had tried, but Everett's brother had known exactly how to get under her skin. Anything she said, he disagreed with. She could have told him the grass was green and he'd have argued it was turquoise with the pure purpose of fucking with her. He clearly thought he was amusing, and she wanted desperately to knock him down a peg or two.

Or ten.

"If you keep glaring at him like that, your face will set," Gemma chuckled as she took Charlie's vacated seat at the table under the patio. The meal had been delicious, as was to be expected when Gemma's brothers hosted, but Sara had spent a lot of it considering how best to dispose of Everett's brother while making it look like an accident. The thoughts had been therapeutic.

The men were across the yard, each clutching a beer (or wine, in Jeff's case) and discussing Brennan's desire to build a little pergola with a hot tub in it. The men gestured, or pointed, or paced out space on the patch of grass, and they were clearly absorbed in trying to work out the best position and plan of attack for the project. Charlie had boasted that he was a builder –which didn't surprise Sara at all, given the man's frame, or his tan, though Sara unkindly wondered how much sun there actually was to bask in in London– and was loudly explaining the way he would approach the task.

Sara huffed and turned her attention back to her friend. "At least he's not treating you like shit anymore," she acknowledged, before jutting her chin towards the end of the table. "Reckon his mummy gave him a talking to?"

"Probably," the other woman agreed with a nod, completely serious in the face of Sara's semi-joking tone, "Everett thought she might."

Sara reached primly for her wine. "Hmmph," she huffed, nose in the air, "as she should have."

Gemma was staring at Sara's glass wistfully but shook herself out of it. "He's not that bad. He was only looking out for Everett. Bren does the same for me."

"Yeah, but you're the one who was left heartbroken and pregnant." Sara wasn't about to give Charlie Rhodes any sort of leeway. She set down her drink and poked a finger in Gemma's direction. "You even told the Abstastic Wonder over there that you didn't want anything from him. He would have told his dickwad brother that."

Her best friend only shook her head. "Come on, Sarz, you're going to have to let it go. I mean, I have, and I'm the one he was a jerk to. If I can smooth things over with him, there's no reason you can't."

Sara's expression turned pinched and she childishly repeated, "There's no reason you can't," in a high pitched, whiny voice.

"Stop it," Gemma laughed and smacked her arm. "I'm serious."

With a long-suffering sigh, Sara gave in. "Fine. I'll try. For you."

"That's all I ask."

* * *

"Hey, babe," Roger greeted Sara outside the restaurant he'd chosen with a quick kiss to her lips.

They were currently 'on again' in their dating cycle. Given that they'd been casually dating again for a few weeks, the cynical part of Sara was waiting for the inevitable break up. Roger was a nice guy –he was an endocrinologist at the hospital where she worked– but he wasn't looking for a serious relationship.

For the most part, Sara was on the same page. She wasn't looking to settle down just yet, but she was thirty-one and she knew she would have to think about her options at some point. Her bestie suddenly becoming a mum had given Sara a tiny internal jolt that she had shoved right down under an imaginary rug in her subconscious, then dragged a metaphorical couch over the top of it for good measure.

She wasn't ready to have those thoughts. She was still in her prime, and she was enjoying dressing up in figure-hugging dresses and being taken out to dinner in upscale restaurants by her wealthy –wannabe playboy– current boyfriend.

But, despite her resolve, it niggled at the back of her brain. Roger was a good guy, and dating him was fun, but he wasn't going to be her Happily Ever After. They both knew it.

His voice shook her from her thoughts. "How are Gemma and…what'd she name the kid again?"

"Zoe," Sara answered, refraining from rolling her eyes. She allowed him to lead her towards their reserved table with a hand at her back, gracefully weaving through tables of other couples. He pulled out her chair for her and she nodded in thanks. "And they're good. They've just spent most of the week getting to know Everett's mum and brother, and I think Gems might actually miss them when they leave."

Roger made a non-committal sound to acknowledge that he had been half-listening while he perused the wine list. The warm yellow lighting bounced off his light brown hair, giving him a sort of halo effect. "Didn't you hate the brother?"

She shrugged, though he wasn't looking. "Yeah, well, I'm not the one who has to get along with him, I guess."

"Really?" her boyfriend finally looked up and across the table, arching a bushy eyebrow at her. "You and Gemma are practically attached at the hip. You're stuck with this guy in your life too, you realise."

She couldn't prevent her eyes from rolling. "Ugh," she huffed, "don't remind me."

He chuckled, flashing his perfectly straight pearly white teeth at her and, not for the first time, she was struck by how handsome he was when he smiled. "Well," he set the wine list down on the white linen tablecloth, "it probably is a bit strange to talk about other men while you're on a date."

Sara snorted inelegantly. "You're the one who asked about him."

"Point," he ceded, still smiling. "But maybe I'm the jealous type."

That almost had her laughing. Roger was many things, but jealous was not one of them. Still, she played along. Batting her lashes with exaggerated coquettishness, she asked, "So, you're just making sure I only have eyes for you?"

"Maybe I am."

Sara could feel her lips twitching with amusement. She shook her head. "Trust me, babe," she assured him, "Charlie –I'm an absolute wank-stain of a person– Rhodes is not my type."

"I'm glad to hear it," he answered, then raised his hand to hail a passing waiter. "Now, do you feel like red wine or white?"

"White," was her response.

He requested a bottle of something that sounded obnoxious and fancy, and then went ahead and ordered their meals for them as well. When they'd first started dating, Sara had considered the action of him ordering for her somewhat condescending and controlling –and it still was both of those things, to an extent– but she'd come to realise that he meant well by it. Roger truly wanted to share the best things in life with her, but he just never stopped to consider that her tastes might be different to his own.

"So, how was your day?" Sara asked him after the waiter left their table. She poured them each a glass from the carafe of sparkling water on the table. "No dramas at work?"

Given that he was a specialist, he had his own suite of offices in the hospital and mostly managed patients with ongoing endocrine disorders or chronic diseases. Roger rarely ever dealt with emergencies. Occasionally he was called in to consult with other specialists in order to diagnose what he referred to as 'curly' cases, but his job wasn't particularly stressful…even if he did consider himself the next *Gregory House M.D.* The biggest drama he'd had recently was his fight to reserve a better parking space.

"It was good," he answered, sipping at the drink she had poured him, "all ongoing patients for standard reviews. Nothing out of the ordinary." He set his glass down and cocked his head at her. "Yours?"

"Fairly standard for me, too," she replied with a half-shrug and fiddled with the corner of the linen napkin in front of her, idly musing that it practically blended into the tablecloth. This place was very on brand for Roger. Modern, sleek, a little pretentious. It didn't have a lot of character, but the food was rumoured to be amazing. (It would want to be for the price.) "Had a kid with a broken arm, and a tradie who had an unfortunate accident with a nail gun, but nothing too out there for me, either. Then I caught up with Gems after my shift, which you already know."

The waiter returned with the wine, pouring a mouthful into a glass for Roger, which he then made a show of sniffing and tasting before inclining his head in approval and gesturing for the other man to pour two proper glasses. Idly, Sara couldn't help but wonder whether her beau could truthfully tell the difference between the ridiculously priced beverage he'd just sampled, or the eight-dollar bottle in the bottom of her fridge at home. Her money was on 'not a chance'.

"And have you given any more thought to going back to uni?" he prodded, taking a sip of his wine after once again dismissing the poor waiter.

Fighting the urge to roll her eyes, she shook her head. "I'm happy working the E.D." Sara informed him, primly sipping from her own glass. *Yeah,* she thought, *the stuff at home's nicer.* "I don't really want to be a doctor."

She wondered if his 'encouragement' for the idea of her furthering her qualifications was all part of his weird superiority complex. After all, he'd love to tell people he was dating another doctor instead of a lowly nurse. Secretly, though, she felt the nurse suited his convertible driving cliché a bit more.

At least he knew to drop the issue, though he was determined to have the last word on the subject, "Of course it's up to you, but you can never have too many qualifications, you know."

Instead of continuing to argue with him, Sara made a noncommittal sound and changed the topic. She had always been good at deflection and had no qualms playing dirty.

Leaning forward to give him an impressive view of her cleavage, she pouted, "Don't you wanna see me in my naughty nurse getup anymore?"

She knew she'd been successful as Roger cleared his throat, his pupils dilating.

At least she knew she'd have some fun tonight. Once the meal was over, at any rate.

* * *

"Tell me, love, does that rod up your arse ever come out, or are you stuck like this permanently?"

Sara rolled her eyes at Charlie's ham-handed attempt at getting under her skin. "When are you leaving again?" Before he could open his mouth, she clarified, "The country, not the restaurant."

She couldn't believe that she would have to put up with this meathead for the rest of her life. Couldn't Gemma have vetted her boy toy's family before he accidentally knocked her up?

"Settle petal," Charlie's smug retort grated on her nerves, "I like your presence here about as much as you like mine."

Despite how well Gemma had taken to Charlie since the barbecue at Brennan's place, Sara couldn't see what was so likable about the man. But she'd come along to the farewell meal, this one held in public at Gemma's favourite Thai restaurant, because Gemma had practically begged her to. At least Beatrice was lovely.

"Charlie," as if to illustrate Sara's mental point, Charlie's mother scolded him like a toddler as she sat between the two of them, "I thought we'd discussed this?"

Sara valiantly fought the urge to lean back in her seat and poke her tongue out at him behind his mother's back.

Across from them, Brennan and Jeff cooed over Zoe, who was staring around at all the bright colours and gold accents with her usual unfocused gaze. It was a conversation between the two men and Sara which had set the elder Rhodes brother off to begin with, butting in to offer his opinion as though Sara had cared to hear it.

When she'd told him that she hadn't, he had bitten back with that lame attempt at an insult.

Now cowed by his mother, Charlie was silent. Sara much preferred him that way. Sitting up a little straighter, she smirked to herself and reached for the menu, catching a glimpse of the disapproving glare on her bestie's face from her seat beside her brother.

Damn it.

Sara feigned innocence. "What?"

Gemma cocked her head to the side with an eyebrow raised. "I think you know what."

Sara had promised to try to be civil, hadn't she? *Ugh.* It was harder than she thought it would be. Jutting her chin higher, she held on to her pride. "Nope," she responded lightly, "no idea."

"Sara..."

Not lifting her eyes from the page in front of her, Sara sassed, "You've really got that cranky mum tone down pat. Bravo."

There was a sigh. "Sarz. Come on."

Fuck it. She hated the defeat in her best friend's voice. "Fine," she exhaled, lowering the menu to glower over the top of it. "But I want it noted that I object. A lot."

"When don't you?" Gemma teased, but her shoulders drooped with obvious relief at the same time as Everett returned from the bar with their drinks.

"I think you'll find there are plenty of things I don't object to," Sara winked at Gemma's baby daddy as he took his seat at the end of the table just offside to Gemma, then laughed as he awkwardly deflected. Her BFF told her to knock it off while fighting off her own amusement. "Alright, alright," Sara took a sip of her wine. "I'll behave."

Even though Sara didn't like Charlie, it was good to see Gems much more at ease than she had been when Everett's family had first entered the country. She had worried for Gemma when Everett had so suddenly burst back onto the scene, especially when it seemed he wanted to be active in the baby's life. The man had a lot more money –and some might argue this meant more stability– to offer a child, and there'd been a moment where Sara had been terrified that his family would demand he apply for custody, potentially whisking Zoe out of the country and out of Gemma's reach.

She thanked all the deities she could think of that Everett had proven her wrong. It would have broken Gemma if he'd been that guy.

"So, tell me," Charlie directed the question her way once she'd made her promise to Gemma, the glint in his eye seemingly payback for her smugness at his own telling off, "why doesn't your boyfriend ever attend these family get-togethers?"

"Roger marches to the beat of his own drum," she answered easily with a shrug. "Sometimes he comes along, other times he doesn't. We don't need to live in each other's pockets."

After a couple of years of doing the whole on-and-off/casual relationship thing, she was used to it. Besides, Roger didn't pressure her to attend events with him, either. Which was a good thing, because his snobby parents couldn't stand her, and vice versa.

Sara felt as though things were pretty equal in that way.

"I couldn't imagine him in a low-key restaurant like this, to be honest," Jeff chimed in, chuckling. He stuck his nose in the air and assumed a haughty tone as he looked down at his menu, "Sara, darling, I don't see a single main here over twenty-five dollars. Outrageous! We're truly dining with the commoners tonight."

Balling up a purple paper napkin, she threw it at her friend, even while she smothered her own giggles. "Stop it," she chastened, "he's not that bad."

Gemma snorted. Sara levelled her with a glare, but all Gemma did was raise her glass of water to her twitching lips and sip primly. "Sorry," she said, sounding anything but apologetic, "but that impression was spot on."

"You both suck," Sara sighed, shaking her head.

"Sounds like you could do with a real man in your life," Charlie was having far too much fun at her expense, and it ruffled her feathers the wrong way.

It was one thing for her friends –who also worked with Roger in the hospital– to playfully tease Sara about him, but altogether different for this random English wanker to do so.

"I hope you're not suggesting you're a viable option," she sassed back, "because I don't think you fall into that category either."

Okay, so it was a bit flat and ridiculous as far as comebacks went, but he scowled back at her, so she took it as a win, nonetheless.

"Don't flatter yourself, love."

"*Aww*, diddums, did I hurt your feelings?"

They were interrupted by their names being snapped on either side of them. He was cowed by his mother's frown, while Sara sighed and apologised to Gemma.

This really was going to be much more difficult than she'd initially thought.

***

READ IT NOW! Find You Can't Hurry Love at **https://books2read.com/ YouCantHurryLove**

About the Author

Anita (A.N.) Verebes is a daydreamer and romance novelist. As a civil marriage celebrant, Anita makes a living telling other people's love stories and celebrating real romance! Also armed with a Bachelor of Education (Secondary), Anita is a qualified -but not practising- High School English teacher who loves to read anything she can get her hands on, including fanfiction. (And, yes, she's written her fair share of that, too.) Living directly between Queensland's sunny Gold and Sunshine coasts, Anita spends her days exploring the Great South East with her husband and their two rambunctious sons. When at home, she's also a slave to two cats and one very spoilt Great Dane X.

You can connect with me on:

 https://anverebesauthor.wordpress.com

 https://www.facebook.com/ANVerebes

Subscribe to my newsletter:

 https://landing.mailerlite.com/webforms/landing/w0o9h1

Also by A.N. Verebes

A.N. Verebes writes Contemporary Romance. Light, feel-good, easy reads that scratch an itch…and turn up the heat!

You Can't Hurry Love

Sara Carlisle and Charlie Rhodes are complete opposites. Oil and water. Chalk and cheese. But, when their relationship turns from reluctant acquaintances to red hot lovers, they find it's good.

Really good.

What could possibly go wrong?

In a slow-burn, standalone romance that follows hot on the heels of *Handle With Care,* Sara and Charlie discover that you really can't rush romance.